THE MURDERS IN PRAED STREET

A Dr Priestley Detective Novel

John Rhode

Spitfire Publishers

CONTENTS

ABOUT 'THE MURDERS IN PRAED STREET'

With a strange and mysterious regularity, murder had come to the squalid, uninviting London neighbourhood of Praed Street. Not one murder, which might have caused a temporary excitement, but a succession of murders – each different from the others, yet all alike in that they seemed without cause. Scotland Yard were alert, but what clues were to be found succeeded in proving false. As a last resort, Dr Lancelot Priestley, whose unusual methods of investigation had solved other baffling problems, was persuaded to lend his assistance. At the very outset, Dr Priestley found that he himself was a marked man – his own life was at stake regardless of his part in the investigation of the serial killer.

About the Author

John Rhode was the pseudonym for the author Cecil Street, one of the best-selling and most popular British authors of the Golden Age of Crime. His most famous literary creation was Dr Lancelot Priestley, a forensic detective who featured in seventy-two novels written over forty years, solving many ingenious and misleading murders. Cecil Street was born in 1884 in Gibraltar to a military family. At sixteen he attended the Royal Military Academy at Woolwich. He served with distinction in the First

World War and then in military intelligence before taking up writing full-time. He was a founding member of the Detection Club, the illustrious dining club of detective story writers, and created the famous 'Eric the Skull' used in the rituals of the organisation. He would write over 140 detective novels (writing also as Miles Burton and Cecil Waye) and died aged 80, in 1964.

Praise for John Rhode's Dr Priestley Detective Novels

The Murders in Praed Street
'An absorbing murder mystery'
New York Times
'A very ingenious tale'
Times Literary Supplement
'Pleasingly original'
Martin Edwards, The Story of Classic Crime in 100 Books
'Thoroughly thrilling'
New York Herald-Tribune
'A mystery story that will keep them sitting up'
Boston Transcript
'Brilliantly conceived, engagingly written'
Somerset Standard

The Ellerby Case
'Highly exciting'
New York Herald-Tribune
'Could there possibly be a more ingenious method of committing a murder?'
The Evening Standard
'Dr Priestley, a scientist with a flair for criminal investigation'
New York Times
'Picturesque and ingenious'
Times Literary Supplement
'Ingeniously worked out and vibrant excitement'
Punch

Mystery at Olympia

'Novel, well-built and surprising, this is a keenly satisfactory tale'
New York Times

Death at Breakfast
'A fine, skilful handling of a neat mystery which is unravelled under Dr Priestley's persuasive but ironic coaching'
Chicago Daily Tribune

Death on the Board
'Undoubtedly, incontestably, incontrovertibly the best thing John Rhode has done'
Manchester Evening News

Proceed with Caution
'A brilliantly simple answer to the conundrum: "How to transport a corpse inconspicuously across the face of England."'
The Sunday Times

Invisible Weapons
'An enthralling mystery'
The Times

Death on the Boat-Train
'Highly enjoyable'
Boston Transcript

The Fourth Bomb
'Technically brilliant'
New Yorker

Death of an Author
'Full of mystery meat and brain-work'
New York Herald-Tribune

Dr Priestley Investigates
'Any time that Dr Priestley takes a hand in a case one can be certain of a diverting evening's reading'
New York Times

Tragedy on the Line
'As usual the advent of the straight-thinking Dr Priestley ensures a good tale'
New York Times

Dr Priestley Lays a Trap
'One of the best of the Priestley series and that is no faint praise'
New York Times

The Claverton Affair
'Scientific investigator, Dr Priestley, is one of the most satisfactory successors to Sherlock Holmes'
New York Times

The Robthorne Mystery
'A genuinely baffling crime puzzle of the first quality'
New York Times

Shot at Dawn
'The story really is excellent'
Chicago Daily Tribune

The Corpse in the Car
'Sound plot... well-knit reasoning'
Dorothy L. Sayers

Tragedy at the Unicorn
'The best detective story of 1928'
Times Literary Supplement

Tragedy on the Line
'One of the neatest of Mr Rhode's very neat puzzles'
The Sunday Times

The Hanging Woman
'Very well constructed, well written, and, above all, convincing'
Times Literary Supplement

PART 1

THE CRIMES

CHAPTER 1 THE STREET

Praed Street is not at any time one of London's brighter thoroughfares. Certainly it ends upon a note of hope, terminating as it does on the fringe of the unquestioned respectability of Bayswater, but for the rest of its course it is frankly lamentable. Narrow, bordered by small and often furtive shops, above which the squalid-looking upper parts are particularly uninviting, it can never have been designed as more than a humble annexe of its more prosperous parent, the Edgware Road. And then, for no apparent reason, the Great Western Railway planted its terminus upon it, and Praed Street found itself called upon to become a main artery of traffic.

It seems to have done very little to adapt itself to its new rôle. Beyond an occasional grudging widening, it has left the unending streams of buses, of heavy railway lorries, of hurrying foot passengers, to shift for themselves as best they can. It almost seems as though Praed Street regarded Paddington Station as an intrusion, and those who throng to and from it as unwelcome strangers. It had its own interests long before the railway came—one of the termini of the Grand Junction Canal lies within a few yards of its sombre limits. Praed Street watches with indifference the thronging crowds which pass along, and they in turn take little heed of the uninviting thoroughfare through which their journey leads them.

Not that these philosophic reflections occupied the mind of

Mr James Tovey, which was far too full of an acute sense of annoyance and discomfort to find room for any other sensations. Mr Tovey was not an inhabitant of Praed Street, although he lived in its neighbourhood. There was nothing secretive about Mr Tovey, you could see his name and occupation painted in bold letters over a shop in Lisson Grove; James Tovey, Fruit and Vegetable Merchant. He was, in fact, a greengrocer, and, years ago, when Mr Tovey had originally employed a small legacy in the purchase of the business, the sign had read: Tovey, Greengrocer, etc. But it was Mr Tovey's proud boast that he always moved with the times, and since his neighbours, the butcher and the grocer, had respectively converted themselves into Meat Purveyors and Provision Dealers, he had abandoned the vulgar term of greengrocer for the more high-sounding appellation.

Sunday was a day of strict observance with Mr Tovey, its presiding deity his own comfort. One can hardly blame him for this indulgence, since the rest of the week left him little leisure for repose. His habit was to rise before six, in order to drive the van to Covent Garden. The van, a second-hand Ford, was the subject of the ribald mirth of his acquaintances. Every non-essential part had long since fallen off, as an aged elm sheds its branches, and the essentials were held together by odd pieces of rope. But to any suggestion of the van's imperfections, Mr Tovey merely shrugged his shoulders. "'Tisn't 'er looks as matters," he would reply. "So long as she does 'er job she'll do for me." And perhaps this phrase, applied to things at large, was a complete summing up of Mr Tovey's philosophy.

He opened the shop as soon as he returned from Covent Garden, and kept it open, winter and summer, till a late hour. Lisson Grove shops late, and it was usually ten o'clock before Mr Tovey could reckon to get his bit of supper. It was therefore natural that so strenuous a week should be rewarded by a relaxation on Sunday. It was his invariable habit to stay in bed till noon, inhaling the savoury smell of the Sunday joint roasting in the kitchen, and only to rise and put on his best suit when the clock struck that hour. The afternoon was usually devoted to the peaceful somnolence of repletion, or sometimes in summer, if Mrs Tovey's legs felt equal to accompanying him, to a walk in the park. And in the evening there were always the thrilling columns of the Sunday paper.

Mr Tovey hated to be disturbed in the evening of this day of rest. Especially on such an evening as the present. The day had been an eminently satisfactory one, from his point of view. The sirloin of beef, carefully selected by Mrs Tovey from the stock of her friend the Meat Purveyor, over the way, had been of uncommon succulence; the Yorkshire pudding crisped to that exact degree of golden delicacy that Mr Tovey's heart desired. True, he had had a slight difference of opinion with Mrs Tovey, but that had merely given a zest to a day which might otherwise have been uneventful. Mr and Mrs Tovey never really quarrelled. For one thing they were neither of them of a quarrelsome disposition, and for another they were both too fond of their own comfort to risk its disturbance by domestic rancour. But sometimes they did not see eye to eye, as in the present case.

It had begun when Mr Tovey had come down to the kitchen and noticed that only two places had been laid at the table. He had raised his eyebrows and glanced towards the massive form of Mrs Tovey, bending over the glowing range.

"Hullo! Where's Ivy, then?" he asked, in an almost querulous tone.

"Gone out with Ted," replied Mrs Tovey quietly, from among the saucepans. "He's taken her home to dinner, and they're going on to the pictures afterwards."

Mr Tovey clicked his tongue, his favourite expression of annoyance. Of course, Ted and Ivy had known one another since they were children. Old Sam Copperdock, Ted's father, was Mr Tovey's oldest friend, and they had been near neighbours ever since the latter, as a newly married man, had bought the greengrocery business. Still, Mr Tovey didn't altogether like it. Ivy was twenty now, and young Ted Copperdock only three years older. Just the sort of age when young folks get the bit between their teeth and go and get married without a thought of the future. Old Sam was a thorough good chap, and his son was a very nice lad; Mr Tovey would not have denied either of these facts for a moment. But Ted's only prospects lay in his father's shop in Praed Street, and Mr Tovey had very different views of his only child's future, very different.

Yet he had never put these views into words. Perhaps he would have found it very difficult to do so, for Mr Tovey's vocabulary was strictly limited. But they were there, just the same—had been ever since Ivy's prowess at school had discovered her to be a "scholar." From that moment Mr Tovey had been at great pains to educate his daughter to an entirely different state of life from that to which it had pleased God to call her. That she was by now tall, distinctly pretty, and extraordinarily self-possessed was not, one supposes, due to the efforts of Mr Tovey. But she certainly owed the fact that she was an extremely competent shorthand typist to the pains he had devoted to her education.

Mr Tovey, though naturally he would have been justifiably annoyed at such a suggestion, had an incurably romantic core to his plodding and material mind. Of course, in common with most of his class, he firmly believed that human happiness varied exactly with the social scale. "As happy as a king" was to him no mere catch-word. He was convinced—and, to do him justice, he drew considerable satisfaction from the conviction—that the members of the Royal Family were the happiest persons in the land, and that this happiness descended in regular gradation through the ranks of the nobility and gentlefolk until it reached acute misery somewhere in the lower strata of those who dwelt in slums. From this outlook on life it necessarily followed that the more he could enable Ivy to better herself, the happier she must ultimately be.

How this betterment was to take place, Mr Tovey never explained. But sometimes he had a vague intangible dream of Ivy, his Ivy, captivating the heart of some susceptible employer, preferably of the Upper Classes. His eye, diverted for the moment from the business of wrapping up a parcel of leeks, often caught sight of the pictures in the newspaper which he was using for the purpose. "Lady Mary Mayfair (right) and the Countess of Piccadilly (left) on the lawn at Ascot." Suppose that one day he should proudly open the paper to find Ivy with a smile like that, gracefully posing under the heading "A leader of Society in the paddock at Goodwood?" After all, why not?

But it was not until after the second helping of roast beef and Yorkshire that he made any further remark about his daughter to Mrs Tovey. "I wouldn't encourage young Ted to hang round Ivy too much, if I was you," he said, as he pushed aside his plate.

"Encourage? He don't want no encouraging," replied Mrs Tovey briskly. "He just comes in, cheerful like, nods to me, asks after you, says a word or two to Ivy, and away they goes together. Things ain't the same now as they was when we was their age, Jim."

"No, it's a fact they ain't," agreed Mr Tovey darkly.

"But let 'em alone," continued Mrs Tovey. "Ivy's not the girl to make a fool of herself, you ought to know that by this time. Now you can go and sit in your chair by the fire. It's not the sort of day for the likes of us to be going out."

Mr Tovey shook his head, as though unconvinced by his wife's words, and looked out of the window. Much as he might disagree with her on the subject of their daughter, there was no doubt that she was right about the weather. It was the beginning of November, and the month was doing its best to live up to its reputation. A thin mist, precursor of the fog that must surely follow, filled the narrow streets, and through it filtered a cold raw drizzle, through which a few passing pedestrians hurried, muffled up to their ears.

Mr Tovey grunted, and drew his chair up closer towards the fire. The weather could do what it liked, as long as it cleared up before the next morning. He certainly was not going out into it. He composed himself for his afternoon nap, from which he arose refreshed and eager for the lurid pages of his favourite Sunday paper. He studied this intently for some minutes, then turned animatedly to Mrs Tovey.

"That brute what cut up the young woman he was walking out with is committed for trial at the Old Bailey," he said.

"I reckoned he would be, the dirty brute," replied Mrs Tovey, who was almost as keen a criminologist as her husband. "And I'd see he didn't get off, neither, if I was on the jury."

Mr Tovey turned and looked at her gravely. "'Tis all very well for you to talk like that," he said reprovingly. "It's a terrible thing to be on a jury when a man's life depends on what you says. Nobody knows that better than I do, I'm sure."

"Yes, I remember the state you was in that time," replied Mrs Tovey. "Dear, dear, best part of a week you was at it, and Ivy just born and all. What was the chap's name? I remember he was a doctor who'd killed one of his patients by giving him a dose of something."

"Morlandson, Dr Morlandson," said Mr Tovey. "Lord, whenever I eats anything as disagrees with me I dreams of his face a' looking at us from the dock. Fair gave me the creeps, it did, for a long time after. We found him guilty, and I couldn't help looking at him when the judge put on his black cap and sentenced him. Ugh!"

"But they didn't 'ang 'im after all," remarked Mrs Tovey.

"No, he was reprieved, I don't rightly know why. Because he'd been a big pot in his way, I suppose. Twenty years hard he got, though, and serve 'im right. This bloke I'm telling you about won't get off so easy, though."

Mr Tovey returned to the perusal of his paper, and the evening wore on, the silence of the cosy kitchen broken only at intervals by the voice of Mr Tovey, reading in a halting voice some more than usually spicy extract to his wife. Tea-time came and went, and still Ivy made no appearance. It was nearly nine o'clock when Mr Tovey referred to her absence. "I can't think where that girl's got to," he said irritably. "She's no call to be out all this time."

"Ted'll have taken her home to have a bite of supper," returned Mrs Tovey equably. "His father likes to have her round there, cheers him up, she does. She'll be back before long, never you worry."

The reply which sprang to Mr Tovey's lips was checked by the urgent ringing of the telephone bell in the shop, separated from the kitchen by a door kept locked on Sundays.

"Hullo! What's that?" he inquired in a startled tone. Mrs Tovey had already moved towards the door. "I'll go and see," she replied shortly. Her husband, listening intently, could hear her steps on the bare boards, the sudden cessation of the ringing as she took up the receiver, her voice as she answered, then a pause.

Then he heard her call him from the other room. "Somebody wants to speak to you, Jim."

With a muttered objurgation he dragged himself from his chair and went into the shop. His wife handed him the instrument. "Hullo!" he said and for a moment stood listening.

"Yes, I'm James Tovey." A long pause, while Mrs Tovey vainly tried to make sense of the faint sounds which reached her ears. "What's that? Oh! a man, you say, thank the Lord for that! I thought for the moment it might be my daughter, she's out a bit late tonight. Yes! I'll be along at once."

He put back the receiver and turned to his wife. "That's a rum show!" he exclaimed, not without a tremor of excitement in his voice. "St Martha's Hospital, that was. There's a fellow been run over, and they can't find out who he is. The only thing in his pocket is a bit of paper with my name an' address on. Now, who the dickens can it be?"

"Why, young Alf, as likely as not," replied Mrs Tovey unemotionally. "Why 'e 'asn't been run over afore, goin' about as he does with his 'ead in the air, is more than I can make out."

Alf was the youth employed by Mr Tovey to deliver the purchases of such of his customers as did not prefer to carry them home wrapped up in newspaper. But Mr Tovey shook his head at the suggestion.

"Not it! Young Alf lives down Camberwell way, and he's not likely to be up this way of a Sunday. Give us my coat, missus, and I'll go along and see who it is."

Mr Tovey struggled into his coat, and turned the collar well up over his ears. It was a most unpleasant evening to be out in, but, after all, it was worth it. His mind had been steeped in sensation all the afternoon, and now he was himself about to take a leading part in some thrilling tragedy. In imagination he could see the account in the next issue of the *Paddington Clarion and Marylebone Recorder*. Headlines first: "Fatal Accident. Man crushed to death by Motor Bus." Then his own name: "The body was identified by Mr Tovey, the well-known Fruit and Vegetable Merchant of Lisson Grove." This was fame indeed!

He stood at the corner of Lisson Grove for a moment, eyeing the buses as they passed him. Through their streaming window panes he could see that they were all full, a row of dejected looking passengers standing in each one of them. There was nothing for it, he would have to walk. It wasn't very far, anyhow, not more than half a mile at most.

Mr Tovey stepped out smartly along Chapel Street, across the Edgware Road, and entered Praed Street. Despite the depressing weather, the pavements seemed to be full of people, groups of whom overflowed into the roadway, only to be driven back helter-skelter by the menacing onrush of the motor-buses. Mr Tovey picked his way through the crowd with the consciousness of the importance of his mission. So intent was he upon reaching his goal, and, having played his part, upon regaining the comfort of his own fireside, that he scarcely spared a glance for the lighted window above Sam Copperdock's shop. Ivy was behind that drawn curtain, no doubt. He might drop in and pick her up on his way home. He certainly could not stop now.

With a due sense of dignity he climbed the steps of the main entrance of St Martha's, and nodded familiarly to the porter in the hall. "My name's Tovey," he said, "you rang me up just now to come and identify an accident case."

The porter looked at him incredulously. "Rang you up? 'Oo rang you up? First I've heard of it."

Mr Tovey clicked his tongue impatiently. "Why, not more than a quarter of an hour ago," he replied. "Man been run over, and you couldn't find out who he was."

"We ain't had no accidents brought in the 'ole blessed day," returned the porter stolidly. "You've made a bloomer, you 'ave. Wait 'ere a moment while I goes and sees if anybody knows anything about it. Tobey, did you say your name was?"

"Tovey!" replied that individual angrily. The porter turned his back upon him and disappeared, his boots clattering noisily upon the tiled floor. Mr Tovey, with a sudden reaction from his excited imaginings, stood cold and miserable in the centre of a puddle formed by the drops from his overcoat.

After what seemed an interminable time the porter returned. "Somebody's bin pulling your leg," he said, with a malicious grin. "We ain't 'ad no accidents, and nobody 'ere aint ever 'eard of you. Didn't get the name of the 'orspital wrong, did you? Wasn't St George's, was it, or maybe St Thomas's?"

Mr Tovey shook his head. "No, it was St Martha's, right enough," he replied. A sudden wave of anger at the hoax which had been played upon him surged through his brain, and without another word he turned and strode out of the hall. It was monstrous that he, a citizen and a ratepayer, should be dragged out into the streets on a fool's errand like this. With his grievance rankling to the exclusion of every other thought, he pushed his way along Praed Street, his head down, his hands crammed into his overcoat pockets. The drizzle had turned to sleet, and the sting of it on his face added to his ill-humour.

Ahead of him was the Express Train, a public-house which had presumably been built and named at the time of the coming of the railway. It was closing time by now, and a stream of gesticulating figures was being disgorged upon the crowded pavement. Mr Tovey looked up as he heard the turmoil. The cold air and comparative darkness, after the warmth and light of the bar, seemed to have had an unsteadying effect upon the ejected guests. They lurched about the pavement singing snatches of ribald songs, arguing heatedly in loud voices.

Mr Tovey frowned. Nice way to spend a Sunday evening! Thank God, he didn't live in Praed Street, anyhow. He wasn't going to be barged off the pavement by a lot of drunken hooligans, not he. Putting his head a trifle further down, like a bull about to charge, he strode straight ahead in an undeviating line. One man lurched into him, another jostled him from behind, and a menacing voice, its effect somewhat marred by a loud hiccough, called out, "'ere, 'oo the 'ell d'yer think your pushin'?"

And then Mr Tovey, with a queer strangled cry, suddenly collapsed in a heap upon the muddy pavement.

CHAPTER 2 THE HERBALIST

It is the proud boast of our modern educationalists that the process of forcing knowledge down unwilling throats, known as compulsory education, has resulted in the triumph of science over superstition. Alchemy and astrology, the magic of the Middle Ages, have given place to chemistry and astronomy, the mysteries of which are displayed before the wondering eyes of the elementary scholar. The Age of Superstition is commonly supposed to have fled before the progress of the Age of Materialism.

This supposition is demonstrably false. At no other age in the earth's history has superstition owned so many votaries. From the most rapt spiritualist to the man who refuses to walk under a ladder, the world is full of people who allow superstition to play an important part in their lives. In the neighbourhood of Praed Street fortune tellers and interpreters of dreams are superstition's most popular ministers, though it may come as a surprise to many that a brass plate nailed to the door of a house in the Harrow Road advertises the existence of the British College of Astrology.

Even Alchemy is not without its devotees, although the alchemist has forsaken the more picturesque apparatus of his stock-in-trade. He now owns a small shop, the darker the better, and fills the windows with a curious assortment of dried herbs, each with a notice affixed to it describing its virtues. You may go in and buy two pennyworth of some dried plant with a high-sounding Latin name, the herbalist assuring you that, mixed with boiling water and drunk as tea, it will cure the most obscure disease. If you have sufficient faith, it probably will.

But this is the least of the herbalist's abilities. It is, in fact, merely the outward sign of an inward and spiritual wisdom. You can consult him, in the little back parlour behind the shop, upon all manner of subjects, which you do not care to mention to your friends. And, for a consideration, he will give you advice, which you may or may not follow. At all events, if the herbalist knows his business, he will contrive to command respect, and, at the same time, earn a surprising number of shillings.

The establishment of Mr Elmer Ludgrove, the herbalist of Praed Street, was almost exactly opposite that of Mr Samuel Copperdock, who dealt in another herb, namely tobacco. There was a considerable contrast between the two shops; that of Mr Copperdock was always newly painted, and its windows full of tins and boxes bearing the brightest labels known to the trade. The herbalist's window, on the other hand, was low and frowning, backed by a matchboard partition which effectually precluded any view into the shop. Between the partition and the glass were displayed the usual bunches of dried plants and dishes containing seeds and shrivelled flowers. The door of the shop closed with a spring, and if you had the curiosity to push this open you found yourself in a dark little room, across the centre of which ran a narrow counter. The noise of your entry would bring Mr Ludgrove through a second door, shrouded by a heavy curtain, and he would ask you politely what he could do for you.

Mr Ludgrove's appearance was certainly in keeping with his calling. He was tall and thin, with a pronounced stoop and a deep but not unpleasant voice. But it was his head that you looked at instinctively. Above the massive forehead and powerfully-chiselled features was a wealth of long, snow-white hair, balanced by a flowing beard of the same colour. His eyes, behind his iron-rimmed spectacles, looked at you benignly, but they conveyed the impression that they saw further into your mind than the eyes of the mere casual stranger. If you were a mere customer for some simple remedy, you came away with the pleasant feeling of having been treated with unusual courtesy. If your business was such that Mr Ludgrove invited you to discuss it with him in the room behind the curtain, you very soon found out that behind Mr Ludgrove's impressive presence there lay a wealth of wisdom and experience.

Praed Street, which beneath its squalor possesses a vein of native shrewdness, had very soon estimated Mr Ludgrove's worth. That neighbourhood had very few secrets, romantic or sordid, which, sooner or later, were not told in halting whispers behind the sound-defying curtain. And, whatever the secret might be, the teller of it never became swallowed up again in the stream of humanity which flowed past Mr Ludgrove's door without some grain of comfort, material or moral, which as often as not had cost the recipient nothing.

Mr Samuel Copperdock had from the first taken a great fancy to old Ludgrove, as he called him. When the name had first appeared over the shop, which had stood empty for years, almost opposite his own premises, he had been intrigued at once. Curiosity—or perhaps it was not mere vulgar curiosity, but a thirst for information—was one of Sam Copperdock's chief characteristics. He must have been one of Mr Ludgrove's first customers, if not the very first, for on the very day the herbalist's shop was opened he had walked across the road, pushed open the door, and thumped upon the counter.

He stared quite frankly at Mr Ludgrove as the latter came into the shop, and opened the conversation without delay. "Look here, you sell medicines, don't you?" he inquired briskly.

Mr Ludgrove smiled, and with a slight gesture seemed to indicate the long rows of drawers behind the counter. "Yes, if you like to call them such," he replied gently. "What particular medicine do you require?"

"Well, I'm terrible troubled with rheumatics," said Mr Copperdock. "Mind, I don't hold with any of them quack mixtures, but I thought I'd just step across and see if you had anything that was any good."

Mr Ludgrove smiled. Certainly Mr Copperdock, short, red-faced, and inclined to stoutness, looked the picture of health. "Rheumatism, eh?" he remarked. "How long have you suffered from it?"

Mr Copperdock laughed. There was something disarming in the attitude of this herbalist fellow. Besides, deception in any form was not Mr Copperdock's strong suit.

"Well, to tell the truth, I don't worry much about them rheumatics," he replied. "I came across neighbour-like, mainly to see what sort of a place you've got here."

"I'm sure you're very welcome," replied Mr Ludgrove courteously. The two men leant on the opposite sides of the counter, chatting for a while. At last Mr Copperdock straightened himself up, half reluctantly. "Well, I must get back to business, I suppose," he said.

"Look here, how serious were you about that rheumatism?" interposed Mr Ludgrove. "Do you ever feel any twinges of it?"

"Oh, sometimes," replied Mr Copperdock nonchalantly. "Can't say as it worries me much, though."

"If you take my advice, you'll stop it before it gets worse," said Mr Ludgrove, opening a drawer and taking from it a scoopful of some parched-looking seeds. "If you put a teaspoonful of these into half a tumbler of boiling water, and drink the liquid twice a day after meals, you won't have any further trouble."

He had poured the seeds into a paper bag as he spoke, and handed them across to Mr Copperdock.

"How much?" asked the latter rather awkwardly, putting his hand in his trouser pocket.

But Mr Ludgrove waved him away. "Try them first, my dear sir," he said. "Then, if you find they do you good and you want some more, we'll talk about payment."

That first introduction had, in the course of years, ripened into friendship. Nearly every morning Mr Copperdock was in the habit of stepping across the road and having a chat with old Ludgrove. Mr Copperdock loved somebody to talk to. If you went into his shop to buy a packet of your favourite cigarettes you were lucky if you got out after less than five minutes' conversation. In the evening, after the shop was closed, a select company in the saloon bar of the Cambridge Arms gave Mr Copperdock the opportunities he sought. Mr Copperdock, who had been a widower for many years, always talked of retiring in favour of his only child Edward.

"Does the lad good to be left in charge of the shop for a bit," was his father's justification for his morning talk with his friend the herbalist. And Mr Ludgrove, whose trade was never very brisk in the mornings, always seemed glad to see him.

Thus, on the Monday following Mr Tovey's adventure it was to Mr Ludgrove that Sam Copperdock hastened to unbosom himself. He was simply bursting with news, and he watched impatiently until the unlocking of Mr Ludgrove's shop door indicated that that gentleman was ready to receive visitors. Then he bustled across the road and into the shop. "Are you there, Ludgrove?" he called out.

"Come in, come in, Mr Copperdock," replied a welcoming voice from behind the curtain, and the tobacconist, with an air of supreme importance, passed into the inner room.

The room was half-parlour, half-laboratory. One side of it was entirely occupied by a long bench, upon which stood a variety of scientific instruments. At the other side, placed round a cheerful fire, were two comfortable arm-chairs, in one of which sat the herbalist himself. With a hospitable gesture he motioned Mr Copperdock towards the other, but the tobacconist was too excited to perceive the invitation.

"I say, have you heard the news about poor Jim Tovey?" he exclaimed, without preliminary.

"My dear sir, I read my paper pretty thoroughly every morning, as you know," replied Mr Ludgrove with a glance at the sheet which lay on the table by his side.

But Sam Copperdock merely snorted impatiently. "Newspaper!" he exclaimed, "why, the newspapers don't know nothing about it! I tell you I've been up three parts of the night over this affair."

"Indeed? Then you probably know all the details," replied the herbalist. "If you can spare the time, I should be very interested if you would sit down and tell me all about it."

This was exactly what Mr Copperdock had meant to do. He sank heavily into the chair with a portentous sigh. "Terrible thing, terrible," he began, shaking his head. "I've known Jim Tovey ever since he first took that shop in Lisson Grove, and to think that a thing like this should happen to him! And his poor daughter Ivy spent the best part of the evening at my place, too."

Mr Ludgrove, who knew his friend's methods of expression, was careful not to interrupt, and after a short pause the tobacconist resumed his relation.

"First I knew of it was from my boy, Ted. You see, it was like this. Ted's very sweet on Ivy, and a nice girl she is, too. None of your fly-away misses, but a nice steady girl what'll make her way in the world. Ted brought her to my place for dinner, then they spends the afternoon at the pictures, and comes back for supper. About half-past nine or maybe quarter to ten Ivy says it's time she was getting home, and she and Ted goes out together. I was thinking Ted was a long time a-seeing of her home, since it was a shocking night, and they weren't likely to dawdle on the way, when in he comes white as a sheet, and all of a tremble. 'Dad,' he says, 'Ivy's father's been murdered.'

"Well, I thought the boy had gone off his head. 'Murdered?' I says. 'Why, what do you mean? Who'd want to murder Jim Tovey, I'd like to know?' Then after a bit I manages to get the whole story out of him. It seems that when he and Ivy got to Lisson Grove, Jim Tovey was out. He'd been called to St Martha's to identify an accident case. He stayed there for a bit, when suddenly the door bell rings. Mrs Tovey answers it, and in comes a policeman, with a message that Mrs Tovey and Ivy were wanted at St Martha's at once. Mrs Tovey goes upstairs to put her things on, and Ivy goes with her. Then the policeman asks Ted if he's a friend of the family, and when he says he is, tells him that

21

poor Jim has just been murdered in this very street, not a couple of hundred yards from where we're sitting now."

Mr Ludgrove nodded. "A most extraordinary affair altogether," he commented.

"Ah, you may well call it extraordinary," agreed Mr Copperdock significantly, "there's more in it than meets the eye, that's what I says. Well, as soon as I hears this I thinks of those two poor women, and off I goes to St Martha's to see if I could be of any use. There I finds a police inspector who asks me who I was. When he hears I was Jim Tovey's oldest friend he tells me all about it. It seems that a policeman who had his eye on the lads coming out of the Express Train—they're a rough crowd, as you know—saw a man fall down and then heard a lot of hollering. Thinking there was a scrap he went over and found Jim Tovey on the ground with a lot of fellows standing round him. It didn't take him long to find out that Jim was dead, but nobody seemed to know how it happened. There was a crowd on the pavement outside the pub, and it was a foggy sort of night that you couldn't see very clearly in."

"I know," put in Mr Ludgrove. "I was out about that time myself. I always go for a walk after supper, rain or fine; it's the only chance of exercise I get."

"Yes, I know you do," agreed Mr Copperdock. "I often wonder you don't catch your death of cold. Well, the policeman calls up the ambulance, and they gets poor Jim round to St Martha's. There they very soon finds out what's the matter. There's a great long knife, in shape rather like a butcher's skewer, but without a handle, sticking into him. And the point's right through his heart."

Mr Copperdock paused dramatically. There was no doubt that he was thoroughly enjoying himself, and Mr Ludgrove was far too good a listener to interrupt him.

"I took Mrs Tovey and Ivy home," he continued, "and the Inspector told me he'd come and have a chat with me later. It was past midnight when he turned up, and then of course he wanted to know all about poor Jim, and whether I knew of anybody who had a grudge against him. He couldn't have come to a better man, for I know a lot about Jim Tovey that I don't suppose he ever told anybody else. You've heard of the Express Train gang, I suppose?"

Mr Ludgrove nodded. "It consists, I believe, of a number of young men who frequent the racecourses, and who meet in the evenings at the Express Train," he replied.

"They were the fellows outside the pub when poor old Jim was murdered," continued Mr Copperdock significantly. "Now the police, who know a lot more than most people give them credit for, know all about that gang. They'd had every man jack of them rounded up before the Inspector came to see me and put them through it. As the Inspector said, if Jim Tovey had been beaten up with bits of iron pipe, or something like that, he could have understood it. But the knife trick didn't sound like the gang, somehow. None of them had the guts for deliberate murder like that, and there seemed no reason why they should have set upon Jim Tovey. He'd nothing to do with racing, and he wasn't likely to be carrying a lot of money about with him."

Again Mr Ludgrove nodded. "I see the point," he said.

"Yes, but you don't know what I know," replied Mr Copperdock darkly. "The leader of the gang is young Wal Snyder. Decent lad he used to be, I knew his father years ago before he died. He and my Ted used to go to school together, and I managed to get him a job as errand boy. Then he got into bad company, run away from his job, and has been hanging about doing nothing ever since. Now, if you please, this young rip had the sauce to walk into Tovey's shop a few weeks ago, and ask if Miss Ivy was in. Jim asks him what he wants her for, and he says that he knew her as a child, and as she'd turned out such a fine girl he'd like to take her out on the spree one fine evening. Jim told me he fair lost his temper at that; I don't know exactly what he said to young Wal, but he let him know pretty straight that if he found him hanging round Ivy he'd put the police on his track. The young scamp cleared out, telling him he'd better look out for himself."

"Ah, this throws a new light upon the matter!" commented Mr

Ludgrove, with polite interest.

"Better look out for himself," repeated Mr Copperdock with careful emphasis. "A regular threat, mark you. Jim didn't say anything about Wal to Ivy or her mother, you never know how women will take these things. Of course, I told the Inspector about it, and he took it all down in his book. He'd already seen Wal, together with the rest of the gang. It seems they'd had a pretty good week, and most of 'em confessed they were a bit on, and didn't remember much after they was chucked out of the pub. But young Wal said he remembered an old chap barging into him—he said he didn't recognise him—and just behind him was a fellow who looked like a seaman. He couldn't say much about this other fellow, except that he had a sort of woollen cap covering his head, a fierce-looking black beard, and a great scar right across his cheek. Said he looked like one of them Russian Bolsheviks. Of course, there was a lot of people on the pavement, but he was the only one he noticed."

Mr Ludgrove smiled. "I am inclined to think that the story does credit to the young man's imagination," he said quietly. "I can't say that I've ever seen a Bolshevik sailor wandering about Praed Street on a Sunday evening."

"Nor hasn't anybody else," replied Mr Copperdock scornfully. "What's more, the policeman, who was on the spot pretty sharp, didn't see anybody like this man in the crowd. There's no question but what Wal Snyder invented this story to cover himself. It's all plain as daylight to me—ah, but there's one thing I haven't told you. Remember I said that poor old Jim had been sent for to St Martha's to identify an accident case? Well, that was all my eye. There hadn't been no accident and St Martha's hadn't rung him up at all. It was just a trick to get him out into Praed Street."

"It ought to be possible for the police to trace where the call came from," suggested Mr Ludgrove.

"Of course. The Inspector told me they'd done that already, but it didn't get them much further. The call came from one of the boxes at Paddington Station, one of them automatic contraptions where you press the button when you're through. If you're sharp with the button, there's nothing to tell the people you're speaking to that you're speaking from a box. And, of course, at a place like Paddington there's no one to see who goes in and out of those boxes."

"I see. And where was Wal Snyder when the call was made?"

"Oh, in the Express Train all right. He'd got his alibi fixed up, no fear of that. Put one of his pals on to that job, the cunning young devil. And then, of course, he'd watch till Jim came past the pub on his way home, and the rest was easy."

"And what did your friend the Inspector think of all this?" inquired Mr Ludgrove.

"He didn't say much," confessed Mr Copperdock. "But the police ain't such fools as you might think. Young Wal Snyder will have to go through it, you mark my words. Well, I'd best be getting back home. You never know when I shan't be wanted to give evidence or something."

And with that he rose and stalked out of the back room, leaving Mr Ludgrove with a thoughtful expression on his face.

CHAPTER 3 THE INQUEST

The inquest upon Mr Tovey, although it was reported at length in all the evening papers, did not throw any further light upon the identity of his murderer. The knife was produced and handed round for examination. There was, however, nothing extraordinary about it, except perhaps its inordinate length and the fact that it had no handle.

A cutler, called as an expert witness, identified it as the blade of a paper-cutter's knife, carefully ground down so as to obliterate the maker's name and also to produce an edge all the way up as well as at the point. Such blades were usually supplied with a wooden handle, into which they fitted loosely, being secured by means of a set-screw. This witness agreed that knives of this type were rarely seen in ordinary use, but that they were made in considerable quantities for use in certain trades. There would be no difficulty in purchasing one.

Wal Snyder, with a mixture of glibness and injured innocence, gave his version of the affair. But the atmosphere of the coroner's court, so painfully reminiscent of the police court, reduced him in a very short time to stuttering incoherence. Yes, he had caught sight of somebody just as the dead man fell. Hadn't never seen him before, biggish fellow with a lot of black hair, and an ugly-looking cut across his cheeks, like as if he'd been slashed with a knife. Asked why he thought he was a sailor, Wal replied that he wore a woollen cap and a coat and trousers like the sailors wear. He knew because he had got pals down the West India Dock Road. Asked again if he had any reason to suppose that this was the man who stabbed the deceased, Wal became more confused than ever. Well, then, had he seen him strike the blow? Wal had not, but incautiously advanced the opinion that he looked just the sort of cove who'd do a thing like that.

This brought the whole weight of the coroner's displeasure upon his unlucky head. He was told to stand down and not talk nonsense. Then his appalled ear was assailed by an exact and monotonous catalogue of the misdemeanours committed by himself in particular and the Express Train gang in general; things which he fondly believed were known only to himself and a few chosen associates. They ranged from petty larceny to assault and battery, but the Inspector who recited them seemed to treat them with contempt. He smiled as he replied to the coroner's questions.

"No, sir, I don't believe any of them have the intelligence or the pluck to plan a murder like this," he said, "nor do I think that they would be likely to play any of their games outside the Express Train, under the very eyes of the police. In fact, sir, we have no evidence that any of them was in any way connected with the crime."

The constable who had been first on the scene proved an excellent witness, and earned the coroner's commendation. He had been standing, at about half-past nine on the previous Sunday evening, on the pavement opposite the Express Train. There had been complaints of disorderliness in Praed Street at closing time. There had been a large number of people passing along the pavement, and the sudden surge of twenty or thirty men from the door of the public house caused a few moments' confusion. He heard a lot of shouting, then saw a man fall on the pavement. A group immediately gathered round the fallen man and hid him from sight until he pushed them aside.

Asked if he could form any estimate of the time which elapsed between his seeing the man fall and his reaching his side, the constable said, it could not have been more than fifteen seconds.

He did not see anybody resembling the black-haired sailor described by a previous witness, but had there been such a man he would have had ample time to disappear in the crowd in the interval. He could not distinguish faces across the street, it was too foggy. His ambulance training had convinced him that the deceased was dead when he reached him.

A house-surgeon at St Martha's described the wound. It would not require the exercise of any great force to drive the knife in, but the location of the blow showed a certain knowledge of anatomy. The knife had passed right through the outer clothing of the deceased; it was only when the body was undressed that it was discovered. It seemed difficult to imagine how a man holding a blade without a handle could have driven it in so far. Death from such a wound would be practically instantaneous, but there would be no external haemorrhage.

The coroner, addressing the jury, made it quite plain that although there was no doubt how deceased met his death there was no evidence as to how the blow was delivered. The jury, taking their clue from his remarks, found that the deceased had been murdered by some person or persons unknown, and added a rider expressing their sympathy with his widow and daughter.

Mr Samuel Copperdock, who had escorted Mrs Tovey and Ivy to the court, brought them back to his place in Praed Street for tea. In Mr Copperdock's mind there still lingered a strong suspicion that Wal Snyder and the Express Train gang were in some way mixed up in the affair. His disappointment that someone had not been brought to book made him unusually silent, and it was not until tea was over, and he and Mrs Tovey were ensconced in arm-chairs in his comfortable parlour, that he resumed his accustomed cheerfulness.

Mrs Tovey, a voluminous figure in the deepest of black, had taken the tragedy with her accustomed philosophy. She was not the sort of woman to give way to despair; and all her life she had faced the ups and downs of fortune with the same outward placidity. Her inner feelings were her own concern; even her husband had never attempted to probe their depth. Besides, Mrs

Tovey belonged to a class which cannot afford to let sentiment interfere with the practical considerations of the moment.

"I shall keep on the business," she was saying. "'Tisn't as though I'd been left without a penny, in a manner of speaking. Jim had a tidy bit put away; he always used to say he was saving it up for our old age. Then there'll be the insurance money. Ivy's a good girl, she hasn't cost us nothing for the last year or two, and it's her I'm thinking of mostly. She'll want a home yet for a bit, and she couldn't have a better one."

Mr Copperdock glanced over his shoulder towards the other end of the room, where Ivy and Ted were holding an earnest conversation in low tones. It was Thursday afternoon, early closing day, and the shop below was shut, a circumstance for which Ted appeared devoutly grateful.

"I shouldn't wonder if you lost Ivy before very long," said Mr Copperdock slyly. "But she's a good girl, as you say. But you'll never manage the business by yourself, Mrs Tovey. Who's going along to do the bit of buying of a morning?"

"I'll manage easy enough," replied Mrs Tovey confidently. "I shall take young Alf into the shop, and get another lad to drive the van. You'll find I'll manage to rub along very comfortable, Mr Copperdock."

They entered upon an earnest discussion of the science of greengrocery, heedless of the equally earnest discussion which was going on behind their backs.

"No, it's no use, Ted, not yet," Ivy was saying. "You none of you seem to understand quite. It's different for Mum; she's got the business to look after, and she doesn't think of anything else. I can't forget how good Dad always was to me, and we just couldn't do anything he wouldn't have liked."

"You mean he wouldn't have liked you to—to walk out with me?" put in Ted, half resentfully.

Ivy blushed in spite of herself. "It wasn't that, exactly," she replied. "Mind, he never said anything to me, but I've got it out of Mum since. He always wanted me to—to get on in the world, and be a credit to the education he's given me. And I feel that even now he's dead, I've got to try and do what he wanted."

"It isn't that there's anybody else?" he suggested with a note of anxiety in his voice.

"There isn't anybody else, Ted," she replied, looking him straight in the face. "But I'm not going to promise anything until I've got over the shock of his being killed like that. Oh, Ted, who can have done it? He hadn't an enemy in the world, not a real enemy, I mean."

Ted shook his head helplessly. "I can't make it out," he replied. "I can't believe Wal Snyder had anything to do with it. After all, if—if he wanted to be friends with you, it wasn't the way to go about it."

"Wal Snyder must have known perfectly well that I'd never have had anything to do with him," exclaimed Ivy indignantly. The disclosure of that episode at the inquest had roused her to a pitch of anger she rarely displayed. "Besides, he's too much of a worm to do a thing like that. I'd like to see him hanged, just the same."

Ted tactfully disregarded this piece of feminine logic. "It must have been some lunatic, or perhaps, whoever it was mistook your father for someone else," he replied vaguely.

"And sent him that telephone message first," she struck in, with a touch of scorn. "No, poor Dad was murdered deliberately. Oh, Ted, if only I were a man, and could find out who did it!"

Ted, looking at her clenched hands and tear-filled eyes, felt suddenly the urge of a great resolve. "Ivy, if I were to find out who it was, would you marry me?" he exclaimed impulsively.

Her eyes dropped before his ardent gaze. "Perhaps," she murmured.

Their further conversation was interrupted by the stately rising of Mrs Tovey from her chair.

"Come along. Ivy," she said. "It's time we were getting along home."

Ivy rose obediently, as Mr Copperdock helped her mother into her cloak. "Ted'll see you home, Mrs Tovey," he said. "I don't like the thought of your being about the streets alone."

"That's very kind of you, Mr Copperdock," replied Mrs Tovey. "I really don't know what I should have done if it hadn't been for all your goodness. You'll come back to our place tomorrow and have a bit of something after the funeral?"

"I'd be very glad to, Mrs Tovey," said Mr Copperdock. He walked with them as far as the door of the shop, and stood there for a few seconds, until he lost sight of Mrs Tovey's ample form among the crowd. Then he walked slowly up the stairs, and flung himself into his own particular chair.

"I wonder if she suspects anything?" he muttered, with a reflective frown. "I'll have to go cautious-like, I can see that."

Mr Copperdock sat for a long time, motionless, his usually cheerful face furrowed in deep thought. He hated being alone at any time, but somehow this evening it was doubly distasteful. Ted was a long time coming back; no doubt Mrs Tovey, hospitable soul, had asked him to step in. It was no good stepping across to Elmer Ludgrove's; Thursday afternoon was that gentleman's busiest day of the week. The herbalist never closed on Thursday. His customers were for the most part people who were engaged in trade, and the weekly half-holiday was their only opportunity for consultations. Also it seemed a long time before it would be his usual hour for going to the Cambridge Arms. Mr Copperdock consoled himself with the thought that, as one who had actually attended the inquest, he would not lack an attentive audience.

In due course Ted came back, with a suppressed light of excitement in his eyes. He said very little until they had finished tea, and then, *à propos* of nothing in particular, he burst out with the subject which occupied his mind. "I say, Dad, I would like to find out who killed poor old Tovey!" he exclaimed.

Mr Copperdock glanced at him in astonishment. "Would you, my lad?" he replied sarcastically. "Think you're a sucking Sherlock Holmes, perhaps? You take it from me, if the police can't lay their hands on the chap, tain't likely you will."

Ted sighed heavily. In his heart of hearts he was of the same opinion himself. But the magnificence of the reward had blinded

31

him to the difficulties which lay in his path. In every thriller which he had ever read the hero had at least the fragment of a clue to work upon. But rack his brains as he would, Ted could not hit upon the faintest idea of how to set about looking for one.

His father continued to look at him with a not unkindly smile. "I dessay you think that Ivy would give a lot to know, eh?" he said, his native shrewdness carrying him straight to the point. "Well, I wouldn't be disheartened if I was you. Women's queer folk, and they often takes the will for the deed, as the saying is. But you stick to the tobacco trade, my boy, and don't go trying no detective tricks on your own, or you'll find yourself in trouble."

It was not until the following evening that Mr Copperdock had a chance of a word with Mr Ludgrove. The excitement engendered by Mr Tovey's funeral had kept him busy all the morning, and on his return from that ceremony he had found the herbalist's shop full of people. But as he was coming back from his evening visit to the Cambridge Arms, he overtook Mr Ludgrove, who was strolling with a leisurely air along the pavement of Praed Street.

They were glad to see one another. "I have been hoping for a chance of a chat with you ever since yesterday," said Mr Ludgrove. "Of course, I read the report of the inquest in the papers, but naturally I should be interested in a fuller description. As you see, I am on my way home from my usual evening stroll. Would you care to come in for a few minutes?"

Mr Copperdock laid his hand on his friend's arm. "No, no, you come over to my place," he replied hospitably. "Ted's sure to have a decent fire going, and there's a bottle of whisky in the cupboard. And it's rarely enough you find time to come and see me, and that's a fact."

Mr Ludgrove agreed, and for the second time the tobacconist went over the story of the inquest. His son listened attentively, not so much to his father's words as to the comments of the herbalist. He had great faith in Mr Ludgrove's wisdom, and he felt that at any time he might suggest some clue which could be followed up.

But Mr Ludgrove disappointed him. "It is really the most remarkable affair," he said as his friend came to the end of his recital. "I confess that I have puzzled over it more than once since last Monday morning. In fact, I have no doubt that I shall amuse myself by speculating upon it during the weekend."

"Going away?" asked Mr Copperdock incuriously.

Mr Ludgrove nodded. "I hope to catch the 12.35 from Liverpool Street tomorrow," he replied.

"Weed hunting, as usual?" said Mr Copperdock facetiously.

"If you like to call it so," answered Mr Ludgrove. "As you know, I employ most of my weekends looking for our rarer English plants. It has become the custom to sneer at the simple remedies of our ancestors, but I assure you that there are plants growing in the hedgerow, if one can only find them, which will cure almost any human complaint, and it is my favourite practice to seek for them."

Mr Copperdock shook his head. "Can't say as I should find much fun in it," he said. "Too lonely a business altogether. I likes to have someone to talk to when I'm on a holiday. And where might you be going this time?"

"A little place I know in Suffolk, not very far from Ipswich. Now why don't you come with me, Mr Copperdock? I shall stay at the inn, a most pleasant little place, and we could go out searching for plants together."

But Mr Copperdock was not to be tempted. "It's very good of you, I'm sure," he replied. "But, as a matter of fact, the country isn't very alive, leastways not at this time of the year. Perhaps I'll come with you some time in the summer, if you're going to stay at a decent little pub. Some of them country pubs ain't half bad if you're thirsty."

After a little further conversation Mr Ludgrove took his departure, and Mr Copperdock, after a final drink, retired to bed. But it is to be feared that his thoughts gave him very little rest. He almost regretted that he had not accepted Ludgrove's invitation. For it was being slowly borne in upon him that his agitation would drive him to confide in the wisdom of the herbalist. Ludgrove could be trusted not to give him away, and would certainly give him good advice.

CHAPTER 4 THE POISONED PIPE-STEM

Mr Ludgrove returned from Suffolk by a late train on Sunday night, burdened with a capacious suitcase, which he laid on the bench in the inner room. He made himself a cup of cocoa, and then proceeded leisurely to unpack the case.

It contained a carefully arranged mass of plants, which he laid out in rows, attaching to each a label upon which he scribbled its name. He was thus busily engaged, when he was interrupted by a loud knocking upon the door of the shop, which he had locked behind him.

The herbalist was not a man who allowed himself to be disturbed by trifles. He merely smiled and glanced at his plants, not a half of which were yet properly classified. Then he went towards the door. It had sometimes happened that one of his clients, in urgent need of his services, had hammered on the door during the hours when the shop was shut. Mr Ludgrove, if he happened to be within, made a point of answering these summonses. At any hour he was prepared to do what he could to relieve pain or anxiety.

The door opened, disclosing a short, stout figure upon the step. The rather austere lines of Mr Ludgrove's face widened into a smile of hospitable welcome.

"Come in, Mr Copperdock!" he exclaimed. "I haven't been back more than a few minutes, but there's a fire in the back room."

Mr Copperdock nodded. "Thanks, Ludgrove," he said, as he

came in. "I know you're just back, I saw you come in. And I thought to myself that this was a very good chance of having a few minutes' chat with you."

"I'm only too glad you came over," replied Mr Ludgrove, leading the way to the back room. "Bring that chair up closer to the fire. I've just made myself a cup of cocoa. Will you have one, too? the kettle's still boiling."

"Not for me, thank you kindly all the same," said Mr Copperdock. "Cocoa's not exactly in my line. A man of my age can't afford to put on weight, you know."

His eyes strayed towards a cupboard in the corner of the room, the door of which his host had already opened. From it appeared a bottle of whisky and a siphon, which were placed on the table within reach of Mr Copperdock's hand. At a gesture from Mr Ludgrove, the tobacconist poured himself out a drink and held it to his lips. It was noticeable that his hand trembled slightly as he did so.

For a minute or so Mr Copperdock sat silently in his chair, glancing nervously about the room. It was obvious that he had something on his mind, but could not find the words in which to unburden himself. His host, skilled in the art of encouraging the tongue-tied, appeared not to notice his confusion, and strolled over towards the bench upon which his harvest was laid out.

Mr Copperdock's eyes followed him. "Hullo, did you bring that lot back with you this time?" he enquired in a tone which he endeavoured to render conversational.

"Yes, they're rather a good collection," replied Mr Ludgrove. "There are one or two quite scarce plants among them, of which I have been anxious to secure specimens for a long time. I had a most enjoyable time. You ought to have come with me, Mr Copperdock."

"I wish I had, I'd have been saved a deal of worry," said Mr Copperdock fervently. Then, with scarcely a pause, he added, "Do you know old Ben Colburn?"

"The baker at the other end of the street?" replied Mr Ludgrove. "I always buy my bread at his shop, but I hardly know

Ben Colburn himself, I have seen his son Dick several times. Isn't Dick a friend of your lad's?"

For an instant Mr Copperdock made no reply. His face grew even redder than usual, and he picked with his fingers at the arms of his chair. Mr Ludgrove, recognising the symptoms, knew that at last he was approaching the point of this late visit. He walked across the room, sat down in the chair on the opposite side of the fire, and waited.

"Old Ben Colburn's dead," blurted out the tobacconist at last, as though the words had been torn from his lips.

Mr Ludgrove raised his eyebrows, "Indeed?" he murmured. "Rather a sudden end, surely? I was in the shop on Friday, talking to Dick, and he said nothing of his father being ill."

"No, he wouldn't," said Mr Copperdock grimly, "He wasn't taken ill until about two o'clock yesterday afternoon, and he was dead by tea-time."

"The usual story in such cases, I suppose?" suggested Mr Ludgrove. "A diseased heart, and a sudden attack ending fatally?"

"Worse than that," replied Mr Copperdock slowly. Then suddenly he raised his eyes and looked fixedly at his host. "What do you know about young Dick?" he asked.

It was the herbalist's turn to hesitate, "I might reply that I am a customer of his," he said at last. "It would be the truth, but not the whole truth. To you, I do not mind admitting in the strictest confidence that he has several times come to me for advice. You will forgive me if I am unable to tell you anything further."

Mr Copperdock nodded. It was well known that Mr Ludgrove had never divulged even a hint of the curious stories which had been told him in hesitating whispers in the privacy of this very room. It was the certain knowledge that this was so which gave so many of his clients the courage to confess to him their most secret troubles.

"Well, put it this way," said Mr Copperdock. "You know that young Dick and his father didn't hit it off quite, don't you?"

"I may as well confess to that knowledge, since neither of

them have made any secret of the fact," replied Mr Ludgrove.

"Old Ben was a bit of a character in his way," continued Mr Copperdock. "He used to drop in sometimes at the Cambridge Arms, and I got to know him quite well, in an off-hand sort of way. He had the idea that he was the only man in London who could bake bread, and he often used to tell me that he spent all day and half the night in the bakehouse. He said it was the finest one of its size anywhere, and he used to take me round and look at it sometimes. I couldn't see anything wonderful about it, but that don't matter. Ever been there yourself?"

"Never into the bakehouse. I have been into the shop at least twice a week for the last four years," replied Mr Ludgrove.

"Well, the bakehouse is away behind, you go up a long passage from the shop to get to it. Old Ben spent most of his time in the bakehouse, leaving the shop to the lad. But he was a suspicious old cove, and he always had it in his mind that Dick was trying to make a bit out of the business. Couldn't blame him if he had, the old man kept him short enough. But Dick hadn't much chance. There's a cash register in the shop, through which every penny of the takings has to pass."

Mr Ludgrove nodded. "I know, I've often noticed it," he agreed.

"Every afternoon between two and three, when he'd had his dinner, old Ben used to come into the shop and sit at the cash register, checking the takings. And he always smoked a pipe while he was doing it. Queer thing he never smoked in the bakehouse, only just this one pipe in the day. He would smoke it through, then refill it and put it on a shelf in the corner of the shop, ready for the next day. I suppose he done the same thing every day for a dozen years or more. Now, you remember that Friday was poor Jim Tovey's funeral?"

"I do," replied Mr Ludgrove. "You remember that I came in to see you that same evening."

"So you did. Well, while I was out, Old Ben comes round to my place to buy a pipe. He only kept one going at a time, and when the old one cracked he bought a new one. Always came to me for them, he did. Ted sold him one of the kind he always has, and out he goes.

"Mind you, this is what Ted tells me. The rest of the story Ted told me last night, after I got back from the Cambridge Arms. Seems young Dick had been in when I was over there and told him all about it. Old Ben goes back to his place, fills his new pipe, and puts it on the shelf ready for his usual smoke on Saturday afternoon. Dick swears nobody touched it in the meantime. The old man was very fussy about his pipe, and it was always left alone.

"On Saturday, yesterday, that is, Ben comes back from his dinner a little after two, and the first thing he does is to pick up his pipe and light it. All at once he takes it out of his mouth and cusses. Dick asks him what's the matter, and he says that the mouthpiece is rough and that he's scratched his tongue on it. They have a look at the pipe together, and the old man finds a tiny splinter of glass stuck to the mouthpiece. He scrapes it off with a knife, lights his pipe again, and Dick goes out to get his dinner, same as he always does when the old man comes into the shop."

Mr Copperdock paused, and the herbalist, who had been listening attentively, took the opportunity of putting in a question. "Mrs Colburn has been dead some little time, I believe?"

"Yes, ten years or more, if my memory serves me right. Dick and his father lived over the shop, with a charwoman to come in and do for them in the morning. When Dick comes back from his dinner, a little before three, the old man was still sitting at the cash register, and Dick sees at once that something is wrong. The old chap can hardly speak, says his tongue's very swollen, and that he feels stiff all over. Dick slips out sharp and gets a doctor, and between them they gets Ben upstairs to bed. Doctor, he did what he could, but it wasn't any use, and poor old Ben dies in two or three hours."

"What an extraordinary thing!" exclaimed Mr Ludgrove.

"That's what the doctor said. He wanted to find the bit of glass which had scratched old Ben's tongue, and he and Dick had a hunt for it, but it must have fallen on the floor of the shop. It was only a tiny piece, anyway. Of course they never found it, but the doctor says there must have been some extraordinary powerful poison on it, and I can't see how a bit of glass like that could get stuck on the mouthpiece of a pipe accidental like."

"Of course, nicotine acts as a poison if it is injected into the blood," suggested Mr Ludgrove. "It is just possible that the fragment of glass was harmless enough, but that the nicotine in the pipe found its way into the scratch." But Mr Copperdock shook his head. "It was a new pipe, what hadn't ever been smoked before," he replied. "Bought at my place the day before, as I told you."

"Did your son examine the pipe before he gave it to Mr Colburn?" asked Mr Ludgrove quickly.

"That's just what I asked him, and he says he can't be sure. Of course, he didn't see any glass or he'd have given old Ben another pipe. We gets them in dozens, each pipe twisted up in a bit of paper. Ted took the first that came out of the box, tore the paper off it, and handed it to Ben, who put it straight into his pocket. I've looked at the rest of the box since, and there's no sign of any glass on any of them."

"You say that Mr Colburn filled the pipe as soon as he got home, and put it in the usual place," said Mr Ludgrove slowly. "It was lying there until two o'clock on Saturday. Anybody might have tampered with it in the meanwhile. The cash register, and I suppose the shelf where the pipe was kept, is within easy reach of anybody coming into the shop."

"I'm afraid that won't work," replied Mr Copperdock, shaking his head, "There's not one in a thousand as goes into the shop that knows the pipe's there. You didn't yourself till I told you just now, yet you say you're a regular customer. No, if that pipe was tampered with, it was somebody on the other side of the counter what did it."

"Then you are quite convinced in your own mind that Mr Colburn was deliberately murdered?" suggested Mr Ludgrove. "But what motive could anybody have for desiring his death?"

"What motive had anybody for murdering poor old Jim Tovey last week?" retorted Mr Copperdock. "There's only one person who gains anything by Ben's death, and who that is you know as well as I do!"

"I can't help thinking that you are taking too grave a view of the case," said Mr Ludgrove. "I admit that it is difficult to account for a piece of poisoned glass finding its way on to Mr Colburn's pipe by accident, but murder is a very grave charge, and there is hardly sufficient evidence at the moment to warrant it."

Mr Copperdock braced himself in his chair as though to give himself the strength to utter his next words. "Ludgrove," he said impressively. "I *know* poor Ben Colburn was murdered, same as I know Jim Tovey was murdered. And it was the same hand as struck them both down."

Mr Ludgrove sank slowly back into his chair, and a faint smile twinkled for a moment at the corner of his lips. But before he could make any remark, Mr Copperdock, who had been watching him closely, continued.

"It's all very well for you to laugh, but neither you nor any other living soul knows what I do. Now just you listen, and see if I'm not right. Last Wednesday, I was in the Cambridge Arms in the evening, same as I almost always am. In comes old Ben Colburn, and comes straight over to me. He puts his hand in his pocket, and slaps an ordinary bone counter down on the table in front of me. 'Now then, Sam, what's the meaning of this little joke?' he says.

"I looks at the counter and I looks at him. 'What do you mean, what's the joke?' I says.

"'Why, didn't you send me this?' he says, suspicious like.

"I told him I hadn't, and then he says that it came to him by post that morning, wrapped up in a bit of blank paper. 'I made sure it was one of your jokes, Sam,' he says. I picked up the counter and looked at it. On one side it had the figure II drawn on it in red ink. 'What does it mean?' I said. 'That's just what I want to know,' says Ben. 'You shove it in your pocket, Sam, you're better at finding out that sort of thing than I am.' So I shoved it in

41

my pocket, and here it is."

Mr Ludgrove took the counter which the tobacconist handed him and looked at it curiously. It was just as Mr Copperdock had described it, a white bone counter, about the size of a halfpenny, with the Roman numeral II, carefully traced upon it in red ink.

"I never thought about it again, until this afternoon," continued Mr Copperdock. "Naturally I didn't connect it with Ben's death. Why should I? But today, being Sunday, I went round to see Mrs Tovey neighbour-like. You see, it was her first Sunday after Jim's death, and I thought that she and Ivy might get brooding over things."

Mr Copperdock looked anxiously at his friend as he spoke, but the expression on the herbalist's face was one of polite interest only. "Very thoughtful of you, I'm sure," he murmured. "I hope that Mrs Tovey is not taking her husband's death too much to heart."

"She's bearing up as well as can be expected," replied Mr Copperdock. "She and I got to talking about Jim, and wondering whoever it could have been that murdered him. She was telling me all about the telephone call, and she went on to say that this was the second queer thing that had happened just before he died. Naturally I asked her what the first was, and she told me that on the Friday morning before his death, a typewritten envelope came addressed to him. He opened it, and all there was inside was a white counter with the number I drawn on it in red ink. Now what do you make of that?"

Mr Ludgrove sat silent for a moment under his friend's triumphant gaze, a thoughtful frown upon his face. "This is most extraordinary," he said at last. "If your facts are correct—not that I doubt them for a moment, but I know how fatally easy it is to find presages after the event—it means that both Mr Tovey and Mr Colburn received, a couple of days or so before their respective deaths, a white counter bearing a numeral in red ink. It is almost certain that both counters were sent by the same person, and, if they were intended as a warning, we may infer, as you said, that both men were murdered by the same hand."

Mr Copperdock nodded rather impatiently. "Just what I told you all along," he said.

"But, my dear sir, look at the difficulties which that theory entails," objected Mr Ludgrove. "We are agreed that it is impossible to think of any motive for the murder of Mr Tovey, and I at least am inclined to say the same regarding the murder of Mr Colburn. Yet now we are faced with the problem of finding a man who had a motive for murdering both of them. By the way, do you happen to know if they were ever associated in any way?"

"Never!" replied Mr Copperdock emphatically. "Although they'd both lived in these parts most of their lives, I don't suppose they even knew one another by sight."

"The fact that they had nothing in common makes it all the more puzzling," said Mr Ludgrove reflectively. "But perhaps you have thought of a way out of the difficulty?"

A cloud came over Mr Copperdock's naturally cheerful face, and there was a marked hesitancy in his tone as he replied. "Aye, I have thought of something, and it's that that's been worrying me. Mind, I don't believe it myself, but I'm in mortal fear lest someone else should see it too."

"I think I can guess what you mean," said Mr Ludgrove gently. "I know as well as you do that it isn't true, but we're both of us too well aware of the mischief that can be caused by whispering tongues to treat it as unimportant. You mean that young Colburn was not on good terms with his father, that he and your son are great friends, and that your son sold Mr Colburn the pipe which is supposed to have been the agency of his death."

"I do mean that," replied Mr Copperdock deliberately. "I mean too that Ted is very sweet on Ivy Tovey, and that poor old Jim wasn't very keen on the idea. Now you see the sort of lying whispers that might get about if all this was known. And I'm blest if I see what I can do about it."

"I think you told me that you had some conversation with a Police Inspector last week on the subject of Mr Tovey's murder?" suggested Mr Ludgrove.

"That's right," replied Mr Copperdock. "Very decent sort of

chap he was, too. What about him?"

"Do you know where and how to get hold of him?"

"Yes, he left me his card. I've got it at home somewhere."

"Well, Mr Copperdock, if you will take my advice you will go and see him, and tell him everything you know, as you have just told me. It's all bound to come out, sooner or later, and if you have already informed the police, your position will be all the stronger. Don't you agree?"

"Yes, I suppose I do," replied Mr Copperdock reluctantly. "But it seems terrible, like giving evidence against my own flesh and blood."

"On the contrary, you will be doing the very best for your son. A frank statement of facts is always the best defence of the innocent. Tell your friend the Inspector everything, not forgetting the curious incident of the numbered discs. He will know better than I do what advice to give you in the matter. And, if you feel that I can be of the slightest assistance to you, do not hesitate to come to me at once."

After some further discussion Mr Copperdock agreed to follow his friend's advice, and, after a parting drink, went home, somewhat comforted. The herbalist, having locked the door behind him, returned to the interrupted classification of his plants. But, from the slight frown which passed across his face from time to time, one might have guessed that he was thinking more of his conversation with Mr Copperdock than of the specimens before him.

CHAPTER 5
INSPECTOR
WHYLAND

The death of Mr Colburn, following so closely upon that of Mr Tovey, caused a distinct sensation in Praed Street and its immediate neighbourhood. Suspicion was, so to speak, in the air, and anybody known to have been intimate with either of the dead men was looked at askance, and became the subject of whispered comment when their backs were turned. Not that this floating suspicion actually settled down upon any individual head. But Praed Street discovered an uneasy feeling that the two inexplicable deaths of which it had been the scene indicated that it harboured a murderer.

On the Wednesday morning following Mr Ludgrove's visit to Suffolk, a man walked into his shop and rapped upon the counter. The herbalist emerged from the back room at the summons, and, as was his habit, glanced gravely at his customer. He saw before him a youngish man, immaculately dressed, who immediately turned towards him interrogatively. "Mr Ludgrove?" he said.

The herbalist bowed. "That is my name," he replied. "Can I be of any service to you?"

The stranger placed a card upon the counter, with an apologetic gesture. "I'm Detective Inspector Whyland, attached to the F Division," he said. "And if you could spare me a few minutes, I should be very grateful. I'm awfully sorry to have to intrude in business hours."

"Oh, pray do not apologise, I am rarely very busy in the morning," replied Mr Ludgrove courteously. "Perhaps you would not mind coming through this door. We shall be able to talk more privately."

Inspector Whyland accepted the invitation, and sat down in the chair offered him. Mr Ludgrove having pressed him to smoke, sat down in the opposite chair, and looked at him inquiringly.

"I dare say that you can guess what I have come to talk about," began the Inspector, with a pleasant smile. "I may as well confess at once that I want your help. We policemen are not the supermen which some people think we ought to be, and most of us are only too anxious to ask for assistance wherever we are likely to get it. And I personally am under a debt of gratitude to you for persuading Mr Copperdock to unburden himself to me."

Mr Ludgrove smiled. "Oh, he told you, did he?" he replied. "It was much the best thing he could do. I hope he convinced you, as he certainly did me, that both he and his son were completely innocent of any knowledge of these queer happenings."

It was the Inspector's turn to smile. "He did. I don't think that Mr Copperdock is of the stuff of which deliberate murderers are made, and from what I have seen of the son, I fancy the same applies to him. But may I, since you appear to be pretty intimate with Mr Copperdock, ask you one or two questions about him? You needn't answer them unless you like."

"Most certainly I will answer them to the best of my ability," replied Mr Ludgrove gravely.

"Thank you. In the first place, can you suggest why he is so obviously confused when any reference is made to the Tovey family? I understand that his son and Tovey's daughter are —well, great friends, but that could hardly account for his manner."

Again Mr Ludgrove smiled, this time with genuine amusement. "My dear sir, haven't you guessed the reason? I did, some days ago. Mrs Tovey is, I believe, a very charming woman, and by no means too old to consider the possibility of marrying again. Mind you, Mr Copperdock is convinced that his secret is safely locked in his own breast, and I should forfeit his friendship if he had any inkling that I shared it."

Inspector Whyland laughed with an obvious air of relief. "Oh, that's the way the wind blows, is it?" he said. "You may rest assured that I shall be the soul of discretion. I had an uncomfortable feeling that he knew something that he did not care to tell me. Now, if I may trouble you with another question, what do you know of the relations between the Copperdocks and the Colburns?"

This time Mr Ludgrove shook his head. "Nothing at first hand," he replied, "only what Mr Copperdock has told me, which is doubtless the same as what he told you."

"You will forgive my pressing the point, Mr Ludgrove," persisted the Inspector. "But I gather from Mr Copperdock's remarks that you are to some extent in the confidence of young Colburn."

Mr Ludgrove looked him straight in the face. "Inspector Whyland," he said gravely, "I should like you fully to realise my position. Many of the inhabitants of this part of London believe, rightly or wrongly, that my experience of the world is greater than theirs. Consequently they frequently seek my advice upon the most personal and intimate matters. I have been the recipient of many confidences, which it has been my invariable rule never to mention to a third person. Dick Colburn has consulted me more than once, and it is only because I believe it to be in his interest that I am prepared to break my rule in his case."

"I fully appreciate your motives, Mr Ludgrove," replied the Inspector. "I will make no use of anything you care to tell me without your permission."

"Thank you, Inspector," said Mr Ludgrove simply. "Dick Colburn informed me some months ago that he found it very difficult to get on with his father. His chief complaint was that although he performed the whole work of the shop, his father treated him as though he were still a child, and refused to allow him any share of the profits of the business. I advised him to persuade his father to admit him into partnership, and if he proved obdurate, to announce his intention of seeking work elsewhere. I think it is only fair to add that the lad came to see me yesterday evening, in order to assure me that he had no share in his father's death."

Inspector Whyland shrugged his shoulders. "In spite of appearances I am inclined to believe him," he replied wearily. "Frankly, Mr Ludgrove, I am completely at a loss. As you know, the jury at the inquest on Mr Colburn returned an open verdict, but I think there can be very little doubt that he was deliberately murdered. We can rule out suicide, people don't take such elaborate steps to kill themselves. And the circumstances seem too remarkable to be accidental, which brings us back to Mr Copperdock and his remarkable story of the numbered discs. What do you make of that, Mr Ludgrove?"

"Very little, although I have puzzled over it a good deal, since I heard it," replied the herbalist. "Of course, it is possible that the receipt by Mr Colburn of the one you have doubtless seen had nothing whatever to do with his death, and that the combined imagination of Mr Copperdock and Mrs Tovey evolved the first out of something equally harmless. Mrs Tovey is the only person who claims to have seen it, I understand."

"And yet her accounts of it are remarkably consistent," said the Inspector. "I went to see her and introduced the subject as tactfully as I could. She described the incident in almost exactly the same words as Mr Copperdock used, and added that her husband, attaching no importance to it, threw counter, envelope and all into the fire. Her daughter, Ivy, was not present at the time. And yet, if we apply the obvious deduction to the sending of these numbered counters, what possible motive could anybody have for murdering two peaceful and elderly tradesmen, apparently strangers to one another, or, still more, for warning them first? It only adds another problem to this extraordinary business."

"Are you going to make the story of the numbered counters public?" asked Mr Ludgrove.

"One of my reasons for coming to see you was to ask you to say nothing about it," replied the Inspector. "We have decided that there is nothing to be gained by letting it be known. Bone counters of this size are very common, and we are not likely to learn where these particular ones originated. On the other hand, the minute the story becomes known, there will be an epidemic of counters bearing the number III in red ink. The Post Office will be overwhelmed by envelopes containing them, and every one of the recipients will come clamouring to us for protection. You may think this is an exaggeration. But you have no idea of the effect of crime upon some people's mentality."

Mr Ludgrove laughed softly. "I think I have," he replied. "I haven't been a sort of confidential adviser to the poorer classes all these years for nothing. Nearly everybody who has been in this room for the last week has had definite knowledge of the murderer of Mr Tovey, for which knowledge they seem to think it is my duty to pay a large sum of money. When I tell them to go to the police their enthusiasm evaporates with amazing rapidity. And since you people offered a reward for Wal Snyder's sailor, the whole neighbourhood appears to have seen him."

"So I imagine," said the Inspector. "There is usually a queue at the police station waiting to claim the reward. But what could we do? I confess I was very sceptical about the existence of this man; but I've bullied the wretched Wal half a dozen times, drunk and sober, and he sticks to the story. 'S'welp me, it's as true as I'm standing here,' he says, 'a big tall bloke, dressed like a sailor, with a black beard, an ugly gash on his cheek, and a woollen cap.' We had no option but to advertise for such a man."

"Well, I hope you'll find him, Inspector," remarked Mr Ludgrove. "But you'll forgive my saying that I have grave doubts about it. Even Mr Copperdock, who spends a large part of his time watching the people who pass his shop, has never seen anybody answering his description. And again I find it difficult to imagine a black-bearded sailor with a scar having a grudge against Mr Tovey. Besides, he doesn't sound the sort of person to deliver numbered counters in typewritten envelopes."

The Inspector rose from his chair with a smile. "It is a maxim of the police never to admit defeat," he said. "I am immensely obliged to you for your courtesy, Mr Ludgrove. Perhaps if you hear of anything which has any possible bearing on the case you will send for me?"

The herbalist willingly consenting to this, Inspector Whyland took his departure. He had scarcely been gone five minutes before Mr Ludgrove, who had returned to the back room, heard Mr Copperdock's voice in the shop.

"Come in, Mr Copperdock," called the herbalist genially.

The curtain was furtively drawn aside, and Mr Copperdock came in, a look of deep anxiety upon his face. "That was Inspector Whyland in here just now, wasn't it?" he inquired.

"It was," replied Mr Ludgrove. "We had quite a long chat." Then, with a sudden change of manner, he laid his hand on his friend's shoulder. "Look here, Mr Copperdock," he said earnestly, "get out of your head all idea that the police have any suspicions of you or your son. I can assure you that they have not, and that your straightforwardness in going to them and telling them all you know has impressed them greatly in your favour.

"Thank God for that!" exclaimed the tobacconist fervently. "I've been terrible worried these last few days. I've laid awake at nights and puzzled over it all again and again. I've even given up going to the Cambridge Arms of an evening. I sort of feel that the fellows there don't talk to me quite in the way they did."

"Oh, nonsense!" exclaimed Mr Ludgrove. "You mustn't let this prey on your mind. We all know as well as you do you have done nothing to reproach yourself with. Now I must ask you to excuse me, for I think I hear a customer in the shop."

As the days went by, and no further developments took place, Mr Copperdock's face regained its accustomed cheerfulness, and he resumed his visits to the Cambridge Arms. The newspapers found fresh sensations with which to fill their columns, and even Praed Street, in the stimulus to trade furnished by the approach of Christmas, began to forget the strange occurrences of which it had been the scene. Ted Copperdock developed a new smartness of appearance and carefulness of speech, no doubt the results of his frequent enjoyment of Ivy's company. It was only natural that on Sundays, when the young people were out at the Pictures, Mr Copperdock should walk over to Lisson Grove to console Mrs Tovey's loneliness. Only Mr Ludgrove, as he regretfully explained to his friends, found himself too busy to spend one of those weekends in the country which he so much enjoyed.

Indeed, it was not until the weekend before Christmas that he found an opportunity for leaving the shop for more than an hour or two at a time. He confided his intentions to Mr Copperdock on the Friday. "I have just heard that a plant of which I have long been in search is to be discovered in a spot not far from Wokingham," he said. "The nearest inn appears to be a village called Penderworth. I propose to go there tomorrow and spend the afternoon and Sunday searching for the herb. As I mean to come up by an early train on Monday, I have taken the liberty of telling Mrs Cooper, who comes in every week-day to tidy my place up, that I have left the key with you. I suppose that it is no use asking you to come with me?"

Mr Copperdock fidgeted uncomfortably. "Leave the key by all means," he replied heartily. "I'll look after it for you. Sorry I can't come with you, but you see about Christmas time I—we—there's a lot of folk comes to the shop and I can't very well leave Ted alone."

"I quite understand," said Mr Ludgrove, without a smile. "I shall leave Waterloo at 1.30 tomorrow, and reach that station again just before ten on Monday. If Mrs Cooper has finished before then, she will bring you back the key."

His arrangements thus made, the herbalist closed his shop at noon on Saturday, and, equipped with a suitcase which he always took with him, took the Tube to Waterloo station. On arrival at Wokingham, he hired a car to drive him to the Cross

Keys at Penderworth. It was after three o'clock when he arrived, and after securing a room, writing his name and address in the register, and arranging for some supper to be ready for him at half-past seven, he went out again immediately, a haversack slung over his shoulder, and an ordnance map in his hand.

It was after seven when he returned, his boots covered with mud, and his haversack bulging with a miscellaneous collection of plants. A fine drizzle had come on during the afternoon, and he was very wet. But trifles like these never dampened his spirits, and he made remarkable headway with the cold beef and pickles produced for his delectation. His meal over, he made his way to the smoking-room fire, and, spreading a newspaper on the table, began to examine the contents of his haversack.

The rain, which by this time was falling steadily, seemed to have kept the regular customers of the Cross Keys at home. The smoking-room was empty, but for Mr Ludgrove; and the landlord, after leaning idly against the bar at one end of the room, and staring inquisitively at his solitary guest, could restrain his curiosity no longer. Lifting the flap, he walked across the room, with the ostensible object of making up the fire.

Mr Ludgrove looked up at his approach. "Good evening," he said pleasantly.

"Good evening, sir," replied the landlord, glancing at the plants laid out on the newspaper. "You've been having a walk round the country this afternoon, then."

"Yes, and a very pleasant country it is for one of my interests," said Mr Ludgrove. "I have secured several very interesting specimens, and I hope to find others tomorrow."

"Ah!" exclaimed the landlord. "Flowers and that aren't much in my line. I've got a bit of garden, but it's mostly vegetables. Pity the rain came on like it did."

"Oh, I don't mind the rain," replied Mr Ludgrove. "Walking about the country as I do, I am compelled to take the weather as it comes. I can only get away from London during the weekends."

"I see you come from London by what you wrote in the book,"

said the landlord slowly. "It's Praed Street you lives in, isn't it?"

Mr Ludgrove smiled. The eagerness in the landlord's voice was very transparent. "Won't you sit down and have a drink with me?" he said. "Yes, I live in Praed Street. Perhaps you saw in the paper that we had some very unusual happenings there a few weeks ago."

"I did, sir, and it was seeing you came from there made me think of them," replied the landlord. He went back to the bar and got the drinks, which he brought to the fire. It immediately appeared that his interest in crime, as reported in the newspapers, was at least as keen as that of the late Mr Tovey. But never before had it been his fortune to meet one who had personally known the victims of two unsolved murders.

"It's a queer thing," he said, "but a couple of days or so before this Mr Tovey was murdered, I was polishing the glasses behind the bar in this very room, when I looked out of the window and sees a sailor, big chap he was, walking past. I didn't rightly catch sight of his face, but he was carrying a bag and going towards London. Looked as if he was on the tramp, I thought. I never thought about it again till I sees the police advertising for this sailor chap, then, of course, I tells the constable at the Police Station up the village. I never heard whether they traced him or not."

"You didn't notice if he had a black beard or a scar?" suggested Mr Ludgrove mildly.

"No, I didn't see his face," replied the landlord, with the air of a man brushing aside an irrelevant detail. "But that's just like the police. You give 'em a bit of valuable information, and they hardly ever says thank you for it."

The landlord, warming to his work, and finding Mr Ludgrove an excellent listener, developed theory after theory, each more far-fetched than the last. It was not until the clock pointed to closing time that he rose from his chair with evident reluctance. "You mark my words, there's more in it than meets the eye," he said darkly, as he leant over the table, "as my old dad, what kept this house afore I did, used to say, if there's anything you can't rightly understand, there's bound to be a woman in it. Look at the things what you sees in the papers every week. How do you know that these two poor chaps as were killed wasn't both running after the same woman? And if she was married couldn't 'er 'usband tell you something about why they was murdered? You think it over, sir, when you gets back to London."

And the landlord, nodding his head with an air of superlative wisdom, disappeared in the direction of the tap-room. By the time he returned, Mr Ludgrove had collected his belongings and retired to bed.

By the following morning the rain had ceased, and Mr Ludgrove was enabled to pursue his explorations in comfort. He went out directly after breakfast and returned to the Inn in time for lunch. In the afternoon he followed a different direction, arriving back shortly after dark. When he repaired to the smoking-room after supper, he found that his fame as a personal acquaintance of the murdered men had preceded him. Mr Ludgrove was before all things a student of human nature, and he seemed almost to enjoy taking part with the leading men of Penderworth in an interminable discussion of the unsolved crimes. Perhaps he reflected that the looker-on sees most of the game, and that these men, viewing the circumstances from a distance, might have hit upon some point in the evidence which had escaped the observers on the spot.

At all events, he went to bed on Sunday night with the remark that he had thoroughly enjoyed his visit to Penderworth. A car had been ordered to take him to Wokingham station early on Monday morning. His first act upon reaching the platform was to buy a paper and open it. Across the top of the centre page lay spread the ominous headline:

ANOTHER TRAGEDY IN PRAED STREET

CHAPTER 6 A MIDDLE-AGED POET

Mr Richard Pargent's public was a very limited one. A few lines of type, of unequal length, would appear from time to time in one of the ultra-artistic magazines, and would be hailed by critics of the new school as yet another deadly blow at the shackles which have hitherto fettered the feet of the muse of poetry. The general public found them incomprehensible, which was perhaps a fortunate circumstance for Mr Pargent's reputation.

But, in spite of Mr Pargent's extreme literary modernity, his surroundings and circumstances were typically mid-Victorian. His age was between fifty and sixty, and he lived with his sister Clara in a tall, narrow house in Bavaria Square, Bayswater. It was, as a matter of fact, the house in which he and his two sisters had been born. On their parents' death he and Miss Clara Pargent had elected to remain where they were and keep house together. Miss Margaret, younger and more adventurous, had taken unto herself a companion—of the female sex—and migrated to a house in the little town of West Laverhurst, in Wiltshire.

It will be gathered from this that the Pargent family were not dependent upon Mr Richard Pargent's literary earnings. Each member of it was comparatively well off, and lived according to the standards of mid-Victorian comfort. In their own phrase, they knew quite a number of nice people, and sometimes they found it difficult to make time in which to perform all their social duties. As a consequence, they had little opportunity left for doing anything useful.

Although many years had elapsed since Miss Margaret had shaken the dust of Bayswater off her feet and retired to the intellectual wilderness of West Laverhurst, her brother and sister had never completely recovered from the shock of such a revolutionary proceeding. Never before, within the memory of man, had any member of the Pargent family done anything but what was expected of them. And even now, when any of their friends asked after Miss Margaret, they replied with an almost imperceptible hesitation, with the apologetic smile we adopt when speaking of anyone who exhibits such remarkable eccentricity.

Not that Miss Margaret's departure had entirely broken the bonds which united the family. She and Miss Clara exchanged letters every day, although it must exceed the comprehension of ordinary mortals what they found to write about. Further than this, West Laverhurst was the object of a regular fortnightly pilgrimage on the part of Richard Pargent. Every other Saturday he caught the 10.45 at Paddington, which reached West Laverhurst at 12.25, giving him ample time to lunch with his sister and catch the 3.10 up, which deposited him at Paddington at 4.55. Miss Clara always had tea ready for him in the drawing-room in Bavaria Square. A No. 15 bus from Paddington took him almost to his door.

The Saturday before Christmas happened to be the occasion for one of these fortnightly visits. It was usual for Mr Pargent to walk the short half mile which separated West Laverhurst from his sister's house, but, the afternoon being wet and Mr Pargent very careful of his health, he asked Miss Margaret to requisition a car to drive him to the station. He arrived there in plenty of time, and in due course the 3.10 came in punctually. Mr Pargent took a corner seat in a first-class non-smoking carriage, and immediately became immersed in a book which he had brought with him for the purpose of reading in the train. He inwardly congratulated himself upon having secured a seat in an empty carriage.

The 3.10 up from West Laverhurst stops twice before reaching Reading, and then runs fast up to London. The stop at Reading is a somewhat long one, owing to the fact that tickets are collected there. On this particular afternoon, the train had run into the station a minute or two before time, and the stop was even longer than usual, giving a tall man in a rather tight-fitting overcoat ample time to walk leisurely the whole length of the train and select an empty first-class smoking carriage close to the engine. The train started at last, Mr Pargent being left in undisputed possession of his compartment.

The train arrived at Paddington punctually at five minutes to five. Mr Pargent had observed that the rain was falling more heavily than ever, but, from his long experience of Paddington Station, he knew how to reach the stopping place of the No. 15 bus, keeping under cover nearly all the way. He had only to follow the subway which leads to the Underground booking-office, and then climb the stairway which leads into Praed Street. The No. 15 bus stops nearly opposite on the further side of the street.

The passenger who had got in at Reading seemed to know his way about as well as did Mr Pargent. This man, who somehow vaguely suggested a retired ship's officer, had an iron-grey beard and a curious patch of crimson, such as is popularly known as a port-wine mark, on his left cheek. He walked slowly down the subway, so slowly that Mr Pargent overtook him before he reached the foot of the stairway. The two ascended it together, only a few steps separating them, Mr Pargent leading.

The mouth of the stairway was blocked, as it so often is in wet weather, by a knot of people unfurling their umbrellas and waiting for an interval in the traffic to dash across to the refuge in the middle of the road. Mr Pargent unfolded his umbrella like the rest, and seizing his opportunity, ran for the island. The interval was a narrow one; an almost unceasing stream of buses and taxis was pouring down Praed Street. Only two or three followed Mr Pargent's example, among them the Reading passenger. In the blinding rain and the flurry of the traffic nobody noticed a swift movement of the latter's arm, nor did they watch him as he left the refuge immediately and gained the far side of the road.

The clock above the entrance of the station showed it to be exactly five o'clock. The Reading passenger glanced at it, walked swiftly a few yards westward up Praed Street, then, seizing his opportunity, crossed the road again. This brought him to the slope leading to the departure platform of Paddington Station. He hurried through the booking office on to No. 1 platform, at which stood the 5.5 train for Bristol, which stops for the first time at Reading. He showed the ticket collector a third-class single ticket for Reading, and the man hastily opened a carriage door and pushed him in. "Near shave that, sir!" he remarked.

The passenger was far too short of breath to do anything but nod his head in reply. He sank down exhausted upon the seat as the guard blew his whistle and the train drew out of the station. There were only two men beside himself in the carriage, and they, with true British indifference, took no further notice of him. The train had nearly reached Reading when he walked down the corridor to the lavatory. He did not return to the carriage, but stepped straight from the corridor to the platform as the train came to rest. He mingled unnoticed with the stream passing the barrier. He noticed that the hands of the clock pointed to ten minutes to six.

Meanwhile Mr Pargent had stood for an instant upon the refuge in the middle of Praed Street, a puzzled expression on his face. An approaching taxi-driver noticed his swaying form and swerved sharply, just in time to avoid him as he crashed forward into the road-way. The taxi-driver's action caused a sudden check to the traffic, and for an instant there was a chaos of skidding vehicles, screeching brakes, and blasphemous language. Then the nearest drivers jumped from their seats and clustered round the prone form. A majestic policeman, setting a calm and undeviating course through the tumult, knelt down and turned the body over. Mr Pargent was dead.

The newspaper which Mr Ludgrove bought at Wokingham

Station and read carefully during the journey to Waterloo contained nothing more than a bare statement that the famous poet, Richard Pargent, had fallen dead in Praed Street, and that, upon the body being conveyed to the mortuary, a blade was found in it, with the point entering the heart. Round these facts a formidable structure of conjecture and reminiscence was built up. There was an obituary notice, in which Mr Pargent's Christian names and the titles of his published works were incorrectly stated. There was a résumé of the case of Mr Tovey, and a photograph of Praed Street, with heavy black crosses marking the places where the murders had taken place. Finally there was a leading article, in which the responsibility for the murders was ingeniously fixed upon the Government, which in consequence came in for severe criticism. In fact, the murder of Mr Pargent was evidently the topic of the day.

Mr Ludgrove sat with his haversack beside him on the carriage seat, even his beloved plants unheeded. He read every bit of the paper over and over again, seeking for some clue which might account for the crime. The description ended with the words "the police are, however, in possession of a clue, the nature of which they are not at present prepared to divulge, but which, they are confident, will lead to startling developments in the near future." Mr Ludgrove smiled rather cynically as he read them. They seemed to him to have a somewhat familiar ring.

He had the paper in his hand as he walked into Mr Copperdock's shop to get his key, and his friend caught sight of it. "So you've seen the news, then?" he said excitedly.

Mr Ludgrove nodded gravely. "I have been reading the account as I came up in the train," he replied.

"We didn't know a thing about it till eight o'clock on Saturday evening," continued Mr Copperdock eagerly. "I was just going across to the Cambridge Arms when Inspector Whyland came in and asked me casual-like what I'd been doing all the afternoon. As a matter of fact neither Ted nor I had hardly left the shop, and so I told him. It wasn't till then that he let on that three hours before a gentleman had been murdered not a hundred yards away, exactly the same as poor Tovey. Then I remembered that a customer had told me something about an accident outside Paddington Station, but, being busy, I hadn't taken any heed of it. And, that reminds me, the Inspector left a message for you, asking if you would let him know when you got back. I'll ring him up from here if you like, I've got his number."

"I wish you would, I have no telephone, as you know," replied Mr Ludgrove. "Has Mrs Cooper brought my key back yet?"

Mr Copperdock felt in his pocket and handed the herbalist a Yale key. "She brought it in ten minutes ago. She was terribly upset, and talked about our all being murdered in our beds next. It's a terrible thing to have happened just before Christmas like this. People will be afraid to go out of doors after dark."

Mr Ludgrove nodded rather absently, and took the key which his friend offered him. "You'll let Inspector Whyland know I'm back?" he said, and, without awaiting Mr Copperdock's reply, he left the shop, crossed the road, and entered his own premises, a thoughtful frown upon his face.

Inspector Whyland lost no time in acting upon Mr Copperdock's message. The murder of Mr Richard Pargent, following so soon upon that of Mr Tovey, and perpetrated by the same method, had made a great sensation, not only among the public, but, which was far more important to the Inspector, at Headquarters. He had been given a pretty direct hint that unless he could find some clue within the next few days, the case would be taken out of his hands and given to some more capable officer. All the machinery at the disposal of the police had been put into action, but so far without the slightest result. And in Inspector Whyland's despair it seemed to him that the only hope left of gaining any information was through the herbalist, with his peculiar inner knowledge of the inhabitants of the district.

He arrived to find Mr Ludgrove busily engaged in writing up descriptions of his botanical trophies in a large, manuscript book. The herbalist greeted him warmly, and invited him to a seat in the best chair. The two sat for a moment in silence, until the Inspector spoke abruptly.

"Look here, Mr Ludgrove, what do you know about this man who's been killed?"

"Richard Pargent?" replied the herbalist quietly. "I know nothing about him personally. I have seen his name mentioned once or twice as a writer of verse, but I doubt if I should have remembered it had it not been recalled to me by what I read in the papers this morning."

"Do you know anything about this poetry of his?" continued the Inspector.

Mr Ludgrove smiled. "I am no judge of poetry," he replied. "But I can hardly imagine that it was bad enough to inspire anyone with a desire to murder him."

Inspector Whyland shrugged his shoulders impatiently. "That's just it!" he exclaimed. "There doesn't seem to have been anything about the man to provide a motive for his murder. Look here, Mr Ludgrove, you're not the sort of man to go round spinning yarns to your friends. I'll make a bargain with you. You get to know all sorts of things that never come to our ears. Tell me your honest opinion about these murders, and I'll tell you what we've found out so far."

For a moment Mr Ludgrove made no reply. When at length he spoke it was with a deep note of earnestness in his voice. "I am honoured by your confidence, Inspector. As you have guessed, I have been very much concerned by these murders. I have feared that they would be traced to one or other of my clients, some of whom, I regret to say, have little respect for the law. I know much of the inner history of Praed Street and its neighbourhood, and I regret to say that much of it is almost incredibly sordid. I refer of course to its underworld, and not to its respectable inhabitants, who are greatly in the majority. But of two facts I can assure you. The first is that in all my experience I have never heard of a crime committed by any of the class to which I refer except for some specific purpose, either gain or revenge, and the second is that none of them would resort to murder except perhaps in a sudden access of passion."

The Inspector nodded. "That's very much my own experience

of regular crooks," he replied. "But you say you've thought a lot about this business. Haven't you any theory of your own?"

"The only theory I can form is that the murders are the work of some irresponsible maniac," said Mr Ludgrove quietly.

"Would an irresponsible maniac have put a piece of poisoned glass on the end of Colburn's pipe?" countered the Inspector quickly. "No, I am afraid that theory won't do, Mr Ludgrove."

"I think it is the only theory which fits in with the assumption that these three men were all murdered by the same hand," replied the herbalist.

"Yet I don't think you can get away from that assumption," said Inspector Whyland. "I don't mind telling you something that worries me a bit, since it's bound to come out at the inquest. One of the first things we found when we searched Pargent's pockets in the mortuary was this."

He put his hand in his pocket, then held it out with extended palm towards Mr Ludgrove.

The herbalist leant forward with an exclamation of surprise. "Ah, a white counter with the figure III drawn on it in red ink!" he exclaimed. "Do you know, Inspector, I wondered if anything of the kind had been found. That is really interesting."

"Interesting!" grumbled the Inspector. "Aye, the reporters will find it interesting enough, you may bet. We couldn't keep it dark, even if we wanted to. This fellow Pargent got it by post on Saturday morning. He told his sister, Miss Clara, that it must be a secret token from some admirer of his work. He was so pleased about it that he took it down to Penderworth to show his other sister. It was on his way back from there that he was killed. Oh yes, it's interesting enough. We shall have to say that Tovey and Colburn got counters like this, and then there'll be a fearful outcry against us for keeping it dark. 'Had the police not displayed this criminal reticence, the victim would have understood the purport of the warning and adequate measures could have been taken to protect him.' Oh yes, I know what's coming all right."

Inspector Whyland gazed savagely at the counter for a few

seconds, then continued abruptly.

"Fortunately the envelope in which this one came had been kept. The counter was wrapped up in a piece of cheap writing paper, and put in a square envelope of the same quality. The address was typewritten. Our people at the Yard are trying to trace the machine it was done with. I wish them joy of the job. They can tell the make all right; but there must be thousands of them scattered through London."

"If you don't mind my suggesting it, it doesn't follow that because Mr Pargent received a counter he was murdered by the same hand that killed Mr Povey or Mr Colburn," said the herbalist quietly.

Inspector Whyland glanced at him quickly. "No, it doesn't exactly follow," he agreed. "But we'll return to that later. I want to show you something else first. Look here."

This time he produced from his pocket a paper packet, which he proceeded to unroll. From it he withdrew two sinister-looking blades, each stained a dull brown.

"These are the knives with which Tovey and Pargent were killed," he said. "Don't touch them, but tell me if you can tell one from the other."

Mr Ludgrove adjusted his spectacles, and bent over the knives. They were exactly similar, thin, with an extremely sharp point, about half an inch wide and eight inches long. Neither of them showed any sign of having ever possessed a handle.

"No, I can see no difference between them," agreed Mr Ludgrove. "I admit that they strengthen the supposition that Mr Tovey and Mr Pargent died by the same hand. But, admitting that this was the case, it only bears out my theory that the murders were the actions of a maniac. If they were not, if both men were killed with some definite motive, you have to discover some connection between them. Yet they moved in entirely distinct orbits, and, I should imagine, had nothing whatever in common."

Inspector Whyland shook his head with a tolerant smile, "Theory's all very well in its way, Mr Ludgrove," he said, as he replaced the knives in his pocket. "I can't waste my time establishing connections. There's evidence enough here to convince a jury that the same man killed all three of them. And I don't fancy it'll be very long before I lay hands upon him."

"I sincerely hope your expectations will be realised, Inspector," replied the herbalist, in a tone of faint irony which was lost upon Whyland. "I suppose it is indiscreet to ask whether you have any suspicions? I confess that for my part I am entirely at a loss. What about young Snyder, for instance?"

"Master Wal Snyder is out of this," returned the Inspector shortly. "He was pinched a week ago for picking pockets in a tube lift, and is safely under lock and key. But I don't mind telling you in confidence, Mr Ludgrove, that I know the murderer lives somewhere in this district."

Mr Ludgrove lifted his eyebrows in real or assumed astonishment. "Indeed?" he exclaimed. "That is indeed a great step forward. Pray, how did you come to that conclusion?"

If the Inspector perceived the irony in his tone, he paid no heed to it. "Well, it's pretty obvious," he replied. "All three men were murdered in Praed Street, to begin with. Then, there's another thing. The envelope in which the counter was sent to Pargent bore the post-mark of this district, London, W2. You can't get away from it, everything points to the murderer living somewhere about here."

Again Inspector Whyland paused. Then suddenly he rose and stood over the herbalist where he sat in his chair. "There's another thing, Mr Ludgrove," he said, almost menacingly. "You said just now that it didn't follow that because Pargent received a counter he was killed by the same man that murdered the other two. Do you see where that leads you? If the third counter was sent by a different hand, it can only have been sent by one of the very few who knew of the receipt of the first two. And all of them live in this district, you will remember."

Mr Ludgrove gazed up at him in mock alarm. "They do, indeed," he replied. "It makes my blood run cold to think that I am one of them. Really, I am quite relieved to think that I have an alibi in the case of this last murder, at least."

Inspector Whyland laughed shortly. "Oh, for that matter, I'm as much under suspicion as you," he said. "But, you see, there are some people we know who couldn't produce an alibi for the time when any of the murders were committed."

And with that he turned abruptly on his heel and strode out of the room.

CHAPTER 7 THE BLACK SAILOR

That afternoon Inspector Whyland wrote in his report: "I had a long interview with Ludgrove. He is a shrewd fellow, and not easy to get anything out of. I am pretty sure that he has no definite knowledge on this matter, but he admits himself that some of his customers are not above petty crime, and it seems to me that he is the most likely man to hear any underground rumours that may be flying about.

"I managed to convey to him a pretty broad hint that I suspected one of his friends. I did this with a double motive. On the one hand, if he thinks that Copperdock or one of the others had anything to do with it, he will probably pass the hint on, and somebody may try to make a bolt for it, which would give them away. On the other hand, if he is convinced of their innocence, he will be all the more anxious to pass on to me any information he may get and which may tend to clear them. It is just a chance, but it may lead to something useful."

The Inspector's strategy was indeed that of forlorn hope. Rack his brains as he would, interrogate as he might everyone who could possibly throw light upon the murder of Richard Pargent, he found himself up against a stone wall. Nobody could swear to having seen and recognised the victim from the time he entered the train at West Laverhurst until he had been seen to stagger and fall on the refuge in Praed Street. The ticket collector at Reading was almost positive about him, but, as he explained, he saw so many passengers in the course of his day's work that he could not be sure of any particular one, unless there was something very remarkable about him or her. All he knew for sure was that if this was the gentleman, he was alone in the carriage when the train left Reading.

Nobody at Paddington had noticed him among the streams flowing from the arrival platforms, and it was impossible to establish whether or not he had left the station alone. The taxi-driver who had seen him fall had not seen the blow struck, could not even say whether anyone else had been standing on the refuge with him or not. It was a nasty, skiddy evening, and dark at that. He had enough to do to watch the traffic without worrying about people on refuges. It wasn't until he had seen the poor man stagger into the road almost under his front wheels that he had even noticed him. And then his attention was fully occupied in pulling up and trying to avoid collisions.

Finally, neither of the Miss Pargents could throw the faintest glimmer of light upon the affair. Their brother was not the type of man to have secrets from his family. Both sisters appeared to know the inner history of every moment of his life since infancy, and insisted upon dispensing the knowledge at great length. As to his having an enemy in the world, the thing was absurd. He was a very retiring man, who lived only for his work, and had never sought adventure beyond the narrow bounds of the family circle. Inspector Whyland came away from his last interview with the sisters—for Miss Margaret had been prevailed upon to come up to London—convinced that it would have been impossible for the dead man to have embarked upon any clandestine enterprise without the knowledge of one or other of them.

He was equally unsuccessful in finding any link between Richard Pargent and any of the inhabitants of Praed Street. Their names were utterly unfamiliar to either of the sisters, and Mr Pargent's only connection with Praed Street appeared to be that he occasionally passed along it in a bus. Inspector Whyland was convinced that the same hand that had struck down Mr Tovey, had killed Richard Pargent, and probably Mr Colburn, though the receipt of the counter was the only link in the latter case. But what could be the motive for the murder of these three men, so entirely disconnected from one another? And, if one adopted the theory of a homicidal maniac, the difficulty was scarcely diminished. Homicidal maniacs either kill indiscriminately, or, as in the classic case of Jack the Ripper, they attack a certain class or type. Yet the receipt of the numbered counters implied some process of definite selection. Upon what possible grounds could such a selection be based?

The inquest helped the authorities not at all. Nothing beyond what Inspector Whyland already knew was elicited, and the only fresh sensation which it provided was the disclosure of the fact that each of the three victims had received a numbered counter. Whyland's forecast of the results of this was proved to have been only slightly exaggerated. Most of the newspapers of the day following the inquest appeared with leading articles discussing the wisdom of official secrecy upon such a matter. A large number of practical jokers despatched counters bearing the number IV to their friends, many of whom arrived hot-foot at Scotland Yard demanding instant police protection. The fatal counter became for the moment a national symbol. The Opposition newspapers contained cartoons depicting the Prime Minister opening an envelope labelled "Public Opinion," and containing a numbered counter. An enterprising Insurance Company issued a poster upon which appeared an enormous representation of the counter, and under it the words, "You need not fear this if you are insured with the Gigantic." To find one in one's Christmas pudding was an omen of bad luck for the ensuing year. Then, having played its part as a nine days' wonder, the vogue of the numbered counter ceased as suddenly as it had begun.

Meanwhile, the police had been by no means idle. To Inspector Whyland it had always seemed that the focus of the whole business had lain in Mr Copperdock's shop. Mr Copperdock had been an intimate friend of Mr Tovey's; Ted Copperdock was on familiar terms with Dick Colburn. It had been through Mr Copperdock that he had first learnt of the receipt of the numbered counters; the pipe which had been responsible for Mr Colburn's death been bought at Mr Copperdock's shop. Inspector Whyland began to regard the three victims as represented by the extremities of the letter Y, which, although they are not connected to one another, are each connected to a central point. But, if Mr Copperdock was the central point, this graphic representation was incomplete until the connection between Richard Pargent and Mr Copperdock could be established. And, try as he would, Inspector Whyland could find absolutely no link between the two.

Nevertheless, Whyland determined to make a very thorough investigation into Mr Copperdock's habits and associates. He was rewarded by the discovery of two very interesting facts. A representative of Scotland Yard, announcing himself as an agent of the Planet Typewriter Company, the manufacturers of the machine owned by Mr Copperdock, and used by his son for writing business letters, called at the tobacconist's shop, ostensibly for the purpose of inspecting the machine. He succeeded in carrying away with him a specimen of its work, which was submitted to experts. They reported that, although there were no perceptible peculiarities in any of the letters which would enable them to identify this specimen with the address on the envelope sent to Richard Pargent, there was, on the other hand no discrepancy between the two types, and that therefore the envelope might well have been typed on Mr Copperdock's machine.

This, though disappointingly inconclusive, was to Whyland's ideas a point to be remembered should any corroborative evidence come to light. Among the circle in whose actions he found himself interested, the Copperdocks were the only people who possessed a typewriter at all. As a matter of fact, Mr Copperdock had only purchased it quite recently, at the instance of Ted, who while stoutly maintaining that no respectable tradesman could be without one, had been suspected by his shrewd father of less disinterested motives. Certainly it had seemed only natural that, the machine once purchased, the expert Ivy should come in of an evening and show Ted how to work it; but Mr Copperdock had a way of winking at his son behind her back which made that ingenuous youth blush most embarrassingly.

The second curious fact was discovered by Inspector Whyland almost by accident. In his study of Mr Copperdock and his associates, he had taken to frequenting the saloon bar of the Cambridge Arms, carefully choosing such times as Mr Copperdock was busy in the shop. There was nothing in any way suspicious about the Cambridge Arms; it lay in one of the streets which run southwards from Praed Street, and was consequently almost hidden in a backwater. Its remarkably cosy little saloon bar was patronised chiefly by the neighbouring small tradesmen, and its habitués were all well-known to the proprietor, with whom Whyland soon became on confidential terms.

A couple of days after the inquest on Richard Pargent, Whyland turned into the Cambridge Arms just as its doors were opened, at five o'clock. The proprietor met him with a smile, and, having executed his order, leant over the bar and entered into conversation.

"I never thought, when I opened up last Saturday, that that poor fellow was being murdered at that very minute," he began. "Just about five o'clock, wasn't it, sir?"

Whyland nodded. "The clock was striking five as they picked him up," he replied.

"I remember the evening well," continued the proprietor. "Though it wasn't until nigh upon seven that I heard anything about it. I says to my wife it was that wet and foggy that even our regulars wouldn't be in till later. But there you are, you never can tell. I hadn't opened this bar, not more than five minutes, when in comes one of my best customers, Sam Copperdock, the tobacconist. You may have met him here, sir?"

Whyland nodded non-committally, and the landlord

proceeded.

"I was a bit surprised to see him, sir, because Sam doesn't usually come along until eight, unless it happens to be Thursday, when he closes early. 'Hullo, Sam, you're on time tonight,' I says, jocular like. 'Oh, I've only come in for a drink,' he says; 'The bottle's empty at home, and I couldn't scrounge one from old Ludgrove opposite, he's away.' He has a double, and goes back to his shop. The bar was pretty nigh empty till about seven, when a fellow comes in and tells me about the murder."

Inspector Whyland deftly turned the conversation. He knew that if he questioned the man his suspicions would be aroused, and this he was anxious to avoid. Without any appearance of haste he finished his drink and left the premises. Once round the corner, he walked swiftly to the spot where Richard Pargent had been murdered, counting his paces as he went.

Could Mr Copperdock have committed the murder? It was quite possible. If he had left his shop a few minutes before five, he would have had plenty of time to reach the exit from Paddington station, plunge the knife into his victim, and be at the Cambridge Arms at five minutes past. But, if he were the criminal, a thousand puzzling questions presented themselves. How did he know that his victim would be arriving at Paddington at 4.55 that evening? Above all, why should Mr Copperdock, the tobacconist, have any grudge against Mr Pargent, the minor poet? And then again, Whyland was convinced that the murderer of Richard Pargent had been the murderer of James Tovey. But, at the moment when Tovey had been killed, Mr Copperdock was in his sitting-room with his son and the murdered man's daughter. The riddle appeared to be insoluble.

Whyland turned abruptly, boarded a bus, and took a ticket to Oxford Circus. Here he dismounted, and turned into the first picture-house which presented itself. He had discovered long ago that this was the surest way of securing freedom from interruption. Here for a couple of hours he sat motionless, neither seeing the pictures nor attentive to the strenuous efforts of the orchestra. And as he sat, a new theory slowly unfolded itself in his brain.

Samuel Copperdock, whom he had studied so carefully, did not appear to him to be a deliberate criminal. He was not of the type which harbours revenge, and he did not seem either clever or painstaking enough to work out the details of a premeditated murder. Although, if it were true that he had formed a design to marry Mrs Tovey, the murder of Mr Tovey might be said to be advantageous to him, it was inconceivable that he had had any hand in it. He could not have struck the blow himself, and, since he was not a rich man, it was difficult to see what inducement he could offer to a hired assassin. In all human probability, Mr Copperdock was innocent of the murder of James Tovey.

But, on the other hand, this murder, followed so closely by the mysterious death of his other acquaintance, Colburn, had made a great impression upon him. He had thought and talked of little else, and, as it happened, he had known every detail. He had seen the knife with which James Tovey had been killed; he, in common with very few others, had known of the receipt of the marked counters. Suppose that the crimes had had such a powerful effect upon his imagination that he had felt an irresistible impulse to imitate them? Such things were known, were in fact a commonplace of the criminal psychologists.

Upon this assumption, the rest was easy. Mr Copperdock had learnt by some accident that this man Richard Pargent would arrive at Paddington at 4.55 on Saturday, and had selected him as a likely victim. His imitative faculty fully developed, he had sent him the numbered counter, and had purchased a knife similar to the one which he had already seen. Then, just before the train was due, he had left his shop, met his victim, committed the crime, had a drink to steady his nerves, and then come home.

The theory was plausible, but Inspector Whyland knew well enough that so far he had not a fragment of real evidence with which to support it. But, unless he were to adopt the suggestion of Mr Ludgrove, that some homicidal maniac was responsible,

Whyland could see no alternative. The lack of motive was so extraordinarily puzzling. The murders had been utterly purposeless, and the only possible theory could be one which took full account of this fact. And then again, how account for the despatch of the numbered counters? If the murders had been inspired by irresponsible impulse, what had been their object?

Still deep in thought. Inspector Whyland left the picture-house and walked slowly back to the police station through the less frequented streets. It was a little past eight on a typical December evening, with a light wet mist which magnified the outlines of the passers-by and covered the pavements with a shining dampness. But the weather never had much effect upon Whyland, and, beyond a passing reflection that on such an evening murder in the streets of London was not, after all, an enterprise presenting any great difficulties to a determined man, he paid no great attention to it.

He reached the police station without adventure, ordered a modest supper, and sat down to deal with the mass of reports which awaited him. He was thus engaged when a sergeant entered the room, with the message that a man giving the name of Copperdock wished to speak to him on the telephone. He rose, walked to the instrument, and picked up the receiver. "Inspector Whyland speaking," he said coldly.

"Is that you, Inspector?" came an excited voice, which Whyland recognised at once. "Can you come and see me at once? I've something very important to tell you."

Whyland hesitated for a moment. Whatever it was that Mr Copperdock had to say to him, a visit to his house would afford him an excellent opportunity for keeping his eyes open for some clue in support of his theory. "Yes, I'll come along straight away," he replied. With a word to the sergeant, he left the station and walked rapidly to Praed Street.

It was about a quarter to ten when he arrived and rang the bell outside Mr Copperdock's shop. The tobacconist was obviously awaiting him, and the door was opened immediately. With a brief word of greeting, Mr Copperdock led the way upstairs to the sitting-room. Then, shutting the door carefully behind him, he turned dramatically, "I've seen that there black sailor!" he exclaimed in a hoarse whisper.

Inspector Whyland looked at him sharply. When the reward had originally been offered he had been overwhelmed by a flood of people who had claimed to have seen the "black sailor," but of late this elusive figure had ceased to occupy the popular imagination. Was this a vindication of his theory, showing that Mr Copperdock's brain was completely under the influence of the crime?

"You have seen the black sailor? Sit down and tell me all about it, Mr Copperdock," he replied gravely.

But Mr Copperdock was far too excited to sit down. "I see him plain as I see you now," he exclaimed. "Just after I left the Cambridge Arms——"

But Inspector Whyland put out his hand and forced him gently into the nearest chair. "Now, look here, Mr Copperdock, if your information is to be of any use to me, you must tell it to me in the proper order. Begin by telling me how you spent the evening."

"Soon as I shut up shop at eight o'clock, I goes off to the Cambridge, same as I always does," replied the tobacconist protestingly. "Ted went out too, he's taking Ivy to the pictures, and they won't be back for an hour or so yet. I has a couple there, sitting in front of the fire, and it wasn't until nigh on closing time that I left. There wasn't anybody there as was coming home my way, so I starts off home alone. And I hadn't gone more than a hundred yards when I runs slap into the black sailor!"

"What do you mean when you say you ran into him?" interrupted Whyland.

"Just what I says. I saw someone come round the corner, and before I could move we ran into one another. He was a great big fellow, and I could see him perfectly plain, we was right under the lamp. He bent down and looked straight at me, and you could have knocked me down with a feather. It was the black sailor, all right. He was muffled up in a great heavy coat, but I could see his beard, and his woollen cap, and a great red scar down the right side of his face. He glared at me as though he were going to hit me, and I hollered out, being sure he was going to do me in. Then all at once he turns his back and walks off at a tremendous pace. After a bit I follows him, hoping to meet a copper. But he suddenly turns in to the Edgware Road, and by the time I gets there I'd lost him."

"H'm," said Inspector Whyland. "That must have been nearly an hour ago now." He paused for a moment, then, realising that in Mr Copperdock's present excited state it would be impossible to get anything coherent out of him, he rose and took his leave.

"Well, good night, Mr Copperdock," he said abruptly. "It's a pity you didn't catch your man. I'd better get back to the station and warn my people to look out for him."

As he left the shop he noticed that Mr Ludgrove's door stood open, and as he crossed the road, the herbalist himself appeared in the entrance. "Good evening, Inspector," he said politely.

Obeying a sudden impulse, Whyland stopped and returned the greeting. "Good evening, Mr Ludgrove," he replied. "May I come in for a moment?"

"By all means, come along," replied the herbalist, leading the way into his sanctum. "I do not drink much myself, but perhaps you will take some refreshment yourself?"

He busied himself with a bottle and a glass, while the Inspector drew up a chair to the blazing fire. Then, when his host had seated himself, Whyland glanced at him with a slight smile playing about his lips.

"Our friend Mr Copperdock has seen the black sailor," he remarked.

"Seen the black sailor!" exclaimed the herbalist incredulously. "When and where—if I may ask?"

"Listen, and I'll tell you all about it," replied Whyland. "About an hour ago outside the Cambridge Arms."

Mr Ludgrove laughed softly at something in the tone of the Inspector's voice, then suddenly became serious.

"I do not think that I should place too great importance

upon this incident," he said. "Mr Copperdock is a most excellent person, and I have the greatest respect for him. But I have often suspected that his visits to the Cambridge Arms have—shall I say, a pernicious effect upon the accuracy of his observations."

"He seemed a bit excited, certainly," replied Whyland. "But he was quite positive that he had seen the man."

Mr Ludgrove shook his head. "Now, this is strictly between ourselves, Inspector," he said. "I make an invariable practice of taking a walk every evening, as soon as my clients give me the opportunity. This evening I went out soon after eight, and walked in the direction of Hyde Park. As it happened, I was returning past the Cambridge Arms, when I saw a figure which was unmistakably that of Mr Copperdock leave the entrance of that house. I hastened my steps to overtake him when suddenly he stopped, shouted, and after a moment or two, set off in the direction of Edgware Road. I could not imagine what was the matter, since but for us two the road was deserted as far as one could see for the mist. I was within twenty or thirty yards of him, and I certainly saw no black sailor."

It was Inspector Whyland's turn to smile significantly. "It does not altogether surprise me to learn that Mr Copperdock suffers from hallucinations," he said.

CHAPTER 8 AT NO. 407, PRAED STREET

Although the unexplained murders which had taken place in Praed Street were soon forgotten by the general public, their shadow hung heavily over the neighbourhood in which they had been committed. The fact that the three deaths had taken place within a comparatively few hundred yards of one another could not fail to have its effect upon the local imagination. A very noticeable change came over the usual cheerful and careless life of Praed Street. The evening pavements were no longer blocked by a strolling, noisy crowd. Women and children were rarely to be seen abroad after dark. Even men, traversing the street upon their lawful occasions, had a way of keeping close to the inner side of the pavements, and crossing the road upon the approach of any unfamiliar form.

Christmas passed in this atmosphere of intangible fear; the old year died and the new year came in with a welcome spell of clear and frosty weather. But, in spite of the fact that no further tragedies occurred, the shadow still lay heavily upon the district. Ludgrove, listening to the whispered and entangled stories of his clients, became more and more certain that, even in the hidden depths of the underworld, there was no knowledge of the agency by which the crimes had been committed.

Had such knowledge existed, it must inevitably have been divulged to him. The police, under the direction of Inspector Whyland, were engaged in passing a fine-toothed comb through the Paddington district, and the minor offenders disturbed in the process were as concerned as a colony of ants unearthed by a spade. Mr Ludgrove was visited furtively late at night by anxious people seeking advice how to conceal the evidence of their misdemeanours from the prying eyes of the police. He questioned each of these closely, but the more he did so the more he became convinced that none of them had the slightest inkling of the perpetrator of the murders.

Another section of his clients, however, equally furtive and mysterious, had clues in plenty, which they seemed to think entitled them to some reward. These, after assuring themselves that no one could overhear them, would produce an incoherent story of how one of their neighbours must be the criminal. He had been heard to utter threats that he would do some one in some day, he had been in Praed Street on the night when Mr Tovey was murdered, in the neighbourhood of Paddington station when Mr Pargent was killed. Others, again, had met a muffled figure brandishing a knife, or had seen a dark man with a beard standing in the shadow thrown by a projecting wall. Two or three searching questions were always sufficient to prove that their suspicions were baseless.

The murders in Praed Street were thus peculiar in the annals of crime. In nearly every case of a crime being committed, there are others besides the criminal who know all the facts. The police know this, but their great difficulty is to secure evidence sufficiently convincing to lead to a conviction. There is a certain *esprit de corps* in the constant strife between the professional criminal and the police, and those who know are careful to keep their knowledge to themselves. But in this case, had there been any of the inhabitants of the district in the secret, Mr Ludgrove would have obtained some hint of it. It seemed conclusive that the criminal was either working alone and independently, or came from some other district.

This was the state of affairs towards the end of January. The police were completely baffled; Inspector Whyland, although he still favoured the theory he had evolved in the picture-house, had failed to find any evidence upon which he could act. He hardly knew whether to attribute Mr Copperdock's story of his meeting with the black sailor to pure hallucination, or to an attempt to divert suspicion from himself. In either case, it could be made to fit in with the theory that he had murdered Richard Pargent under the influence of what the psychologists called an imitative complex. Whyland redoubled his activities, and a most accurate watch was kept upon Mr Copperdock's movements. A month had elapsed since the murder of Richard Pargent when Mr Jacob Martin, the prosperous wine merchant of the Barbican, opening his morning post in his comfortable office, came upon a typewritten envelope, marked "Private and Confidential." He ripped it open with the paper cutter which lay upon his desk, and unfolded the letter it contained. It also was typewritten, on plain paper. Only the signature "John Lacey" was in ink.

Mr Martin, a portly, grey-haired man of between fifty and sixty, read the letter through twice, with a gathering frown upon his face. He had prospered exceedingly since the day when he had first set up in business for himself as a wine merchant, so much so that his competitors wondered at his success. There had, from time to time, been rumours, quickly suppressed, to the effect that Mr Martin had other means of livelihood than his ostensible business. But Mr Martin was a remarkably astute man, and had hitherto managed to avoid undue inquisitiveness.

And now, like a bolt from the blue, came this extraordinary letter. Confound John Lacey, and his prying habits, whoever he might be. That little cellar under the back office! How well he remembered it. It had been the scene of many most profitable transactions, had harboured treasures for which the police of two continents had searched in vain. For Mr Martin was a receiver of stolen goods, not a mere general practitioner of the art, but a specialist whose services were utilised only by the aristocracy of thieves, and whose particular function was turning into cash only the most valuable jewellery.

With an exclamation of annoyance Mr Martin turned once more to the letter. "Dear Sir, I venture to address you upon a subject which will no doubt interest you," it ran. "I have recently acquired a lease of the premises No. 407, Praed Street, which, I understand, were in your occupation up till some fifteen years ago. Since you vacated them, these premises have been occupied by a clothier, who did not require the extensive cellarage, which was boarded up. In the course of certain alterations which I am having made to the premises, the entrance to the cellars has once again been opened. In the course of my investigations I have made a most interesting discovery in the small cellar beneath the back office.

"I should perhaps report this discovery to the authorities, but I have thought it best to consult you upon the matter before doing so. This letter should reach you by the first post tomorrow (Saturday) morning. I should be glad if you could make it convenient to meet me on the premises at 2 p.m. that day, when the workmen who are at present employed there will have gone. I can then show you my discovery, and we can consult upon the most suitable steps to be taken in the matter. Should you not find this convenient, I shall assume that the subject does not interest you, and shall report the matter forthwith to the police. Yours faithfully, John Lacey."

A blackmailing letter, without a doubt, Mr Martin could see that at a glance. But what on earth could the fellow have discovered? Fifteen years ago, when Mr Martin moved from Praed Street to the Barbican, he had taken the utmost care to destroy every trace of the purpose to which that little cellar had been put. He racked his brains to try and think of anything that could possibly have been overlooked, but without success. Even those ingeniously contrived recesses in the walls had been torn out, leaving nothing but the bare brick. Mr Martin had done the work with his own hands, not caring to trust anyone else with so delicate a matter. Yet, after all, in spite of all his care, he must have left some clue, which this infernal fellow Lacey had somehow blundered upon.

He brushed aside as absurd the suggestion that "Lacey" could conceal the identity of one of those with whom he had done business, who knew the secret of the cellar and had adopted this clumsy plan to blackmail him. The circle of his secret clients was a very narrow one; he knew them all and was well aware that blackmail was neither in their line nor in their interest. The expert in acquiring jewellery concentrated upon his particular art; he did not descend to blackmail, especially of the one man through whose agency he was able to dispose of his spoil. No, there was no doubt about it, a slip had been made, a slip which had lain undiscovered all these years, through the circumstance that his successor, the clothier, had found no use for the cellars and had boarded up the entrance to them.

There was nothing for it but to carry out the suggestion contained in the letter, and meet the man in Praed Street at two o'clock. He must find out the nature of this mysterious discovery and take steps to ensure that all evidence of it be securely destroyed. Lacey, of course, would demand some compensation for holding his tongue. The sum he demanded would depend upon the importance of what he had found. Well, they would discuss terms, alone in that empty house, in the very cellar which Mr Martin remembered so well.

Mr Martin stroked his chin reflectively. What sort of fellow was this Lacey, he wondered? He himself was a powerful man, proud of his own powers of intimidation. It ought to be simple enough for him to destroy the evidence first, then to tell Lacey to go to the devil and do his worst. He unlocked a drawer of his desk and drew from it a small automatic pistol, which he slipped into his pocket. It was with a smile that he remembered that Praed Street had recently acquired a sinister reputation. Well, if any accident should happen——

Mr Martin's office closed at one o'clock on Saturdays. He left a few minutes before that hour, having put John Lacey's letter in his pocket and examined the mechanism of his automatic. Then he consumed a hasty lunch at a chop-house near-by, and walked down the street to Aldersgate Metropolitan station, where he took a ticket to Paddington. He emerged into Praed Street at about five minutes to two, and began to walk along that thoroughfare in the direction of Number 407.

Praed Street, at this time on a fine afternoon, wore its usual air of busy activity. The exodus from central London was still at its height, the crowds still passed along in bus or taxi towards the portals of Paddington station. On the other hand, the inhabitants of the neighbourhood, released from work, were beginning their weekend shopping. The pavement was crowded, and Mr Martin, who had some distance to walk to his destination, looked about him curiously. Since he had put up his shutters for the last time, fifteen years ago, he had rarely revisited Praed Street, and even then he had only traversed it in a taxi, going to or from Paddington. The street had changed a little since he had been an inhabitant of it. Certainly there were fresh names over many of the shops, and here and there there had been alterations to the buildings he remembered. He glanced at a board on the opposite side of the street. Elmer Ludgrove. That was new since his day. The rather musty-looking shop was conspicuous among its neighbours by being closed. Praed Street, as a rule, does most of its business on Saturday afternoon.

Mr Martin walked on a step or two, then hesitated for an instant. So Sam Copperdock, from whom he bought his cigarettes in those early days, was still here. Mr Martin had long ago abandoned cigarettes for cigars, but he felt a momentary impulse to go in and renew the old acquaintance. Sam Copperdock had been a good customer of his, he remembered. Many a bottle of whisky had he sold him. But on second thoughts he refrained. Perhaps it would be just as well, in the light of what might happen during the next half hour or so, that his visit to Praed Street remained unsuspected.

Mr Martin walked on, and in a few minutes found himself outside Number 407. It was much as he remembered it, but that it was lying empty, and showed signs of being refitted for a new tenant. The windows were almost obscured with patches of whitewash, but peering through them he could see trestles, timber, shavings, all the litter which betrays the presence of the carpenter. So far, then, the letter was correct. Mr Martin, after a furtive glance round about him, walked up to the door and tried it. It was locked.

He drew out his watch and consulted it. It was nearly five minutes past two, but he remembered that he had noticed that morning that it was a trifle fast. Lacey, whoever he was, would doubtless be along in a moment. Mr Martin hoped he would be quick; he had no wish to be recognised outside the premises by any of his old acquaintances. A sudden thought struck him. Perhaps Lacey was already inside, waiting for him. There was an electric bellpush by the side of the door. Mr Martin pressed it firmly, but could hear no answering ring above the roar of the traffic. Then all at once he became aware that a small girl was standing by his side, looking up at him with an appraising expression.

As he turned to look at her, she made up her mind and spoke. "Is your name Mr Martin?" she asked.

Mr Martin frowned down at her. "What's that got to do with you?" he replied.

"'Cos if you are, Dad told me to give you the key," she continued, quite unabashed. "And there's a message from Mr Lacey that you're to go in and wait for him, as he'll be a few minutes late."

"Oh, I see," said Mr Martin with a smile. "Yes, my dear, I am Mr Martin. How did your father come to have the key?"

She jerked her head towards a sweetshop two or three doors away. "We lives there," she replied curtly. "Mr Briggs the builder, what's working here, leaves it with us because he's my uncle. His men come and get it in the morning. And Mr Lacey, him what's coming here, telephoned just now to say you was coming to see the drains and I was to give you the key."

"Oh yes, that's right," said Mr Martin, completely reassured. "Thank you, my dear. I'll see that either Mr Lacey or myself brings you back the key so that your uncle's men may get in on Monday morning. That's the shop, there, isn't it?"

He waited until the child had disappeared into the shop, then opened the door of Number 407 with the key which she had given him, walked in and closed the door behind him. Here, he paused for a moment, thinking rapidly. He felt that he was up against a brain as agile as his own, and that the coming interview would demand all his skill if he were to bring it to a favourable issue. This man Lacey had taken steps to advertise the fact that Mr Martin had entered the premises, obviously as a precaution against foul play. His automatic would be no use to him, he would have to rely upon his brains instead.

Then suddenly it flashed upon him that he had been given a very fortunate opportunity. It was not to be supposed that Lacey had left his discovery, whatever it was, lying about the cellar in full view of the workmen who had been there that morning. But, if he could have a quiet look round by himself, he might gain some clue to the nature of the discovery, and so be prepared to meet Lacey when he arrived.

Mr Martin was not anxious for Lacey to come upon him unawares while he was searching the cellar. Fortunately, the possibility of such an event could easily be guarded against. He bolted the door top and bottom, and noticed with satisfaction that the bolts were brand new, evidently part of the alterations which the new tenant was making to the premises. Then, after glancing round the ground floor, and making sure that nobody was hidden there, he made his way to the top of the stairway which led down to the cellars. The upper part of the house had no connection with the shop, and was approached by a separate entrance.

He saw at once that the letter had been correct as to the alterations being made. During his tenancy the cellars had been lighted by gas, but now electric light was being installed throughout. Mr Martin could see the run of the wires and the fittings for the lamps, but he noticed that the lamps themselves had not yet been inserted. This fact did not worry him. He had a box full of matches in his pocket, and one of these he lit as he cautiously descended the stairs. The builders' litter was here, as everywhere, and he picked his way among it until he stood in the main vault below the shop. It smelt close and musty, as though it had only recently been opened up after a long period of disuse. Mr Martin, holding a lighted match above his head, glanced rapidly round. Nothing had been altered here since he remembered it, except that a new brass switch stood behind the door, and two empty lamp sockets projected downwards from the ceiling.

The way to the little cellar below the back office lay along a narrow passage, and this Mr Martin followed, striking a fresh match as he went. Every detail came back to him, as though he had last passed this way yesterday, instead of fifteen years ago. The door of the little cellar closed with a spring; as he pushed it open the spring creaked with a note which he remembered so well, and the door closed behind him with the same muffled bang. Again he raised his match and looked around him anxiously. The cellar appeared to be the same as he had left it, even to a mildewed packing case against the wall, which had sometimes been used as a table. Only here, as in the larger cellar, the electricians had been at work. There was a lamp holder on the ceiling, but this time it held a lamp. It was evidently by the light of this lamp that Lacey had made his discovery. There was no reason why he should not use it too.

The match had burnt down very near his fingers, but as he dropped it he caught sight of the switch. Without troubling to light another match he groped his way towards it and turned it on. There was a flash and a sharp report, but the cellar remained in complete darkness. Mr Martin, with a gasp, leapt for the door in sudden panic. Someone hidden in the cellar must have fired at him. Then, after a moment, the absurdity of the idea forced itself upon him. The report had not been nearly loud enough for a pistol, and the cellar was far too small to conceal anybody. With a short laugh, but with trembling fingers, he felt for his matchbox and struck a light.

Then at once he saw what had happened. The globe had burst as he turned on the current, and only the butt remained in the holder. He turned to look at the switch, and then for the first time he noticed that something white was hanging from it by a string. He bent down and held his match close to it. It was a white counter, bearing the figure IV in red ink.

With a sudden access of fear he clutched at it, in order to examine it more closely. The string broke, and he stared at the counter in his hand, fascinated. He began to realise his position. He had been lured to this empty house, and the assassin was no doubt even now in the passage outside, waiting to plunge his deadly knife into him as he emerged. Thank heaven, he had brought his automatic with him!

Mr Martin was no coward. His plan of defence was quickly made. Throwing the match away, he took his stand on the far side of the cellar, facing the door, his automatic in his hand. If his assailant came in, he would hear the creak of the spring, and could fire before the man could reach him.

For a second or two he waited, tense and with ears strained for the slightest sound. It was very quiet in the cellar; the rumble of the traffic in Praed Street came to him but faintly. Then, all at once, he caught his breath as a pungent and unfamiliar smell reached him. Suddenly he found himself choking, dizzy, his senses leaving him. An overpowering impulse to escape from the cellar swept through him, drowning his fear of what might be awaiting him outside. He staggered towards the door, his hands clawing wildly over its damp surface. There used to be a string by which one pulled it open, but Mr Martin could not find it. Vainly he strove against the awful numbness which closed in upon him. He must find the string, must——

With a crash Mr Martin fell down at the foot of the door. The little cellar resumed its accustomed silence.

CHAPTER 9 A STRANGE AFFAIR

It was not until shortly after eight o'clock on Monday morning that Inspector Whyland, who had arrived early at the police station, received the startling intelligence that there was a dead man lying in the cellar of Number 407, Praed Street. He immediately jumped into a taxi, and was met on the doorway of the empty house by a man who introduced himself as Mr Houlder, the builder who was carrying out certain alterations for the new tenant, Mr Lacey.

"My men found him when they came in this morning," he said. "They telephoned to me and I told them to fetch a policeman. He rang you up, I understand. I think I can explain how the man got in, and who he is."

"Thanks very much, Mr Houlder," replied Whyland. "I think we'll have a look at him first, if you don't mind. Will you lead the way?"

They descended to the cellar together, Mr Houlder leading the way with an electric torch. As they arrived at the passage leading to the small cellar, a constable appeared and saluted.

"Ah, you're in charge here, I suppose?" said the Inspector. "You haven't touched anything, I hope?"

"Not since I've been here, sir, but I understand that the body was moved accidentally before I came. I've got the man who found him here, sir."

A man, who had been hidden in the gloom behind the

policeman, came forward at this. He explained that he was the electrician who had been wiring the cellars. He had very nearly finished the job on the previous Saturday, and had left about noon. The carpenters were still working on the ground floor when he left. He returned just before eight this very morning, found the carpenters already at work, and went down to the cellars to put the finishing touches to the job. The door of the small cellar appeared to be jammed, and he pushed against it to open it. When he had got it open far enough to squeeze through, he found the body of a man lying against it. He had immediately run upstairs and told the foreman, and had waited there till the constable came and asked him to show him the body.

Inspector Whyland dismissed Mr Houlder and the electricians, and went on into the cellar with the constable. "There's something queer about this business, sir," said the latter, as soon as they were alone. "I had a look round while I was waiting for you, and the first thing I saw was one of them white counters, same as the others had. There it lies, sir, I didn't touch it."

They were in the cellar by now, and Whyland glanced at the counter, lying in the beam of light which the constable had thrown upon it. "With the figure IV on it, I'll wager," he muttered. "Yes, I thought so. We'll try for finger marks, but I'll bet it's no good. Now, let's have a look at this dead man."

The constable turned his lamp on the prostrate form, and Whyland knelt down and gazed at it intently. The body was lying doubled up as it had fallen, and was quite cold.

"H'm," said Whyland, rising to his feet. "We can't do much more till the doctor comes. You don't know who he is, I suppose?"

"Mr Houlder said he believed his name was Martin, sir," replied the constable cautiously.

"Well, you stay here till the doctor comes. I'll go and have a chat with Houlder. Just throw your light over the floor for a minute. Hullo, what's this?"

He strode across the cellar and carefully picked up a small

automatic. "Hasn't been fired," he muttered. "Now I wonder who that belongs to? Just see if you can spot anything else. Don't touch it, if you do."

He went upstairs again, and drew Mr Houlder aside into a quiet corner. Mr Houlder's story was a very simple one. His foreman had orders to leave the key of the house with Mr Briggs, the confectioner, three doors off. Mr Briggs was Houlder's brother-in-law. The reason for this arrangement was that whoever came on the scene first could get the key and start work. On Saturday the key had been left as usual, about 12.30.

On Saturday morning, about nine o'clock, Mr Briggs had come to his place and told him that Mr Lacey, who knew about the key arrangement, had rung him up to say that a Mr Martin was coming to inspect the drains. Mr Lacey was to have met him at two o'clock, but would be delayed. Would Mr Briggs keep a look out for him and give him the keys. Mr Briggs had promised to do so, and his daughter Marjorie had seen Mr Martin, who had promised to bring back the keys, but had not done so. Mr Briggs had forgotten all about them until the evening, and then, finding that the door of Number 407 was securely locked, had supposed that Mr Martin had gone away with the keys in his pocket. Mr Houlder had agreed with this theory, and had given Mr Briggs a duplicate key which he happened to have.

The foreman had called on Mr Briggs, and had been given the duplicate key. But when he came to try the door, it would not open. He made several attempts, but, finding them unavailing, desisted and made his way in through a window at the back. He then discovered that the door was bolted on the inside, a circumstance which puzzled him tremendously. Shortly afterwards the electrician arrived, and his thoughts were diverted into other channels.

Inspector Whyland spent a few minutes talking to the foreman, who confirmed the latter part of Houlder's story, and had barely finished his enquiries when the doctor arrived. The two went down to the cellar together, and the doctor, without wasting words, proceeded to examine the body, Whyland watching him intently.

"Poisoned!" pronounced the doctor, after a short interval. "Prussic acid, by all the signs of it, but I can't be sure till I've made a post-mortem. You'll have him taken to the mortuary, of course? Queer place to choose for suicide. How did he get in here?"

Inspector Whyland shook his head. "I don't think it's a case of suicide, doctor. Look here!"

He pointed to the numbered counter. The doctor glanced at it and sniffed contemptuously. "You fellows have got counters on the brain since that business last month," he said. "How do you know he didn't put it there himself to throw you off the scent? It's not uncommon for suicides to try and make their deaths look like murder. You'll find there's some question of insurance behind it. Well, I'll be along at the mortuary and let you know the result of the PM."

The doctor bustled away, and Whyland, having made arrangements for the removal of the body, made a very careful examination of the cellar. This done, he sent the constable for the electrician, and asked him to look round and see if he could find anything which had not been there when he left on Saturday.

The man looked about him carefully, and suddenly pointed to the ceiling with an exclamation of astonishment. "Why, there's the butt of a broken lamp in that holder, sir," he said. "I didn't put no lamps in before I left. That's one of the things I came here to do today."

"Well, take it out and put in a fresh lamp," replied Whyland. "I didn't know the current was on. We'll be able to see what we're doing."

The electrician obeyed him, and no sooner had he put the new lamp in the holder than the cellar was flooded with light. "Hullo!" he exclaimed. "The switch is on. I'll swear I left it off on Saturday. Why, that's queer! This isn't the butt of an ordinary lamp at all. Looks to me more like one of them electric detonator things, made to go into a lamp-socket. And it's gone off, too. You can see where it's blackened, sir."

"Was the current on on Saturday?" asked Whyland, quickly.

"Yes, sir, I connected up in the morning," replied the electrician. "Somebody must have put that thing in the lamp-holder, then turned the switch on. Well, that's a rum go, and no mistake."

Whyland, having cautioned the man to say nothing until the inquest, left the house and walked into the confectioner's shop. Here he interviewed Mr Briggs and his daughter, Marjorie, and obtained from them the story of Mr Martin's arrival at Number 407, and of the telephone message from Mr Lacey. By this time the body had been conveyed to the mortuary, and Whyland set to work to examine the contents of the dead man's pockets. His most interesting discoveries were the letter which he had received on Saturday morning and the missing key of Number 407.

The doctor arrived and performed his post-mortem, which confirmed the suspicions he had already formed. "Prussic acid, right enough, and a pretty powerful dose by the look of it. The queer thing about it is that he seems to have died from breathing the vapour rather than from swallowing the stuff. Looks as if he'd uncorked a bottle of the strong acid and sniffed at it. You didn't see anything of the kind lying about the cellar, I suppose?"

Whyland shook his head. "No, I didn't," he replied. "The only thing I found lying about was a loaded automatic which hadn't been fired."

"What did I tell you?" said the doctor triumphantly. "Suicide, without a doubt. He took a pistol with him in case the stuff didn't act. You're suggesting that anybody murdered a powerful man like that by making him inhale prussic acid against his will, are you? Why, the idea's absurd."

Inspector Whyland left the mortuary in a very thoughtful frame of mind, and returned to the police station. Here he set the telephone to work and invoked the aid of his colleagues. By the middle of the afternoon he had collected some interesting information respecting both Martin and Lacey, upon which he began to build up his own theory as to the former's death.

Mr Martin had carried on a wine merchant's business at 407, Praed Street, until fifteen years before. He had then moved to the Barbican, where he employed two clerks and a couple of packers. He had never married, and lived at a boarding house in Streatham. He had more than once gone away for the weekend without notice, and his absence had therefore caused no concern. He was not known to have any enemies, although more than once there had been some unsavoury rumours in circulation as to his dealings with girls whom he had engaged as his secretaries. His movements on Saturday morning were traced from the time he left his office to his reaching Aldersgate station. Finally, as a result of the hint contained in the letter signed John Lacey, the police had searched his office, and had found there certain papers which threw a flood of light upon a long sequence of jewel robberies extending back for the last twenty years.

Mr Lacey was the owner of a group of grocer's shops scattered about West London. He had acquired the lease of Number 407, when the premises were given up by the late tenant, a clothier. He had never heard of Mr Martin, and had certainly never written to him. He always signed himself John R. Lacey, and the signature on the letter found on Mr Martin's body bore no resemblance whatever to his handwriting. He had only once entered the cellars of Number 407, and had made no discoveries there of any kind. On Saturday he had left Liverpool Street at ten o'clock, to stay with his brother in Ipswich, and had not returned until the first train on Monday morning. He had sent no telephone message to Mr Briggs, nor had he made any appointment with anybody to inspect the drains of Number 407. He had no key of the premises, having given the only two which so far as he knew existed, to Houlder, the builder. He was utterly unable to throw any light whatever upon the incident, since more than a week had passed since he had visited Praed Street.

Two other facts did Inspector Whyland discover. The first, which did not astonish him, was that the letter signed John

Lacey had in all probability been typed upon the same machine as had been the envelope in which the numbered counter had been sent to Richard Pargent. The second, which was distinctly perplexing, was that the call to Mr Briggs had been made from a call-box at Aldersgate station, apparently at the very time when Mr Martin was known to have been there. Lastly, the automatic was identified as the property of Mr Martin, and a finger-mark on the counter corresponded to an imprint taken from the dead man's hand.

The significance of the curious butt found by the electrician in the lamp-holder was not so clear. It seemed reasonable to assume that nobody but the dead man had entered the premises after they had been locked by the foreman on Saturday morning. Whyland had examined all the doors and windows very carefully, and had satisfied himself that they bore no signs of violence. He could account for both keys, and although it was possible that a third key existed, it seemed unlikely that anyone had used it between 12.30 and two. Again, since the door had been found bolted on Monday morning, it was probable that the dead man had bolted it behind him, and that he was alone in the house when he died. The foreman had assured him that he had found the windows fastened inside, and that it was only by the use of a special tool that he had been enabled to open the one at the back. It looked very much as if Martin had himself fixed the butt in the lamp-holder. But why?

Certainly it looked very like a case of suicide. But against this theory was the letter found in the dead man's pocket and the numbered counter. Martin himself might have deposited the latter, as the doctor had suggested, but would he have gone so far as to write a letter which must certainly put the police on the alert when it was found? It seemed highly improbable. Inspector Whyland felt convinced that the death of Mr Martin was merely another link in the mysterious chain of murders in Praed Street.

The evening papers were, of course, full of it, though naturally somewhat guarded. "Another tragedy in Praed Street. City Man found poisoned in Empty House"—such was the general trend of their headlines. And Praed Street, which had begun to breathe again during the respite of the past month, felt once more the cold touch of almost superstitious horror. The killer was abroad again, unknown, unrecognised, and no man could tell when he might feel the dread hand of death upon his shoulder.

Inspector Whyland, walking through Praed Street that evening about ten o'clock, heard a cheerful voice bid him good evening, and turned to find Mr Ludgrove by his side.

"Hullo, Mr Ludgrove!" he exclaimed. "I called at your place just now, and found it shut up. I thought you were away."

"I have been taking my usual evening stroll," replied the herbalist. "Won't you come in? I'm on my way home now."

With scarcely a moment's hesitation, Whyland accepted the invitation. There was always the chance that the herbalist might make some suggestion which would throw light on this latest problem. He waited until they were seated in the familiar back room before he asked the inevitable question. "You've heard what happened here this morning, I suppose?"

"I have, indeed," replied Mr Ludgrove gravely. "The papers contain little beyond the bare facts, but I gather that this unfortunate Mr Martin was undoubtedly murdered?"

"I'm afraid so," replied the Inspector. "And I fancy by the same hand which committed the previous murders. We found a typed letter on him, suggesting that he should call at Number 407, which had been posted in this district, and there was a counter bearing the number IV lying by his side. You don't happen to know anything about this Mr Martin, I suppose?"

Mr Ludgrove shook his head. "I understand that he left Praed Street fifteen years ago," he replied. "That was long before I came here. In those days I was leading a very quiet life in Devonshire." He paused, and a curious look of sadness came into his eyes, as of some painful memory. Then he continued briskly, as if ashamed of his momentary lapse. "I dare say that Mr Copperdock remembers him, he has a wonderful memory for everybody who has ever lived in the neighbourhood."

Inspector Whyland's eyes contracted slightly as he replied.

"Yes, he remembers him all right. They did a certain amount of business together, he tells me. In fact, Mr Copperdock is the only person about here who will admit to knowing anything about this fellow Martin."

"Well, I suppose that we are all under suspicion once more," said Mr Ludgrove, with a kindly smile. "No, Inspector, it's no use protesting; I know exactly how I should look at the matter if I were in your place. Until you have some definite clue to the perpetrator of the crimes, the whole neighbourhood is equally guilty in your eyes. I may say that I left here about one o'clock on Saturday, caught the 1.55 from Fenchurch, spent the day in Essex and did not return until after dark. Not, I gather, that an alibi is much use in this case, since it appears that this Mr Martin was alone in the house, in any event."

"I wish everybody in Praed Street would deal with me as frankly as you have, Mr Ludgrove," replied Whyland. "There seems to be a sort of dread in the minds of most of them that the police will in some way take advantage of everything they say. Take Copperdock, for example. I've been talking to him, and he tells me he was at the Cambridge Arms for half an hour or so some time between one and two. Yet neither he nor his son will tell me exactly what time he left his shop or returned to it. They didn't notice, they say."

"Mr Copperdock is not blessed with a very exact mind," said Mr Ludgrove soothingly. "You remember the curious incident of his meeting with the black sailor some time ago. By the way, I suppose that rather intangible person has not yet appeared in connection with the present case, has he? Although nearly everybody whom I have seen this evening has some theory to account for the facts, I have so far heard no reference to the black sailor."

Inspector Whyland smiled as he rose to take his departure. "I'm so certain that the black sailor will never be found that I would willingly double the reward out of my own pocket," he said. "He's a myth, originating in the fertile imagination of that young scoundrel Wal Snyder. Well, good night, Mr Ludgrove. Let me know if you hear any useful hint, won't you?"

It was not until he was some yards down the street that he laughed shortly to himself. "That old chap suspects Copperdock as much as I do," he muttered. "But if it is Copperdock, what the devil is his game, I wonder?"

CHAPTER 10 AT SCOTLAND YARD

The experts to whom the curious device found by the electrician in the little cellar had been sent duly made their report. In their opinion the butt was all that remained of an ingenious poison-bomb. The original machine consisted of a socket made to fit into an ordinary lamp-holder, but the place of the filament had been taken by a piece of fine wire, round which had been wrapped a thread of gun-cotton. Attached to the socket, and in contact with the gun-cotton, had been a sealed celluloid bulb containing pure prussic acid.

The action of such a bomb would be perfectly simple. It had only to be placed in a lamp-holder, and the switch turned on. The current would heat the fine wire, and so ignite the strand of gun-cotton. This in turn would set fire to the celluloid bulb, and its contents would be released in the form of vapour. Although some of this vapour would become ignited, enough would be available to permeate the atmosphere of a room far larger than the small cellar. And, of course, the inhalation of the vapour would rapidly produce death.

This opinion, the report stated, was purely speculative, since only the socket of the bomb remained for examination. Inspector Whyland, after consultation with his Chief at Scotland Yard, decided that it had better not be made public. The idea, though it was probably correct, was hypothetical, and altogether too vague to be put before a coroner's jury. It certainly strengthened Whyland's conviction that Mr Martin had been murdered, for no man would go to the trouble of constructing an elaborate poison-bomb with which to kill himself when he might just as easily have inhaled the acid outright. When the electrician left the cellar on the Saturday the bomb had not been there. Whyland was convinced that the man was speaking the truth upon this point. The only two alternatives remaining were that somebody had entered the house between the departure of the foreman and the arrival of Mr Martin, or that Martin had placed the bomb in position himself. The field of speculation opened by these alternatives was so vast and barren of any clue that their exploration must be a matter of considerable time.

As a matter of fact, the Assistant Commissioner was by no means convinced that Mr Martin has been murdered. "We all know what a difficult job you're up against in trying to trace the murders of these two fellows, Tovey and Pargent," he said to Whyland in an interview to which he had summoned him. "But don't you think you're rather too much inclined to see the hand of the murderer in everything that happens in that district? Now, honestly, assuming that Martin was murdered, have you the slightest clue which could possibly lead to the conviction of the murderer?"

"No, sir, I haven't," replied Whyland. "But I've got my suspicions of this man Copperdock, whom I've mentioned to you."

"Suspicions aren't evidence," said the Assistant Commissioner shortly. "Bring home the original murders to him by all means and then perhaps you'll be able to link him up with the death of this man Martin. At present, so far as I can see, you'll find it difficult to convince a jury that Martin was murdered. That poison-bomb theory is a bit far-fetched, you must admit."

"It is, rather, sir," agreed Whyland. "Still we've got the letter and the numbered counter——"

"It's just that letter that worries me," interrupted the Chief. "It was through the letter that you discovered that Martin was a receiver of stolen goods—a very smart piece of work, Whyland, upon which I congratulate you. But, until we have rounded them all up, we don't want the gentlemen with whom Martin dealt to become aware of our knowledge. If the existence of that letter becomes known, they'll tumble to it at once. I should very much prefer the letter to be kept secret, for the present, at all events."

The Assistant Commissioner paused, and Whyland glanced at him quickly. "I see no reason why it should be mentioned at the inquest, sir," he said. "Nobody knows of its existence outside of the police."

"Then I should be inclined to say nothing about it," remarked the Assistant Commissioner. "Nor, I imagine, will it be necessary to bring into prominence the hypothesis of the poison-bomb, or the fact that you have any suspicions of foul play. I am not suggesting that you should wilfully mislead the coroner, mind. But it is usually a mistake to volunteer information when no useful purpose can be served by so doing."

So it happened that the doctor's evidence at the inquest remained unchallenged. The theory was that Martin, having decided to take his own life, was attracted to his old premises, knowing them to be empty. In order to obtain access, he telephoned himself from Aldersgate station to Mr Briggs, using Mr Lacey's name. Having thus secured the key, he bolted the door behind him to prevent any interruption, then went into the cellar and inhaled the vapour of the prussic acid. The automatic he had brought with him in case the poison should prove ineffective. The numbered counter, which he had also brought with him, as the finger-marks upon it showed, merely emphasised the morbid state of mind which had prompted him to the deed.

The jury returned a verdict of suicide during temporary insanity, in accordance with this theory, and, to all outward appearances, the case of Mr Martin was disposed of. But Inspector Whyland, although relieved to feel that yet another unsolved crime had not been added to his already mounting debit account, knew well enough at heart that once again his mysterious adversary had scored a point against him. But again, there was this insoluble riddle of motive. It was possible to suggest more than one motive for the murder of Mr Martin. He might, for instance, have fallen out with one of the jewel thieves with whom he had such intimate relations. Or again, his dealings with women might have been at the bottom of it. But, assuming one of these suppositions to be correct, how was the death of Mr Martin to be linked up with the previous murders? Or were they indeed all the work of separate persons, who imitated one another's methods with a view to confusing the issue?

Inspector Whyland recalled his mind from such unprofitable speculations. He felt that the solution of the whole mystery lay close under his hand, if he could but devise the means to unearth it. Somehow Mr Copperdock's name always came up in connection with these murders. He had been Tovey's most intimate friend. The pipe which had been the cause of Colborn's death had been bought at his shop. He must have been within a few yards of the scene when Pargent was murdered. And Whyland had no doubt that he would discover some point of contact between Mr Copperdock and the present case.

He was not disappointed. It came out, in the course of a conversation between him and Houlder, the builder. It seemed that Houlder, who was an occasional frequenter of the Cambridge Arms, had mentioned, early in the month, that a new tenant had taken Number 407, and that he had got the job of altering the premises for him. Mr Copperdock had displayed great interest in this remark, and as a result Houlder had invited him to come and look over the place. Mr Copperdock had accepted, and he and Houlder had been over every inch of it. This might have been pure curiosity on Mr Copperdock's part, but at least the fact was significant. Inspector Whyland stored it in the mental pigeon-hole which already contained the note that Martin and Copperdock had done considerable business together in the past.

Thus, putting the case mathematically, Mr Copperdock was the highest common factor of the terms representing the four dead men. Inspector Whyland had spent much time and care in investigating their histories and their actions, and he could find no other factor common to them all. They had been, so far as he had been able to ascertain, complete strangers to one another, and they could never consciously have met one another. The only characteristics which they had in common were that they had all received counters numbered in the order of their deaths, that they were all males, and that their ages had all been over fifty.

Naturally, the mind of Praed Street was not greatly relieved by the verdict on the death of Mr Martin. Violent death was becoming far too frequent an incident for any of the local community to feel safe. Men wondered when it would be their turn to find the fatal counter, and how they should ward off the death which so swiftly followed. It was not as though one could tell exactly what one had to guard against. The knife had been used twice, certainly, but poison in one form or another had accounted for two of the deaths.

The numbered counters were the characteristic feature of the case which appealed most strongly to the popular imagination. Inexplicable murders were common enough, even murders in which no motive nor criminal had ever been found. But a series of murders, each prefixed by a definite warning, were an entirely novel sensation. The theory of the counters was publicly discussed from every possible point of view, without any really satisfactory theory being arrived at. Quite a large proportion of the population of London opened their morning papers in expectation of finding news of the delivery of counter number V.

The news, when it came, illustrated the hold which the subject had upon men's minds, and the moral effect which it had produced. Mr Ludgrove read the story as he consumed his frugal breakfast, and he was not surprised to hear Mr Copperdock's voice in the shop a few minutes later.

"Come in, Mr Copperdock," he called, and the tobacconist, paper in hand, the light of excitement in his eyes, entered through the curtained door.

"Have you seen this about this old chap Goodwin?" he inquired without preliminary.

"I have indeed," replied Mr Ludgrove gravely. "I imagine that the whole thing was an utterly heartless practical joke. I only hope the police will be able to trace the sender."

"Aye, practical joke, maybe, but it killed him all the same," said Mr Copperdock doubtfully. "Fancy an old chap like that, what couldn't have had more than a year or two to live! The paper says that he couldn't even walk from one room to another, had to be wheeled in a chair. This daughter of his what was looking after him says here that the doctor had told her that any shock might be fatal. Wonder if she sent it herself, being tired of waiting for his money? Listen, this is what she says: 'My father's chief amusement was to read the papers. He took the keenest interest in every item of news, and often discussed them with me. We often talked about the murders which have taken place recently in Praed Street, and my father always maintained that the curious episode of the numbered counters proved that they were not the work of a maniac.'"

"Yes. It is easy to understand what a shock the receipt of the counter must have been to him," replied Mr Ludgrove reflectively. "It would be interesting to know who, besides his daughter, knew of this passion for news on his part. I see by the account in my paper that three letters arrived for him by the morning post, and that his daughter brought them in to him on his breakfast tray. He opened the first one, and a counter numbered V fell out of it."

"Then he fell back on his pillow and never spoke again," put in Mr Copperdock excitedly. "The shock killed him right enough, as the doctors had said it would. I wouldn't like to be in the shoes of the person what sent it him."

Mr Ludgrove glanced at his friend sharply. "I cannot understand it, except upon the assumption of a practical joke, and a particularly cruel one at that," he said. "Here was this Mr Goodwin, a retired manufacturer, who had been living in this house at Highgate for many years past. All his acquaintances knew that, his heart was very seriously affected, and that he had only a short time to live. Of course, we know nothing of his past history, but, whatever motive there may have been, to murder a man in his condition would merely be to anticipate the course of nature by a few months. And, in our experience, the receipt of the counter has always been followed by violent death. I say we know nothing about him; I certainly do not. I suppose that you have never heard of him before, have you, Mr Copperdock?"

Mr Copperdock shook his head. "Never!" he replied emphatically. "Seems to me it's just like that poet chap, Pargent. Somebody sends him the counter, and his number's up. Well, thank heaven, it didn't happen in Praed Street this time."

It was not long after Mr Copperdock's departure that Inspector Whyland came in to see the herbalist. He said nothing, but glanced at Mr Ludgrove inquiringly.

"Yes, I've seen it in the paper," said Mr Ludgrove. "As a matter of fact, I've just been discussing it with Mr Copperdock. He came over here as soon as he read about it."

"Oh, he did, did he?" replied Whyland. "And what do you make of it, may I ask?"

Mr Ludgrove shrugged his shoulders. "I know no more than what the paper contains," he said. "It looks to me like a practical joke. I shouldn't wonder if some idiot derives amusement from sending these counters broadcast. I dare say he gets the names of people to send them to from the telephone directory."

"Practical joke? H'm," said Whyland. "Mind, I'm not denying that a lot of fools do send out these counters to their friends. The Yard has had dozens of cases reported to them. I always said that would happen as soon as people heard about them. But in this case I have seen the envelope in which the counter was sent. It was typed on the same machine as the others, and it was posted in this district, exactly as the others were. Your practical joker has followed his original model pretty closely, don't you think?"

The ardent seekers after sensation redoubled their eagerness for news of the next counter. Although opinion on the whole followed Mr Ludgrove in attributing the counter sent to Mr

Goodwin to some irresponsible practical joker, the fact that death had undoubtedly followed its receipt caused many to shake their heads knowingly. If Mr Martin's death had been due to suicide, and Mr Goodwin's to a practical joke, how would the original sender of the counters number his next one? It was not to be supposed that he would claim credit for these spurious imitations of his work. If the next number were to be VI, public opinion was quite prepared to credit him with having compassed the last two deaths. But most people anticipated that it would bear the number IV.

The fact that such discussion was possible showed clearly that the theory of the existence of some mysterious assassin had captured the popular imagination. There was really no reason why any murderer should not send a numbered counter to his prospective victim, but people argued, quite correctly, that murders were far more often the result of sudden impulse than of deliberate intention. It was for this reason that the "counter deaths" as they were sometimes called, attracted so much attention. Yet the weeks drew into months, and the cold winds of spring took the place of the misty drizzle of winter, without any news of another numbered counter being received. The arm-chair criminologists gave it as their opinion that the last had been heard of them, that the mysterious criminal had either fulfilled his vengeance or had died unrecognised in some lunatic asylum. The murders in Praed Street were added to the long list of undiscovered crimes, and slowly they began to be forgotten.

One evening towards the end of April, Mr Copperdock was sitting in the herbalist's back room, enjoying a generous whisky and soda. He was on his way home from the Cambridge Arms, and, seeing his friend's door still open, had looked in for a chat. The night was warm, one of those nights which London sometimes experiences in early spring, conveying the promise, so rarely fulfilled, of a fine summer.

The liquor which he had consumed made Mr Copperdock even more communicative than usual. Some reference to his son had led him on to speak of Ivy, and thus, by a simple association of ideas, to the murder of Mr Tovey.

"You know, Ludgrove, that fellow Whyland always suspected me of having to do with that business," he said. "I don't believe he's satisfied yet, between ourselves. At one time he was always hanging about, coming into my place at all hours, and asking all sorts of questions. I used to see chaps lounging about outside, and sometimes they followed me when I went out. It was jolly uncomfortable, I can tell you."

Mr Ludgrove smiled. "I don't suppose you were any more under suspicion than the rest of us," he replied. "Whyland had an idea that somebody in this neighbourhood was responsible, and I don't know that I don't agree with him. He came in here, too, and asked questions, for that matter. For all I know he may have suspected me."

But Mr Copperdock shook his head. "No, Ludgrove, that won't do," he said. "There was something about the way he spoke to me that gave him away. He still comes in sometimes, and asks me all sorts of questions about those poor fellows who were killed. Very often they're the same things, as he's asked before. Trying to catch me out, I suppose. And he's always asking me if I've ever seen the black sailor again."

"I suppose you really did see him?" asked Mr Ludgrove casually.

"See him? I saw him as plain as I see you now," replied Mr Copperdock, with some indignation. "What would I want to say I'd seen him for if I hadn't? I wish now I'd never said anything about it. I wouldn't have, but I thought it would be doing Whyland a good turn."

"Well, it's all over now," said Mr Ludgrove soothingly. "We haven't had any of these mysterious deaths for nearly three months now. I don't expect that Inspector Whyland will worry his head about the matter much longer."

"I hope he won't," replied Mr Copperdock truculently. "I'll give him a piece of mind if he comes round worrying me much more. I'm as respectable a man as any in this street, I'd have him know."

He finished his drink, and rose to go. Mr Ludgrove saw him off the premises, then settled himself down once more in his chair to read.

Five minutes later he heard a heavy step hurrying through the shop, and the form of Mr Copperdock appeared unceremoniously through the curtain that covered the door of the inner room. Mr Ludgrove rose to his feet in concern. The tobacconist's face was deathly pale, and his hands were trembling violently. He staggered across the room, and sank down into the chair he had so lately quitted.

He held out one shaking hand open towards the herbalist. "Here, look at this!" he exclaimed in a queer hoarse voice.

The herbalist bent over the outstretched hand. In the palm of it lay a white counter, upon which the figure VI had been roughly drawn in red ink.

CHAPTER 11 THE SIXTH COUNTER

Mr Ludgrove looked at the counter and then raised his eyes to Mr Copperdock's face. The tobacconist was staring at him with an expression of complete bewilderment and terror, very different from his truculent demeanour of a few minutes earlier. The herbalist checked the slow smile which had begun to twitch the corner of his lips, and sat down quietly opposite Mr Copperdock.

"Where did you find this?" he asked.

"On my bed, after I left you just now," replied the tobacconist. "It wasn't there when I went out to the Cambridge Arms this evening, I'll swear. I always goes upstairs to have a wash before I goes out, and I'd have been bound to have seen it. It's that black sailor. I always thought he'd get me."

"Well, he hasn't got you yet," said Mr Ludgrove soothingly. "Now that you have been warned, we can take the proper precautions. How do you suppose this counter came into your room?"

Mr Copperdock shook his head helplessly. "It beats me," he replied. "I locked the door behind me when I went out, and nobody couldn't have got in till I went back just now, seeing as I had the key in my pocket all the time."

"You locked the door when you went out? Was Ted out, too, then?"

"Yes, Ted and I went out together, about half-past eight. He was going to spend the evening with the Toveys. I don't expect him back till nigh on eleven. I goes round to the Cambridge Arms, where I stays until I comes in to you just now. And when I gets back, there was this counter, right in the middle of my bed. I just picks it up and comes over to you. I daren't stay no longer in the house alone."

"You didn't notice if anything else in the house had been disturbed, I suppose?"

"I didn't stop to look. It gave me such a turn seeing that thing there, I didn't hardly know what I was doing."

"Well, you'd better stay here until your son comes back," said Mr Ludgrove. "It is very nearly eleven now. I suppose you shut the door behind you when you came over here? How will Ted get in?"

"We both has our keys," replied Mr Copperdock. "Ted's a good boy. I wouldn't have minded so much if he'd been there."

"Well, I'll go to the door and watch for him," said Mr Ludgrove cheerfully. "You'll be all right here, Mr Copperdock."

"Don't you go no further than the door!" exclaimed the tobacconist fearfully. "For all I know that black sailor chap may be on the look out, and seen me come across here. He'll get me, for sure."

"He won't get you here, I promise you," said Mr Ludgrove reassuringly. He mixed a strong whisky and water, and placed it in the trembling hand of his guest. "You drink this while I go into the shop and keep an eye open for your son."

Mr Ludgrove had not been at his post for many minutes before Ted came swinging along the opposite pavement. He stopped at the sound of the herbalist's voice, and crossed the road towards him. In a few whispered words Mr Ludgrove acquainted him with what had happened.

Ted said nothing, but jerked his elbow upwards and winked suggestively.

"No, I don't think so," said Mr Ludgrove. "But you had better come in and talk to him."

The two entered the back room together, and Mr Copperdock looked up anxiously as they came in.

"Ah, Ted, my boy. I'm glad to see you," he said dolefully. "The black sailor's on my track, and he'll get me for sure."

"Nonsense, Dad," replied Ted heartily. "Somebody put that counter on your bed for a joke; one of your pals at the Cambridge Arms, I'll be bound. You come along home with me, and we'll soon find out who it was."

But Mr Copperdock shook his head. "I wouldn't go into that house again not tonight, no, not if you was to pay me," he replied firmly. "I'd sooner go and spend the night at the police station."

"You needn't do that," said Mr Ludgrove. "You can spend the night here on my bed upstairs. I have no objection to sleeping on the chair."

"I daren't be left alone," lamented Mr Copperdock. "Anybody might have seen me cross the road and come in here. Do you think Inspector Whyland would send a couple of coppers along if Ted was to ring him up? I'd feel a lot safer if they was about."

"I hardly think he would," replied Mr Ludgrove. "But if you like we will spend the night together in this room. You can have one chair, and I will have the other. I can put a mattress on the floor for Ted if he cares to join us."

"Not I, I'm going home to bed," put in Ted heartily, with a wink at the herbalist. "Somebody ought to be on guard over at our place in case the black sailor breaks in, you know, Dad."

Rather reluctantly Mr Copperdock agreed to this arrangement. After a few more minutes' conversation, Ted went home, and the two settled themselves down in the chairs. A further strong whisky and water produced its effect upon Mr Copperdock, and he was very soon dozing restlessly. To Mr Ludgrove sleep seemed an unnecessary luxury. He moved quietly over to his bench, and spent the greater part of the night absorbed in his herbs and his microscope, apparently entirely oblivious of the presence of his guest. The only sign he manifested of interest in his affairs was to pick up the counter and examine it very carefully through a powerful lens.

It was not until seven o'clock in the morning that he gently shook the sleeping form. Mr Copperdock woke with a start, and stared about him with puzzled eyes.

"I've got a cup of tea ready for you, Mr Copperdock," said the herbalist. "I thought it was time to wake you, as Mrs Cooper will be here presently, and if she found you here she might talk. We don't want that, do we?"

The tobacconist rose stiffly to his feet and shook himself. "Very kind of you, I'm sure, Ludgrove," he said. "Yes, I remember. What did you do with that counter?"

"I have it here," replied the herbalist. "You are still quite sure that you found it on your bed last night? It wasn't by any chance slipped into your pocket by somebody at the Cambridge Arms?"

"As sure as I live. I found it on my bed, same as I told you," affirmed Mr Copperdock earnestly. "I wasn't tight last night, if that's what you're getting at."

"No, no, of course not," replied Mr Ludgrove soothingly. "Now, shall we go across and see if your son heard anything during the night?"

Mr Copperdock agreeing, they crossed the road to the tobacconist's shop, and let themselves in. Ted was still asleep, and they had some difficulty in waking him. When they had done so, he reported that he had had a good look round the place before he went to bed, and had found nothing unusual. After that—well, he had gone to sleep, and had heard nothing until they had awakened him.

The light of morning appeared to have instilled rather more courage into Mr Copperdock's heart. He announced his determination to carry on business as usual, but insisted that Inspector Whyland should be communicated with and told of his discovery of the numbered counter. It was about ten o'clock when Whyland arrived in Praed Street, but instead of going straight to Copperdock's shop, he went first to the herbalist's.

"What's this story about Copperdock having found a numbered counter?" he asked, as soon as they were safely hidden in the back room from prying ears.

Mr Ludgrove recounted his experiences of the past night, and as he came to a conclusion Whyland laughed contemptuously.

"Is this another of Copperdock's hallucinations, like that meeting of his with the black sailor?" he enquired.

"Not altogether," replied Mr Ludgrove with a smile. "The counter is real enough, at all events. He left it here last night. Here it is."

Whyland examined the counter in silence. He had very little doubt that Mr Copperdock had staged the whole affair, had written the figure VI upon it in red ink himself, and had placed it on his bed. But why? What was his game? Was this a feeble scheme to draw suspicion from himself? The series of murders appeared to have come to an end. What was the point of reviving the memory of them like this?

Mr Ludgrove broke in upon his meditations. "I took the liberty of examining it under a powerful glass," he said, nodding his head towards the bench. "It seems to be an ordinary bone counter and the figure VI has been drawn upon it with a steel pen and red ink."

"Just as the others were," agreed Whyland. "I'll keep this counter, if you don't mind. I want to add it to my collection. Now I suppose I had better step across and see Copperdock. I should like you to come with me, if you can spare the time."

"I think I can risk shutting the shop for a few minutes," replied the herbalist. "I get very few customers in the morning. Most of the people who require my services are at work all day."

"Dishonest work, I'll be bound," said Whyland chaffingly. "Well, come along, then."

They went across to Mr Copperdock's shop together, and were shown by the tobacconist into the room behind the shop, which was used as an office. At one side was a table upon which stood a Planet typewriter, at the other a desk. Inspector Whyland seated himself at the latter, selected one of the pens before him, and dipped it into an inkpot, which happened to contain red ink.

"Now then, Mr Copperdock," he said. "Tell me exactly what happened yesterday evening."

The tobacconist immediately launched into an account of his adventure, Whyland listened patiently, occasionally making a brief note with the pen. "You say that nobody could have entered the house while you were out?" he asked, as Mr Copperdock came to the end of his story.

"Quite impossible," replied Mr Copperdock emphatically. "There's only one door, with a spring lock which catches when you shuts it."

"H'm. I'd like to have a look round, if you don't mind," said the Inspector.

He examined the house carefully. On the ground floor was the shop, and behind it the office and a little kitchen containing a gas stove. The windows of these did not open, and were high up in the wall, and covered with a stout iron grating. There was no back entrance. From a narrow passage a staircase ran up to the first floor, upon which were two bedrooms, occupied respectively by Mr Copperdock and his son, and a sitting-room. The bedrooms were over the shop, and looked out upon Praed Street. The sitting-room was at the back, and looked out over an enclosed yard, belonging to a transport contractor, and used for storing vans at night. The windows on the first floor were obviously inaccessible without the aid of a ladder. Above the first floor were a couple of attics, lighted only by skylights, which were closed and padlocked. From the cobwebs which covered them, it was obvious that they had not been opened for a long time.

Inspector Whyland returned to the first floor. "Were these windows closed and fastened while you were out last night?" he enquired.

"The sitting-room was," replied Ted, who had followed them upstairs. "I looked at it when I came in. It hasn't been touched since."

Whyland looked at it, and satisfied himself that it showed no signs of having been forced. "What about the bedroom windows?" he asked.

"Both Dad's and mine were open at the top," replied Ted. "But nobody could have got in through them, unless they had put up a ladder in the middle of Praed Street."

"Even the black sailor isn't likely to have done that," observed Whyland sarcastically. "Well, Mr Copperdock, the best advice I can give you is not to go about alone at night too much. I'll have a man watch outside the premises for a bit, if that's any comfort to you. But, if you ask me, I don't think you're in any immediate danger."

It seemed that the Inspector was right. Several days passed without anything untoward happening to Mr Copperdock. The tobacconist resumed his normal routine, with the modification that he took care never to be alone. His son walked with him as far as the Cambridge Arms, and at least one of his cronies there walked back with him to the shop. Mr Ludgrove, watching with some amusement, recognised every night the watcher which Whyland had promised to provide. It struck him that the man's instructions were probably to keep an eye on Mr Copperdock's movements rather than to provide for his safety. But upon the tobacconist, who, now he had got over his fright, appeared to regard himself as something of a hero, the man's presence produced an impression of importance and of security.

The only aspect of the incident which appealed to Whyland was the counter itself. He had submitted it to the experts at Scotland Yard, together with the notes which he had made in red ink in Mr Copperdock's office, and they had given it as their opinion that the figure upon it had been drawn with the same ink as that in which the notes had been written, and by a similar pen. Further, this pen and ink corresponded with those which had been used on the previous counters, in the cases in which they had been preserved. The more the Inspector considered it, the more convinced he became that Mr Copperdock was at the bottom of the business. But how to bring it home to him? That was the difficulty.

Mr Copperdock had found the numbered counter on Tuesday evening. On the following Saturday Ted had arranged to take Ivy to a dance, from which he was not likely to return until after midnight. It had been suggested that Mr Copperdock, in order that he should not be left alone, should spend the time between the closing of the Cambridge Arms and the return of his son in Mr Ludgrove's sanctum.

But, deriving courage from the fact that four days had elapsed without anything happening, Mr Copperdock refused to consider any such proposal. He must have detected the general scepticism with which his story of the finding of the counter had been received, and had resolved to say no more about it. He went to the Cambridge Arms at his usual hour, stayed there until closing time, and was then accompanied home by two friends of his, who lived in the Edgware Road, and who had to pass the door on their way home. He invited these two to come in and have a last drink with him, and they accepted, on the grounds that it was a beautiful night, and very thirsty work walking.

The story of the finding of the counter was by this time familiar to all the clientele of the Cambridge Arms, each individual member of which suspected some other member of having somehow conveyed it into Mr Copperdock's possession. It was absurd to think, as one of them remarked in his absence, that anybody could have a grudge against Sam Copperdock. Somebody must be pulling his leg, that was the only possible explanation. It was with some considerable interest, therefore, that his two friends followed the tobacconist as he took them into his bedroom and showed them the exact place where he found the counter.

It was not until nearly eleven that Mr Copperdock's party broke up. Inspector Whyland's deputy, strolling past on the other side of the road, noticed the parting on the doorstep, and observed that after the departure of his friends, Mr Copperdock shut the door of his shop. A few minutes later he saw a light switched on in one of the front rooms upstairs. This he knew, from his experience of previous nights, was the signal that Mr Copperdock was going to bed.

Mr Ludgrove, since the tobacconist had refused his offer of hospitality, spent the evening by himself. The room above his shop was littered with innumerable boxes containing all manner of dried herbs and similar items of the stock-in-trade of his calling. He spent several hours between that room and his sanctum. His work bench became strewed with specimens to which from time to time he affixed labels with high-sounding names. The door of his shop was ajar until about half-past ten, up till which hour an occasional customer interrupted his labours. After that time it was closed, and he was able to devote his whole attention to his plants.

He was still working at midnight. He appeared to require very little sleep, and rarely went to bed before the early hours of the morning. He had just brewed himself a cup of his favourite cocoa, when suddenly he heard a violent hammering upon the door of the shop. Instinctively he glanced at the clock upon the mantelpiece. The hands pointed to twenty past twelve.

Surely no customer could be seeking admittance at such an hour! Besides, the knocking was clamorous, insistent, not in the least like the furtive taps which usually proclaimed the visit of some client, anxious to hide his errand under the cover of darkness. With a shrug of his shoulders Mr Ludgrove put down his cup and went to the door. He drew back the bolts and put out his head, to find Ted Copperdock standing on the pavement outside.

The young man gave him no chance to ask questions. He threw out his hand and caught Mr Ludgrove by the arm, as though to drag him forcibly into the street. "For God's sake come and see Dad!" he exclaimed.

"Why, what has happened?" enquired Mr Ludgrove quickly.

"I don't know, he's dead, I think," replied Ted incoherently. "I've only just come back and found him. Something terrible's happened——"

Mr Ludgrove was not the man to be carried off his feet by a sudden crisis. "Certainly, Ted, I'll come over," he said quietly. "But you appear to want a doctor rather than me. You probably know that a detective has been patrolling the street for the last few nights. I think I see him coming towards us now. You go and fetch the doctor, while he and I attend to your father."

Ted, after a moment's hesitation, ran off down the road,

and Mr Ludgrove walked swiftly towards the advancing figure, which he had already recognised. "Something has happened to Mr Copperdock," he said as he reached him. "I have sent his son for a doctor, and said that you and I would go in."

"Something happened, eh?" replied the man, as the two strode swiftly towards the door of the tobacconist's shop. "You don't know what it is, I suppose? I've had my eye on the place all the evening, and there's been nobody near it between eleven, when two fellows whom Copperdock took in came out, and five minutes ago, when his son let himself in with a key. And there's been a light in the front window upstairs all that time."

"No, I know nothing," replied Mr Ludgrove anxiously. They had reached the shop by this time. The door had been left open by Ted in his haste to call the herbalist, and they hurried on through the shop and up the staircase to the first floor. The door of Mr Copperdock's bedroom stood open, and they rushed in together. On the threshold they halted, moved by a simultaneous impulse. Before them, in the middle of the floor, lay Mr Copperdock, stripped to the waist, with an expression of innocent surprise upon his face.

CHAPTER 12 A HYPODERMIC NEEDLE

For a moment the two men stood still, rooted to the ground with horror. Then Mr Ludgrove stepped forward and fell on his knees by Mr Copperdock's side. He put his finger on his wrist for a moment, then slowly rose to his feet and shook his head.

"Dead?" said the detective enquiringly. "By jove, this is a bad business. Will you stay here for a moment while I go down into the shop and telephone? I'll ring up the station and get them to send for Whyland. Don't touch anything, whatever you do."

Mr Ludgrove nodded. He stood motionless in the doorway when voices below proclaimed the arrival on the scene of Ted and the doctor. The detective, who had sent his message, came upstairs with them, and the three joined Mr Ludgrove.

The doctor took in the situation at a glance. Mr Copperdock was lying on his back, his legs drawn up close to his body. The doctor examined him in silence for a while, then beckoned to the detective.

"I don't understand this at all," he said. "I shall have to make a more thorough examination than is possible while he is lying in this position. I'm afraid there's nothing to be done. I don't want to move him until your Inspector comes. He won't be long, I suppose?"

"He's living close to the station," replied the detective. "They've sent a man with a motor-cycle and side-car round to fetch him and bring him here. It oughtn't to take him more than a few minutes. I'd rather you waited, if you don't mind."

The doctor nodded and continued his examination, while the other three stood where they were, looking keenly about them. It was obvious that when death overtook Mr Copperdock he had been preparing for bed. His coat, waistcoat, shirt and vest lay on a chair, and the basin on the washing stand was half full of soapy water. A towel lay on the floor near it.

The minutes seemed to pass with leaden slowness until a faint throbbing reached their ears, which rapidly grew in intensity until it resolved itself into the sound of a motor-cycle. The noise ceased suddenly as it reached the door, and in a few seconds Inspector Whyland appeared, half dressed, with a stern expression on his face.

"How did this happen, Waters?" he inquired sharply, turning to the detective.

"I don't know, sir," replied the latter. "I've been watching the house all the evening——"

"Well, never mind, you can tell me about that later," interrupted Whyland. "Good evening, Doctor. Can you tell me what this man died of?"

"No, I can't," replied the doctor. "It looks as if he had been bitten by a snake, or something of that kind. I was waiting till you came to make a thorough examination."

"Right. Stand fast a minute while I look round." He made a swift survey of the room, then, taking a piece of chalk from his pocket, marked on the carpet the position in which the body was lying.

"Now then, doctor, I'm ready," he said. "What do you want to do?"

"I want him laid on his side, if you'll bear a hand," replied the doctor. "That's right. Hullo, look at that!"

They had moved Mr Copperdock's body until his back was visible. There, just below the left shoulder-blade, was an almost circular patch, covered with a curious white powdery incrustation. In the centre of this patch was an angry-looking purple spot.

The doctor bent over this and uttered an exclamation of amazement. Opening the case which he had laid down by his side he took from it a pair of forceps, and applied them to the spot on Mr Copperdock's back. From this he withdrew something, which he carried over to the light, and beckoned to Whyland to inspect.

"See that?" he said. "That's the end of a fine hypodermic needle. I'm beginning to see what happened, now. He was injected with some powerful toxic agent by means of a hypodermic syringe, the needle of which broke off in the process. The nature of the poison we shall be able to determine by an examination of this fragment. But I don't understand that white incrustration. Let me have another look at it."

He selected a small phial from his case, put the fragment of the needle into it, and labelled it. Then he turned once more to Mr Copperdock's body, and examined the patch once more with a lens. Finally he removed some of the white powder and put it in another phial, which he also sealed and labelled.

Then he beckoned Whyland aside, and the two conversed for a moment in low whispers.

"This is really most extraordinary," said the doctor. "This man undoubtedly died from an injection of poison administered hypodermically. You remember the case of Colborn, the baker, last year?"

"Yes, I remember it well," replied Whyland. "What about it, doctor?"

"Well, of course I can't say definitely as yet," replied the doctor guardedly. "But it seems to me that the symptoms in the two cases are remarkably similar. I would go so far as to hazard the opinion that the same poison was employed in both cases. Now, in the present case, you, I take it, are chiefly interested in the agency by which the poison was administered. Well, it is possible that in this case it was self-administered. One can just manage to run a hypodermic needle into oneself below the left shoulder-blade. Here's a syringe. There's no needle in it. Hold it in your left hand. That's right. Now, see if you can press the nozzle against your back in the place corresponding to the spot on Mr Copperdock's body.

Whyland obeyed, and after some fumbling contrived to reach the exact spot. "Yes, it can be done, but it's precious awkward," he remarked, handing the syringe back.

"Exactly," agreed the doctor. "That may account for the needle having broken off. Mind, I'm only suggesting a possibility, not laying down a theory. That's your job. Now we come to the white incrustation round the puncture. Unless I'm greatly mistaken, it is potassium carbonate. Should it prove to be so, the fact would be of considerable significance."

"Why?" inquired Whyland. "I'm afraid I don't quite follow you, doctor."

"Potassium carbonate has no particular properties of its own," replied the doctor. "But, if a piece of caustic potash had been applied to the puncture, say an hour or two ago, it would by now have been converted into potassium carbonate. You see what this suggests. Caustic substances are employed to burn out poisoned surfaces. In this case caustic potash may have been employed in an attempt to counteract the poison. Of course, it would be ineffectual, as it had been injected far too deeply. But that it has been so applied I am pretty certain. You can see for yourself that the skin shows traces of burning under the incrustation. Whether the same hand that injected the poison applied this ineffectual antidote, I cannot say."

Whyland nodded, and then a sudden thought struck him. "But look here, if he injected the poison himself the syringe ought to be lying about somewhere!" he exclaimed. "How long would it take for the poison to act, doctor?"

The doctor shook his head. "I can't say, since I do not yet know its nature," he replied. "If it was the same as was employed in Colborn's case, we can make a rough guess, however. A very small quantity, applied to a scratch in his tongue, caused death in two hours and a half. We may assume that a very much larger quantity would be contained in a syringe, and it was driven well into the tissues. Death might well have occurred within a few minutes. But in any case, there would have been time to dispose of the syringe."

The doctor turned and pointed to the window. "That's open at the top, as you see, and the curtains do not meet by a couple of feet or more. He could have thrown it out there without the slightest difficulty."

Whyland turned to the three men, who had been standing by the door. "Slip down below, Waters, and search the pavement and roadway outside this window for a hypodermic syringe," he said. "Sharp, now. Mr Ludgrove, come to this window for a moment; you know this street better than I do. That's your place opposite, isn't it? What's behind that window over the shop?"

"A room I use for storing herbs in," replied Mr Ludgrove. "As it happens, I have been in there once or twice this evening."

"You didn't see anything of what was happening in here, I suppose?" asked Whyland quickly.

"No, I did not," replied Mr Ludgrove. "I was only in the room for a moment or two, selecting bundles of herbs to take downstairs. I did happen to notice about eleven o'clock that there was a light in here, but that was all."

"What about the windows to the right and left of your place?"

"I believe that they belong to offices occupied only in the day-time. I do not think it at all likely that anyone could have overlooked this room from them at night."

"No," agreed Whyland. "We're not likely to be lucky enough to find an actual witness. All right, Mr Ludgrove, thank you. Now, young man, do you know if your father possessed a hypodermic syringe?"

Ted Copperdock, thus addressed, shook his head. "I don't think so, Inspector," he replied. "But I shouldn't know one if I saw it. There's a cupboard over there by the washing stand where he kept a lot of bottles of stuff."

Whyland strode over to the cupboard and opened it. It contained about a dozen bottles of various sizes, each half full of some patent medicine or other. But of a hypodermic syringe, or even any caustic potash, there was no trace.

"If he did it himself, he must have thrown the syringe away," muttered Whyland. "Waters ought to find it; there isn't a lot of traffic along here at this time of night. Well, doctor, I don't think we need keep you out of bed any longer. I'll have the body taken to the mortuary, and perhaps you'll ring me up at the station later in the morning?"

The doctor nodded, picked up his bag, which contained the broken needle and the sample of the incrustation, and left the house. When he had gone, Whyland turned once again to Ted.

"Can you suggest any reason why your father should wish to take his life?" he inquired.

"No, Inspector, I can't," replied Ted frankly. "The business is doing very well, and father was only saying the other day that we'd got a tidy bit put away in the bank. I keep the books myself, and I know everything's all right."

"I see. No money troubles, in fact. You don't know of any disappointment which he may have experienced, or anything like that?"

A faint smile passed across Ted's face. "I don't think he had any disappointment, Inspector," he replied. "In fact, I should say it was rather the other way."

"What do you mean?" said Whyland sharply.

"Why, he always reckoned that nobody knew, but I fancy that we all guessed sharp enough. He's hinted to me once or twice lately that he wasn't too old to marry again. And—— well, from what her daughter lets drop, Mrs Tovey wouldn't mind. He went round there pretty often, and she always seemed glad to see him."

Whyland shot a quick glance at Mr Ludgrove. It was from him that he had first learnt of this attachment. Ludgrove nodded almost imperceptibly and Whyland turned once more to Ted.

"There was nothing preying on his mind, was there?" he asked.

"Well, I've thought sometimes that he fair had the wind up about this black sailor," replied Ted reluctantly. "I never knew what to make of that. He told me one day that he'd met him coming out of the Cambridge Arms, but I never could quite believe it somehow."

"As it happens, I share your scepticism," said Whyland. "Mr Ludgrove here was in the street at the time, and saw your father come out of the Cambridge Arms. There was nobody but himself and your father in sight, he assures me."

"That is so," assented Mr Ludgrove gravely.

"Well, I'm not surprised," said Ted. "It's a funny thing, but these things always happen when he'd been to the Cambridge Arms of an evening. It was when he came home from there that he found that counter the other day."

"Have you ever seen your father definitely under the influence of liquor?" asked Whyland.

"Why no, not to say actually squiffy. He'd talk freer than usual, and imagine all sorts of yarns about things that never happened. I think he got the black sailor on his brain sometimes. When he first got the counter he made up his mind that the black sailor was going to get him. But the last day or two he's been much more cheerful. Of course, it's possible that this evening, when he was alone, it got on his mind again."

The conversation was interrupted by the return of Waters, the detective. "I've searched as best I can for that syringe, sir, and I can't find it," he reported. "I'll have another good look as soon as it gets light, if you like, sir."

"Yes, do," replied Whyland. "Now, you were supposed to be watching this place all the evening. What time did Mr Copperdock come in?"

"Between nine and ten, sir. Two fellows came with him, and the three stood talking at the door for a minute or two. Then they all went in, and the door was shut behind them. It was close on eleven when it opened again, and the two men came out. Mr Copperdock came downstairs with them, I saw him just inside the door talking to them. Then they went away, and the door was shut again. A few minutes after they had gone I saw a light come on in this room."

"You can't see into the room from the opposite pavement, I

123

suppose?"

"Only a bit of ceiling, sir. I noticed the window was open at the top, and the curtains not properly drawn, like you see them now, sir. They've never been properly drawn since I've been watching the house. The next thing that happened was that Mr Copperdock's son came along at about a quarter past twelve, and let himself in with a key."

Inspector Whyland turned to Ted. "What time did you go out?" he asked.

"About eight o'clock. Dad was just getting ready to go round to the Cambridge Arms."

"Where were you between eight and a quarter past twelve?"

"With Miss Tovey," replied Ted, readily enough, but with an awkward blush. "We went to a dance, then we had some supper. After that I saw her home, and stayed there a few minutes. I walked home from Lisson Grove, found Dad like this, and ran straight across to fetch Mr Ludgrove."

"Nobody but you and your father had a key to the premises, I suppose?"

"No. One of us always came down to let the charwoman in in the morning."

"You are perfectly certain, Waters, that nobody came to the house between eleven and a quarter past twelve?" inquired Whyland.

"Certain, sir. I was in the street outside all the time, and never took my eyes off the place."

"Very well. You stay here with the body. I'll arrange for it to be taken to the mortuary as soon as I can. As for you, young man, you had better go to bed and try to get some sleep. We shall want you in the morning. Mr Ludgrove, if you've nothing better to do, I should like you to come round the house with me. I want to make certain that nobody can have broken in."

Mr Ludgrove nodded, and the two left the room together. Whyland examined the sitting-room window. It was shut and fastened, and bore no traces of violence. They then went downstairs and looked over the ground floor, without discovering anything in any way out of the ordinary.

When they reached the office behind the shop, Whyland closed the door and sank wearily into a chair. "Well, Mr Ludgrove, what do you make of it?" he said.

"I couldn't help overhearing snatches of your conversation with the doctor," replied the herbalist. "I confess that I cannot understand why, if Mr Copperdock wished to poison himself with a hypodermic injection, he should select his back for the purpose, unless he had some confused idea of a lumbar puncture. Yet, on the other hand, he is not likely to have let someone else drive a needle into him without a struggle, and of that there is no trace, so far as I could see."

"And how did that person get in?" put in Whyland quickly. "That is, if both Waters and young Ted are telling the truth. Waters is a good man, and I haven't the least reason to suspect him. But it's just possible that he was dozing somewhere between eleven and twelve, and that Ted came home before he said he did. His father wouldn't be surprised to see him, and he might have walked up behind him and jabbed the needle in. Then, when his father found out what he'd done, he got a bit of caustic potash from somewhere and clapped it on. I know there are lots of difficulties, but at least it's possible. At all events, I can't think of another alternative to the suicide theory."

"The case is extraordinarily puzzling," said Mr Ludgrove sympathetically. "If you feel disposed to discuss it, Inspector, I suggest that you do so in comfort over at my place. I can make you a cup of cocoa, or, if you prefer it, I can supply you with something stronger. I always kept a bottle of whisky in reserve for poor Mr Copperdock."

"Well, it's very good of you, Mr Ludgrove," replied Whyland gratefully. "What's the time? After two? I want to stay about here until it's light. I'll just tell Waters where I'm to be found in case he wants me. Then I shall be very glad to accept your kind hospitality."

He left the room and returned after an absence of a couple of minutes. "I can't make it out," he said. "Waters swears he never had his eyes off the place. Still, it won't do any harm to make inquiries into young Ted's movements and verify his statement. It beats me, but then everything Copperdock did was a puzzle. His name seemed to crop up in connection with each of these deaths, somehow. Then there was that yarn about the black sailor, the counter which he said he found on his bed, and now his amazing death. Well, I'm ready to go across if you are, Mr Ludgrove."

The two passed through the shop into the road. As they crossed it, Mr Ludgrove uttered an exclamation of surprise. "Why, the door of my shop is open!" he said. "I must have forgotten to shut it in my haste when Ted Copperdock came over for me."

"Let's hope no inquisitive visitor has been in to have a look round while we've been over the way," replied Whyland.

Mr Ludgrove smiled. "He will have found very little of value to reward him if he has," he said. "No, I'm not afraid of burglars. In any case, it's a very old-fashioned lock which anyone could force without any difficulty."

They had reached the door by now, and Mr Ludgrove pushed it open. "Come along, Inspector, we'll go into the back room," he said, leading the way.

At the door of the inner room he paused, and switched on the light. At a first glance the room appeared to be exactly as he had left it to answer Ted's urgent summons. Then suddenly he clutched Whyland's arm, and pointed straight in front of him with a shaking finger.

On the mantelpiece, propped conspicuously against the clock so that it could not fail to attract attention, was a white bone counter, upon which the figure VII had been carefully traced.

PART 2

THE CRIMINAL

CHAPTER 13 ENTER DR PRIESTLEY

That eccentric scientist, Dr Priestley, sat in his study on the Monday morning following the death of Mr Copperdock, busily engaged in sorting out a mass of untidy-looking papers. Most of them he tore up and placed in the waste-paper basket by his side; a few he glanced at and put aside. The April sun lit up the room with a pale radiance, lending an air of Spring even to this dignified but rather gloomy house in Westbourne Terrace.

Dr Priestley was thus engaged when the door opened and his secretary, Harold Merefield, came into the room. There was an air of heaviness about both men, the old and the young, as though the Spring had not yet touched them, and Winter held them still in its grip. One might have guessed that some absorbing work had monopolised their energies, leaving them no leisure for any tiring but the utmost concentration. And one would have guessed right. For the last six months Dr Priestley had been engaged upon the writing of a book which was to enhance his already brilliant reputation. Its title was *Some Aspects of Modern Thought*, and in it Dr Priestley had, with his usual incontrovertible logic, shattered the majority of the pet theories of orthodox science. It was, as the reviews were to say, a brilliant achievement, all the more entertaining from the vein of biting sarcasm which ran through it.

When Dr Priestley settled down to writing a book, he concentrated his whole attention upon it, to the exclusion of everything else. He allowed nothing whatever to distract his mind, even for a few minutes. He lived entirely in his subject, refusing even to read the newspapers, except certain scientific periodicals which might happen to contain something relevant to the work he had in hand. As he expected his secretary to follow his example, it was hardly to be wondered at that both of them looked jaded and worn out.

"I took the manuscript to the Post Office myself, sir," said Harold Merefield listlessly. "Here is the registration receipt."

"Excellent, my boy, excellent," replied the Professor, looking up. "So the work is finished at last, eh? I have been destroying such notes as we shall not require again. The rest you can file at your leisure. Dear me, you look as if you needed a change of occupation."

He stared at his secretary through his spectacles, as though he had seen him that morning for the first time for many months. "Yes, I think we both need a change of occupation," he continued. "I feel that I should welcome some enticing problem, mathematical or human. It is time we stepped from our recent absorption back into the world. Let me see. What is the date?"

"April 28th, sir," replied Harold with a smile. He knew well enough that the Professor would have accepted any other day he chose to mention.

"Dear me! Then the world is six months older than when we retired from it. No doubt many interesting problems have arisen in the interval, but I fear that their solutions lie in other hands than ours. By the way, when does our friend Inspector Hanslet return from America?"

Harold turned to one of the big presses which lined the walls of the room, and took from it a folder marked "Inspector Hanslet." He consulted this for a moment, then looked up towards his employer. "At the end of this month, sir. There is no definite date mentioned. I dare say he is in London already."

"Perhaps so," agreed the Professor. "It does not really matter. My thoughts turned to him naturally, as to one who has in the past supplied us with some very satisfactory problems. Well, we must be patient, my boy. I have no doubt that we shall very soon succeed in finding some congenial work with which to occupy our minds."

He returned to the business of sorting his papers, while Harold sat down at the table reserved for his use, thankful to be able to do absolutely nothing for a few minutes. His idea of a change of occupation was not to plunge at once into some abstruse mathematical investigation which would involve him in the writing up of endless notes. If only Hanslet would come back and divert the Professor's thoughts into some other channel! But of Hanslet, since he had departed for New York during the previous year to co-operate with the American police in running to earth a gang of international swindlers, nothing had been heard.

Inspector Hanslet was rapidly becoming the foremost figure at Scotland Yard. He was a man who, without being brilliant, possessed more than the usual quickness of perception. He could, in his own phrase, see as far through a brick wall as most people, and to this attribute he added an agility of mind remarkable in a man whose training had been of a stereotyped kind. Early in his career he had become acquainted with Dr Priestley, and the Professor, to whom a problem of any kind was as the breath of his body, had since encouraged him to come to Westbourne Terrace and discuss his difficulties. To many of these the Professor's logical mind had suggested the solution. Since he refused to allow his name to be mentioned, the credit for his deductions descended upon Hanslet. As a matter of fact, the authorities knew very well how matters stood, and Hanslet was always employed upon those cases which promised to be complicated, since it was an open secret that he could call upon the advice and assistance of Dr Priestley.

It was evident that the sudden reaction of having nothing to do, after his unremitting labours of the past six months, was having an unfavourable effect upon Dr Priestley's temper. He roamed about the study, pulling out a file from time to time, and finding fault with Harold because some item did not come immediately to his hand. It was not until it was time to dress for dinner that he desisted from this irritating occupation. And even at dinner he was silent and morose, obviously seeking in vain for some new interest which should occupy his restless thoughts. But hardly had he and Harold finished their coffee, which they always had in the study after dinner, than Mary the parlourmaid opened the door softly. "Inspector Hanslet to see you, sir," she announced.

The Professor turned so abruptly in his chair as seriously to endanger the coffee cup he was holding. "Inspector Hanslet!" he exclaimed. "Why, show him in, of course. Good evening, Inspector, it was only this morning that Harold and I were speaking of you. I hope that you enjoyed yourself in America."

"I did indeed, Professor," replied Hanslet, shaking hands warmly with Dr Priestley, and nodding cheerily to Harold. "Not that I'm not very glad to be home again; one's own country's best, after all. I landed at Southampton last Wednesday."

"And now you have come back to tell us of your experiences," said the Professor. "I am sure we shall be most interested to hear them. Did you succeed in your object?"

"Oh, yes, we rounded them up all right," replied Hanslet. "My word, Professor, you ought to go over to New York and see the things the fellows do over there. As far as scientific detection goes, they've got us beat to a frazzle. You'd appreciate their methods. And they're a cheery crowd, too. They gave me no end of a good time while I was over there."

"Well, sit down, and tell us all about it," said the Professor, motioning Hanslet towards a comfortable chair. "You will relieve the tedium I am feeling at having nothing to do."

Hanslet sat down, and, as he did so, looked inquiringly at the Professor. "You say you've nothing to do, sir? Well, I'm very glad to hear that. The truth is that I didn't come here to tell you my experiences. As a matter of fact, I meant to take a month's leave when I got back, but the Chief asked me to wait a bit and take over a case which has been puzzling the Yard for several months. And I wanted to ask your advice, if you would be good enough to listen."

The Professor rubbed his hands together briskly. "Excellent, excellent!" he exclaimed. "I told you this morning, Harold, that a problem was bound to turn up before long. By all means tell me your difficulties, Inspector. But let me beg of you to keep to facts, and not to digress into conjecture."

Hanslet smiled. The Professor's passion for facts was well-known to him from past experience. "Well, I expect you know as much about it as I do," he began. "Ever since Tovey the greengrocer was killed last November, there's been a lot in the papers——"

But the Professor interrupted him. "I should perhaps have explained, Inspector, that since last October I have scarcely opened a newspaper. My whole mind has been concentrated upon a task which is now happily finished. The name of Tovey the greengrocer is, I regret to say, utterly unfamiliar to me. I should be glad if you would treat me as one who has only lately reached this world from the planet Mars, and give me the facts without presuming that I have any previous knowledge of them."

"Very well, Professor," replied Hanslet. "You must have heard of a series of deaths under peculiar circumstances which have occurred in Praed Street, not half a mile away from here? Why, I read about them in New York! They caused a great sensation."

"I am not concerned with popular sensations," said the Professor coldly. "I admit that some rumours of such happenings penetrated the isolation with which I have endeavoured to surround myself, but I dismissed them from my mind as likely to introduce a disturbing factor. I repeat that you had better repeat the facts, as briefly as possible."

"Very well. Professor, I will tell you the story exactly as it was told to me at the Yard," replied Hanslet. "You will be able to see how much is fact and how much conjecture. As I was not on the spot myself, I cannot vouch for the details. Will that do?"

The Professor nodded, and turned to Harold. "Make a note of the names and dates mentioned by Inspector Hanslet," he said.

"Now, Inspector, you may proceed."

Hanslet, whose memory for names and facts was rarely at fault, recounted as briefly as he could the course of events from the murder of Mr Tovey in November, to the finding of Martin's body in the cellar of Number 407, in January. The Professor interrupted him now and then to ask a question, but in the main he allowed him to tell the story in his own way. When he had finished, and the Professor had expressed himself satisfied, Hanslet continued.

"The man who's been in charge of the case is a fellow called Whyland, keen enough on his job, but a bit lacking in imagination. I had a chat with him yesterday, and he confessed that he was completely at the end of his tether. Up till last Saturday evening, he told me, he was pretty sure that he could lay his hand on the criminal, but that night something happened which entirely upset his calculations."

"What was that?" inquired the Professor, who was listening intently.

"Why, for one thing, the man whom he suspected of the murders was killed himself," replied Hanslet. "Not that there was anything amazing in that, for he seems to have been a trifle unbalanced in any case, and his death may possibly have been due to suicide. No, what altogether upset Whyland's apple-cart was that another man received a counter, some time after the death of the man whom Whyland suspected of delivering them."

"It is remarkable how frequently hypotheses founded upon pure conjecture are upset by one simple fact," remarked the Professor acidly. "Now, what was the name of this man whom Whyland suspected, and who so inconsiderately spoilt the theory by his premature death?"

"Samuel Copperdock," replied Hanslet, turning to Harold, who wrote the name on his pad.

"Copperdock?" repeated the Professor. "An unusual name, and yet I seem to have heard it before in some connection. Copperdock, Copperdock! Let me think——"

"You've probably seen the name above his shop. Professor,"

said Hanslet. "He was a tobacconist in Praed Street. Or you may have seen it some months ago in the paper. He was a witness at the inquest on Tovey, who was the first man murdered."

But the Professor shook his head. "No, if my memory serves me, I heard the name many years ago, in some connection which escapes me for the moment. However, the point would not appear to have any importance. I must apologise for interrupting you, Inspector. You were saying that another man received a counter after this man Copperdock's death, but I do not think you mentioned his name?"

"Ludgrove. Elmer Ludgrove," said Hanslet. "Rather an interesting personality, from what Whyland tells me. He keeps a herbalist's shop, and is a bit of a character in his way. He's a man of some education, between fifty and sixty, a very dignified old boy with a striking white beard, which I expect is a bit of an asset in his trade. He doesn't say much about himself, but does a lot of good in his own quiet way. All the poorer people in the neighbourhood come to him if they're in any sort of trouble, and he freely admits he hears a good many secrets. Whyland thought he would be a useful chap to get on the right side of, and often used to drop in to see him. He says he got more than one valuable hint from him. He was also pretty certain that this chap Ludgrove shared his suspicions of Copperdock, but he would never say so outright. You see, Copperdock was a friend of his."

The Professor nodded. "I see," he said. "And it was this Mr Ludgrove who received the counter, you say?"

"Yes, and, what's more, Whyland was with him when he found it. The poor old boy was terribly shaken for the moment, Whyland says, but after a bit he pretended to treat it as a joke. I've seen him since, and he's pretty plucky about it, knowing as he does that everybody who has received one of these infernal numbered counters has died a sudden death. He says that he is an old man, anyhow, alone in the world and with only a few more years to live in any case, so that his death will be no great blow to anybody."

"A most philosophic attitude," agreed the Professor. "But to return to Mr Copperdock. I should like to hear the circumstances under which he met his death."

Hanslet related the events of the previous Saturday night in considerable detail, up to the time when Whyland and Ludgrove entered the latter's sanctum. "There's not much more to add," he continued, "except that the doctor's suspicions were confirmed as to the poison. The Home office people examined the fragment of broken needle, and I heard this afternoon that they found traces of a remarkable virulent synthetic alkaloid. You'll know what that is better than I do. Professor."

"Yes, I know," replied the Professor grimly. "I have reason to. It was with one of these synthetic alkaloids—there are a number of them—that Farwell tipped the spines of the hedgehog to which I so nearly fell a victim. (See *The Ellerby Case* by John Rhode). You remember that incident, I dare say?"

"I do, indeed," said Hanslet warmly. "What's more, the Home Office people say that a dose of the stuff would produce almost immediate paralysis, and death within a few minutes. The incrustation was potassium carbonate all right, almost certainly the result of putting caustic potash on the place. But that only makes the business more puzzling. If Copperdock poisoned himself, how did he have time to apply the caustic potash before he was paralysed? If someone else did it, why should they apply the caustic, and how did they get in and out of the house? Remember, Whyland's man Waters had the place under observation all the time."

"Then you are inclined to favour the theory of suicide?" asked the Professor.

"On the whole, yes," replied Hanslet. "Oh, by the way, I forgot to tell you that soon after daylight Waters found the syringe, with the other part of the needle still in it, by the side of the road under Copperdock's window. There had been a heavy shower of rain about half past three, and the syringe was covered with mud and filth. The analysts could not find any traces remaining of the poison, but the end of the needle proved that it was the one that had been used. That points to suicide, a murderer wouldn't chuck away his weapon like that where anyone could see it.

"Besides, if you come to think of it, suicide fits in best with what we know. It is a fact that Copperdock's mind was to some extent unhinged. He declared that he met the black sailor, when a reliable witness declares that no such person was about. In fact, the only person besides Copperdock who seriously claims to have seen this black sailor is a degenerate youth who is also a convicted pick-pocket. It is highly probable that the counters were numbered, and the envelopes containing them typed in Mr Copperdock's office. Whyland assures me that the only link between the victims was Copperdock, not in any definite form, certainly, but still definite enough to make the coincidence remarkable. I am inclined to believe that Copperdock was at the bottom of it all somehow. My difficulty will be to prove it."

"You think, I gather, that this Mr Copperdock suffered from a peculiar form of homicidal mania, which finally culminated in his taking his own life?" suggested the Professor. "I admit that such cases are not unknown, but the theory involves you in many difficulties. I mention only one of them, the first that occurs to me. Where did he obtain this synthetic alkaloid? These substances are not articles of commerce, they are not, so far as I am aware, used in medicine. They are only produced experimentally in research laboratories. Farwell had a well-equipped laboratory, as you probably remember, which accounts for his use of such a poison. But how could a man in Copperdock's position procure it?"

Hanslet shrugged his shoulders. "I don't know, Professor," he replied. "I confess that I turn to the theory of Copperdock as the murderer because it seems to present fewer difficulties than any other. The whole thing seems to me to involve a mass of contradictions, whichever way you look at it. It's for that very reason I came to see you, Professor. But you must at least admit that madness in some form must be responsible. What rational motive could there be for the murder of half a dozen men entirely unconnected with one another, and whose deaths could be of no possible benefit to the murderer?"

"I am prepared to admit nothing until I have further examined the facts," replied the Professor severely. "Now, Harold, will you read me your notes upon the first murder? Thank you. I should like all details relating to Mr Tovey, please, Inspector."

It was long past midnight before they reached the end of the catalogue, and the Professor was satisfied that he knew everything which Hanslet could tell him.

"You will, of course, let me know if any fresh facts come to light," he said, as Hanslet rose to take his leave. "Meanwhile, I will consider the matter. If I come to any definite conclusions I will let you know. Good night, and pray accept my most sincere thanks for presenting me with a most absorbing problem."

CHAPTER 14 THE MORLANDSON TRIAL

The Professor came down to breakfast next morning looking even more weary than on the previous day. Harold, looking at him anxiously, guessed that he had hardly slept at all during the night. Some absorbing train of thought, whether started by Hanslet's story of the previous evening or not, had taken possession of his brain. But, in spite of his weariness, there was a queer gleam in the piercing eyes behind the powerful spectacles, which Harold knew from past experience to be the light of battle.

"I have some work for you today, my boy," he said, as soon as the meal was over. "I want you to go to the British Museum and look up the reports of the trials for murder at the Old Bailey during the first ten years of the present century. Among them you will find the trial of a doctor for the murder of one of his patients by giving him an overdose of morphia. I believe that the doctor's name began with an M, and I fancy that his patient had a title. More than this I cannot tell you; my memory, I regret to say, is not what it used to be. I want you to make a précis of that trial and of the sentence."

"Very good, sir," replied Harold, and forthwith started on his quest. He could not guess the purpose for which the Professor required this information, but it could obviously have nothing to do with these intriguing murders in Praed Street which Hanslet had described. Unless, perhaps, the Professor had seen some parallel between the methods of the unknown criminal and those of this vague doctor whose name began with an M. You never could predict the direction from which the Professor would approach a problem. All that you could be certain of was that it would be different from the one you anticipated.

Arrived at the Museum, where he was a frequent visitor on similar errands, he went carefully through the index to the Law Reports. It was not until he came to the year 1906 that he met with anything which corresponded to the data which the Professor had given him. Then he found a reference to the trial of one Doctor Morlandson for the murder of Lord Whatley. This must be the case to which his employer had referred. He turned up the records, and proceeded to make a careful abstract.

It appeared that Lord Whatley had been a man of middle age, and of some considerable wealth. Dr Morlandson was his regular medical attendant, and in 1905 he had been compelled to warn his patient that he was suffering from cancer, and that though an operation might be successful, there was grave doubt that it would permanently remove the source of the trouble. However, Lord Whatley consented to undergo the operation. He was removed to a nursing home, and a specialist was called in. The patient went through the ordeal satisfactorily, and after a while he returned home.

But, by the beginning of the following year, the symptoms reasserted themselves, and Dr Morlandson informed his patient, who insisted that he should be told the truth, that nothing more could be done, and that Lord Whatley had nothing to look forward to but perhaps a year or two of suffering. The relations between the two men were rather those of close friendship than of doctor and patient and, subsequent to Dr Morlandson's pronouncement, they saw a great deal of one another. Morlandson devoted as much time as he could spare from his practice to sitting with Lord Whatley, who was a childless widower and did not encourage the visits of his friends and relations.

By the end of February it appeared that the disease

was progressing even more rapidly than Dr Morlandson had anticipated. He administered frequent injections of morphia, and his patient was rarely conscious. Morlandson continued to spend the greater part of his time with him, and in Lord Whatley's brief intervals of consciousness his doctor, and the nurses who had been called in, were the only people he spoke to.

He died early in March, in the presence of Dr Morlandson and one of the nurses, without regaining consciousness. A cousin of Lord Whatley's, who happened to be his nearest relative, was in the house, and Morlandson informed him that he would return home and bring the necessary certificate with him later in the day. Morlandson, who lived about a mile away, started to walk home. When he had almost reached his own house, he heard a sound of confused shouting, and saw a runaway horse attached to a milk-cart coming towards him. Without a moment's hesitation he rushed for the horse's head, and had almost succeeded in stopping him, when he slipped and fell. One of the horse's hoofs struck him on the head and he was left unconscious on the road.

The spectators of the accident picked him up, and he was carried into his own house. A colleague was summoned, and declared that he was suffering from severe concussion. This diagnosis proved correct, and Morlandson lay in a state of semi-consciousness for nearly a week. On his recovery, he found the house in possession of the police.

Lord Whatley's cousin, hearing of the accident to Dr Morlandson, and learning that he could not possibly attend to his duties for some time to come, was at a loss for the want of a death certificate. He therefore sent for another doctor—not the man who was attending Morlandson—and asked him to sign the certificate. This the doctor would have done, had not one of the nurses, whom Morlandson had reprimanded for some breach of duty, made some vague insinuation that everything was not as it should be. The doctor insisted upon examining the body, and as a result of this examination he communicated with the authorities. A post-mortem was held, and Lord Whatley was proved to have died of an overdose of morphia. The experts gave it as their opinion that the deceased would not have died of the disease from which he was suffering for another year at least. A warrant was immediately issued for Dr Morlandson's arrest.

When Lord Whatley's will came to be read, it was found that he had left the sum of ten thousand pounds to Morlandson, conditional upon his being his medical attendant at the time of his death. This bequest was contained in a codicil executed early in February.

Morlandson came up for trial at the Old Bailey in July. The prosecution alleged that the codicil disclosed the motive for the murder, and submitted that Morlandson, fearing lest Lord Whatley should change his doctor before he died, had made certain of securing the legacy by poisoning him. They pointed out that, but for Morlandson's accident, he would have been able to certify cancer as the cause of Lord Whatley's death, and no suspicion would have been aroused.

Dr Morlandson's counsel put in a very striking defence. In effect, he pleaded guilty to the act of poisoning, but affirmed that this was done at Lord Whatley's express command. He had already suffered considerably and undergone an ineffectual operation, and refused to contemplate the further agony to which he was condemned. As soon as Morlandson had informed him that his case was hopeless, he had begged him to put an end to his sufferings at once, pointing out that such a course could cause no grief or inconvenience to anyone. Morlandson had at first refused, but at last, upon the solemn assurance of Lord Whatley that he would find some means of committing suicide unless his wishes were complied with, he consented to inject morphia in increasing doses. This Lord Whatley agreed to, and whenever he was conscious Morlandson begged him to reconsider his determination. Finally, knowing that the disease was incurable, and that the man he cared for as his friend could only endure months of suffering under his very eyes, he bade him farewell and administered the fatal dose. The news of the bequest came as a complete surprise to him.

Morlandson's defence raised in an acute form a controversy which had been going on for many years. Many people held that he was completely justified in his action, that his offence was purely technical, and that at the most it merited a short term of imprisonment. But the jury, in spite of a hint from the judge, found Morlandson guilty of murder and refused to add a rider recommending him to mercy. Sentence of death was duly pronounced, but the Home Secretary, the Court of Criminal Appeal not being then in existence, ordered a reprieve, and the sentence was commuted to one of twenty years' penal servitude. Morlandson's wife, to whom he was deeply attached, died before a year of it had expired.

This was the substance of the notes which Harold Merefield brought back to Dr Priestley. The latter read them through carefully, then gave them back to his secretary. "Yes, I thought that I was not mistaken," he said. "The facts of the case come back to me very clearly now. It made a considerable sensation at the time, owing to the principle involved. Right or wrong, Morlandson was acting in accordance with his lights. His evidence, I remember, was given with an air of passionate conviction. This Lord Whatley was his friend, and he had saved him from suffering at the expense of twenty years of his own life. I wonder whether he survived his sentence? It would be most interesting to learn."

The Professor relapsed into his favourite attitude of thought, his eyes fixed upon the ceiling, his hands, with the tips of the fingers touching, laid upon the table in front of him. He remained like this for many minutes before he spoke again.

"It would be so interesting that I feel impelled to take steps to discover the facts," he said. "After lunch I shall visit the record department at Scotland Yard. While I am away you can complete the filing of those papers I gave you yesterday relating to the work which we have just completed."

Harold received these instructions without any great enthusiasm. He was not greatly interested in the case of this Dr Morlandson, since it had occurred so many years ago and could have no possible bearing upon any problem of the present day. In his recollection of this forgotten trial the Professor seemed to be neglecting entirely the problems presented by the murders in Praed Street. Perhaps he had decided that they were not worthy of his notice. It was not every problem submitted to him which appealed to him sufficiently to induce him to devote his energies to its solution.

He spent the afternoon in the study, working half-heartedly and awaiting the Professor's return. But it was not until nearly dinner-time that his employer came in, and then he could see by his expression that the result of his search had in some way disappointed him. Dinner was passed through in almost complete silence, and the two returned once more to the study.

"I have discovered the subsequent history of Dr Morlandson," announced the Professor abruptly, as soon as he had finished his coffee. "I shall recount to you the result of my researches at Scotland Yard. You can make notes of them, and file them with your précis of his trial."

Harold produced pencil and paper, and the Professor proceeded to give an account of how he had spent the afternoon. After some delay the authorities at Scotland Yard, who were always anxious to carry out any of Dr Priestley's requests, even though they were ignorant of the motive behind them, had found the record of Morlandson's career after his sentence. He had been sent to Dartmoor, and had served his time there. He had been released on licence in 1920, having undergone fourteen years of his sentence. He had then remained for a short time in London, arranging his affairs, but had not communicated with anybody but his solicitor, to whom he had expressed his intention of spending the rest of his life in the most complete seclusion, and devoting himself to chemical research for which he had always had a bent during the period in which he was in practice.

Before the catastrophe which had overtaken him, Morlandson had been a tall, spare man, clean-shaven, and with carefully brushed dark hair. Upon his release he had developed a slight stoop, and although he was still clean-shaven and smart in appearance, his hair had gone nearly white. He told his solicitor that he knew he had only a few years longer to live, but that he hoped that during that period his researches would confer some benefit upon suffering humanity. He proposed to commence them as soon as he could find a suitable spot for the purpose, where he could live entirely alone.

A few weeks after his release, he found a half-ruined cottage which answered to his requirements, situated in a peculiarly desolate part of the Isle of Purbeck, in Dorsetshire. He took up his residence there, repaired the cottage, and added to it a laboratory, built of concrete. Under the terms of his licence he was compelled to report to the police, and they kept an eye upon his movements. They might have saved themselves the trouble. Once he was established in his cottage, his furthest excursion was to Corfe Castle, the nearest town, to obtain supplies. He lived entirely alone, and invariably walked across the heath to and from his cottage. But, even while living this hermit existence, he was always carefully dressed and shaved. He made no attempt to conceal his identity, but called himself Mr Morlandson, having dropped the prefix "Doctor." He had, of course, been struck off the register, and could not have practised as a doctor even had he desired to do so.

The local superintendent to whom he reported conceived a liking for him, and occasionally walked across the heath to visit him. He invariably found him at work in his laboratory, which was plentifully stocked with chemicals of various kinds. He would never allow smoking in the laboratory, for, as he pointed out to the superintendent, the substances with which he was experimenting were highly inflammable, and that there was consequently grave risk of fire unless proper precautions were taken.

One night, rather more than a year after Morlandson's release, flames were seen from Corfe Castle across the heath in the direction of his cottage. The superintendent leapt on his bicycle, and dashed off to the scene. When he arrived, he found the laboratory burning like a furnace, and quite unapproachable. The flames had caught the cottage, which was by then past saving, especially as the only available water supply was from a well fitted with a small bucket. The superintendent, at considerable risk to himself, managed to enter the sitting-room of the cottage, but could see no trace of Morlandson.

By morning the fire had burnt itself out. The cottage had been completely destroyed, only two or three feet of the outer walls remaining. The laboratory, being built of concrete, had fared rather better. The greater part of the walls remained, as did the steel door, which formed the only entrance. The place had no windows, but had been lighted from above through sky-lights in the roof. These and the roof itself had completely disappeared. The iron door was found to be locked upon the inside.

When it had been broken down, the interior of the laboratory showed how fierce the fire had been. Every trace of wood had been consumed, and solid metal fittings had been melted into unrecognisable shapes. Among the debris on the floor lay a charred human skeleton, upon one of the fingers of which was a half-melted gold ring, of which enough remained for the superintendent to identify it as having been habitually worn by Morlandson. The remains of the unfortunate man were huddled up by the door, the key of which was in the lock. It was clear that Morlandson had tried to make his way out when the fire broke out, but had been overcome by the fumes of the burning chemicals before he could achieve his purpose. He had been in the habit of locking the door in order to secure himself from interruption.

"You have made notes upon this?" asked the Professor. "Good. File them away. I confess that there are many things about this man Morlandson which I do not yet understand. I was able to supplement your account of the trial by an examination of the original records, which I was allowed to make. These gave me considerable food for thought. I believe that, through a pure accident, I have stumbled upon one of the most curious occurrences of modern times. I can, as yet, only conjecture, and so far my conjectures are wholly unsupported by fact. Much research will be necessary before these facts can be established, and it is possible that I may not be spared for a sufficient time to carry out this research."

"Not be spared, sir!" exclaimed Harold, startled by the grave tone of the Professor's voice. "Why, you have many years before you yet, I hope."

"Death comes to us all, sooner, perhaps, than we expect," replied Dr Priestley. "And I feel, this evening, that death may be closer to me than I have supposed. Ah, do I hear someone in the hall?"

With a nervous movement, entirely foreign to him, Dr Priestley rose from his chair and stood facing the door. Harold, with a queer feeling of expectation, walked towards it and opened it. In the hall stood Inspector Hanslet, handing his coat and hat to Mary.

"Good evening, Mr Merefield, I thought I'd look round and see if the Professor had any information for me," he said. "May I see him?"

"Yes, come in by all means," replied Harold, with a sudden sense of relief. "But I shouldn't stay too long, if I were you. He's rather tired and nervy tonight."

Hanslet nodded, and Harold led the way into the study. "It's Inspector Hanslet, sir," he said.

The Professor appeared to have entirely recovered his usual equanimity. "Ah, good evening. Inspector," he said blandly. "I half expected that you would be round this evening. I am very glad to see you."

"I thought I would come round, on the chance that you had some hint to give me," replied Hanslet. "I can't make head or tail of the business I told you about last night. The more I think about it, the more puzzling it seems. It's the utter lack of motive that makes it all so inexplicable."

"I believe, mind, I say only that I believe, that I have discovered the motive," said the Professor quietly.

"You have!" exclaimed Hanslet excitedly. Then, seeing the

slow movement of the Professor's head, he smiled. "I know you won't tell me until you are certain," he continued. "But at least tell me this. Are there likely to be any more of these mysterious deaths?"

"There will be one more, unless I am able to prevent it," replied the Professor.

CHAPTER 15 THE BONE COUNTERS

Mr Ludgrove, as Hanslet had said to Dr Priestley, bore the shock of the finding of the numbered counter extremely well. He had refused to make any alteration in his usual habits, and it was with the greatest difficulty that Whyland could persuade him to allow a constable to sleep in the house at night.

"I can assure you that this mysterious warning does not terrify me," he had said. "I am an old man, and death cannot be far off in any case. I am not sure that I should not prefer a violent end to some lingering illness which might leave me helpless for months before it killed me. But, if you think that by keeping a close watch over me you can gain some clue to the distributor of these counters, by all means do so."

He was in this frame of mind when Hanslet came to see him on the Sunday afternoon. Whyland brought him round and introduced him, and Mr Ludgrove welcomed him with his usual courtesy.

"I have heard of you, Inspector Hanslet, and I am indeed proud to make your acquaintance. Sit down, and make yourself comfortable."

"Thank you, Mr Ludgrove," Hanslet replied. "I thought you wouldn't mind my coming to have a chat with you. Whyland here has told me all about these queer happenings in this street of yours, and of the help which you have been to him."

"I am afraid that I have been of very little help," said Mr

Ludgrove with a smile. "Inspector Whyland has been kind enough to appreciate beyond their value any suggestions I have made."

"Well, that's as may be," replied Hanslet. "Now, Mr Ludgrove, I am going to ask for further assistance on your part. You know as much about these counters as I do. They seem to have been sent, so far, to six men, all of whom have died shortly after they received them. Whyland tells me that he had utterly failed to establish any connection between these men. Except for the fact that Tovey and Copperdock were close friends, they all seem to be comparative strangers to one another, and have never been associated in any common enterprise. You see what I mean, of course?"

"I do, indeed. In fact, Inspector Whyland and I discussed the point, long ago. It might be possible to imagine a motive for the murder of a group of men who were inspired by a common motive or who belonged to some common society. The difficulty is, assuming that the agency which compassed their deaths was the same in each case, to imagine a motive for the actions of that agency."

"Exactly!" exclaimed Hanslet warmly. "I see that you appreciate my point as clearly as I do myself. But now we have a fresh line of investigation. You yourself are added to the list of those who have received the counter. Can you explain why you should have been singled out?"

Mr Ludgrove shook his head. "As you may suppose, the subject has occupied my thoughts ever since I found the counter," he replied. "I am an old man, as I have said before, and for the last twenty years or more I have led a retired life, retired, I mean, in the sense that I have taken no part in the affairs of the world. I have had enemies as well as friends, few men who have reached my years could say otherwise. But most of the contemporaries of my youth are dead, and in any case I do not believe that any of the enemies I may have made would be so vindictive as to seek my life."

"Let us look at it another way, then," said Hanslet. "Can

you imagine any way in which you, in common with the six men who have already died, could have made an unconscious enemy?"

"I cannot," replied Mr Ludgrove. "Of those six men, I knew only two personally, Mr Copperdock fairly well, and Mr Colburn slightly. Both of these I have known only since I came to live in Praed Street, five years ago. Tovey, I had heard Copperdock speak of. The name of Richard Pargent, I had seen mentioned in the newspapers. The other two were complete strangers to me. I cannot imagine how we could have committed any act in common which would draw down upon us the vengeance of a single assassin."

"Then you do not believe that these deaths are the work of a single assassin, Mr Ludgrove?" inquired Hanslet with interest.

"Not of a single man, acting upon any rational motive," replied Mr Ludgrove. "Even in the brain of a homicidal maniac there is usually traceable some dim guiding principle. He either conceives a hatred for a certain class of person, or he kills indiscriminately, usually selecting the people nearest to hand. In this case the selection was anything but indiscriminate. Mind, I am assuming for the moment, as apparently you are yourself, that the death of all six was the direct sequel of their receipt of a numbered counter. If you adopt the theory that a single man is responsible, you may as well believe in the existence of the black sailor."

"I am afraid that we are already committed to him," said Hanslet with a smile. "You see, we offered a reward for him, and it would never do for the police to admit that they had offered a reward for a ghost. Whyland, what is your honest opinion of this black sailor?"

"Entirely between ourselves and this most comfortable room, I have never believed in his existence for a moment," replied Whyland readily. "But what could I do? That young rip, Wal Snyder, swore to having seen him, and I couldn't shake him."

"Whether young Snyder saw him or not," remarked the herbalist, "your reward has made him a very real person to the poorer classes of this district. One or other of my customers sees him every night, usually during the hour which immediately follows the closing of the public houses. And, as a rule, they come here hot-foot to tell me about it."

"I'm sorry, Mr Ludgrove," laughed Whyland. "I wouldn't have done it if I could have helped it. By the way, I suppose that you are perfectly satisfied that none of these odd customers of yours know anything about this business?"

"Perfectly," replied Mr Ludgrove. "They are a strange lot, I admit, professing a code of morals which in some respects would shock the conscience of a savage, and many of them are not above any petty dishonesty. But murder, deliberate and planned murder, that is, is outside their imagination. Besides, the way they know one another's most secret actions is almost uncanny. If one of them knew anything about these deaths, they would all know within a very short time, and the secret would be a secret no longer. Of course, they all come to me with long and complicated tales of how they could tell me the name of the man who did it, if I will give them the money in advance. But I am well accustomed to that, it is a symptom which follows every crime committed in this district."

"You're quite right, Mr Ludgrove, I know something of the ways of these people," said Hanslet. "When they talk like that, you may be sure that they know nothing. It's when they avoid the subject that you may learn something. Well, I'm very glad to have met you. There's just one thing I should like to say. You have received this counter, which was evidently slipped in here while all of you were thinking of nothing but the death of Mr Copperdock. You, and those whose business it is to guard you, are therefore fore-warned. As long as you do what we ask you to, I do not believe that you are in any danger."

Mr Ludgrove smiled. "Mr Copperdock was also guarded and fore-warned," he said quietly.

Whyland swore softly. "I believe Copperdock committed suicide out of sheer funk," he said. "Anyhow, I can't see any way in which he can possibly have been murdered."

"Well, I shall not commit suicide just yet, I promise you that," replied Mr Ludgrove.

It was not more than five minutes after the departure of Hanslet and Whyland that the herbalist heard a soft knock upon the door of the shop. He went to open it, and found Ted and Ivy standing on the step, closely scrutinized by the man in plain clothes who had been deputed to look after Mr Ludgrove's safety.

Mr Ludgrove glanced at Ivy, and welcomed Ted warmly. "Come in," he said hospitably. "I was going to look in later and ask you if you would care to spend the evening here. I am very glad you came over."

"Thank you, Mr Ludgrove," replied Ted awkwardly. "This is Miss Tovey. You have heard poor Dad and me mention her."

"I have, indeed. I am very glad to meet you, Miss Tovey. I think that is the best chair. Won't you sit down and make yourself comfortable?"

The young people sat down in silence. It was evident that they had come with a purpose, but now they had arrived they did not quite know how to state it. Curiously enough, it was Ivy who made the plunge.

"I've heard so much about you, Mr Ludgrove, that I felt that Ted and I simply must come and ask your advice," she began. "We both feel we must do something. First of all my father is murdered, and now Ted's. We just can't sit still and wait any longer. Mr Ludgrove, can't *something* be done to punish the man?"

The herbalist looked at her gravely. "My dear young lady, I sympathise with you entirely," he said. "I, too, have felt the desire to do something in the face of these extraordinary happenings. But let me assure you that the very best brains in the police are at work in the matter. Inspector Hanslet, who was here just now, has the matter in hand, and he has unravelled almost as tangled skeins as this appears to be."

"That was Inspector Hanslet, was it?" inquired Ted, with interest. "We saw two men, one of whom we knew was Inspector Whyland, come in to see you, and we waited until they went away. I've heard of Inspector Hanslet before, seen his name in the papers, often enough. I'm glad he's on the job, I shall feel that something's being done at last. The other chap always seemed to be hanging round the poor old Dad, and doing nothing."

"It is very difficult for the police to do anything without evidence," said Mr Ludgrove gravely. "Now, since you have come to ask my advice, I am going to take an old man's liberty and ask you both a question which you may consider impertinent. Have either of you any knowledge, concerning your dead parents, which you have not imparted to the police? Or, perhaps, I should have put it another way. Have either of you any suspicions, which you have thought it better to keep to yourselves, as to the motive which anyone might have had for committing these murders?"

He looked at Ivy as he spoke, but she shook her head emphatically. "I can think of nothing which I have not already told Inspector Whyland," she replied. "Daddy was a dear, and I don't believe he had an enemy in the world," she replied. "He was a little hot-tempered at times, but everybody knew that he meant nothing by it." She paused for a moment, then continued with downcast eyes. "I can imagine what may have passed through your mind, Mr Ludgrove, but Daddy wasn't that sort of man. I won't say that he was above a mild flirtation, but I am sure that no woman was the cause of his being murdered."

"Thank you, Miss Tovey," replied the herbalist gravely. "That is a franker statement than I had any right to expect and you, Ted?"

"No, I've told the police everything," replied Ted wearily. "I know they think that Dad committed suicide. I believe they want people to think so, so that there won't be another undetected murder up against them. But I know he didn't. Dad wasn't the sort of man to do a thing like that. I know he got a bit tight sometimes, but why shouldn't he? It never did him or anybody else any harm. But even when he was tight he never got morbid, like some fellows do. Besides, he never used one of them syringe things. I don't suppose he'd ever seen one in his life, and he wouldn't know how to use it. No, Dad was murdered, right enough, though I'm blest if I can see how it was done."

"Can't you help us, Mr Ludgrove?" broke in Ivy. "Surely there must be some way of finding out who killed Daddy and Ted's father. It must have been some lunatic, for no sane person could possibly have a grudge against either of them."

"The only way to find out seems to be to learn something about these counters," replied Mr Ludgrove. "Your father, I am told, received the first. Did you see it, Miss Tovey?"

"No. I only know what mother told me," replied Ivy. "Daddy was a bit late coming back from Covent Garden that morning, and I had finished my breakfast and gone to work before he came in. Of course, he had no idea what it meant, poor dear. He thought it was one of these advertising dodges, and threw it into the fire, envelope and all."

"Well, that is a pity," said Mr Ludgrove. "The police have seen all the others, and they say that they are all exactly similar, and that the numbers seem to have been written on them with the same pen and ink, just an ordinary steel pen and red ink that one can buy at any stationers. And, whenever they have been sent by post, the envelopes have been of the same sort, the address typed with the same machine, a Planet, and posted in this district, London, W2. This looks as though they had been sent out by the same hand."

"Typed on a Planet, were they?" remarked Ted. "That's the same machine as we've got."

"Yes, it is a fairly popular make, I am told," replied Mr Ludgrove. "But I have never used a typewriter in my life, and know very little about them. No doubt Miss Tovey can tell us if Planet machines are used extensively?"

"I had never used one until Ted asked me to teach him to use his, nearly a year ago now," replied Ivy. "There were none at the school I was at, and we haven't any at the office. But I believe that some firms have several of them. They have not been sold in England for very long."

"Thank you, Miss Tovey," said Mr Ludgrove. "Now there is another curious thing which I should like to mention. One day, when I was in your place, talking to your father, I saw you sending out what I took to be accounts, Ted. Was I right?"

"I expect so," said Ted, readily. "I always look after that side of the business."

"Would you mind running across and getting me one of the envelopes that you use?"

"Of course." Ted left the room, and returned within a couple of minutes, holding an envelope which he handed to Mr Ludgrove. "Those are what we always use," he said. "We've had them for nearly two years now."

"Do you know where they came from?" asked Mr Ludgrove, examining the envelope with great interest.

"Dad bought a large quantity of them, ten thousand, I believe, from a wholesale stationer somewhere in the Harrow Road," replied Ted. "I forget the name of the people. They were going out of business, or something, and were selling the stuff off cheap. Dad had an idea of sending out a lot of circulars, and thought these would do to send them in. But the scheme fell through, and I've been using them for ordinary business purposes ever since."

"I see," said Mr Ludgrove thoughtfully. "Now, it is a very extraordinary thing that the envelopes which have been shown me as having contained these numbered counters, are exactly the same in every respect as this that you have just given me."

This remark was received in horrified silence. It was Ivy who broke it. "Mr Ludgrove!" she exclaimed. "You don't mean——"

"I mean nothing," replied Mr Ludgrove swiftly. "I am trying to make you both see one aspect of this matter which has caused me much anxiety for some time. The counters were marked with a pen and ink exactly similar to those you have in your office, Ted. The envelopes in which they were sent are exactly the same as the ones you possess and have used for many years. The addresses were typed with a Planet machine, which, according to Miss Tovey, are not to be found in every office. Finally, the letters were posted in this district, W2. You cannot fail to see the inference which must infallibly be drawn."

"But, good heavens, the idea's absurd!" broke in Ted. "You mean that the counters were sent out from our place!" He laughed mirthlessly, while Ivy stared at the grave face of the old herbalist, only half comprehending.

"You, Ted, have seen at least one of these counters," continued Mr Ludgrove, in a quiet and solemn voice. "Do you remember ever seeing anything like it before?"

Ted stared at Mr Ludgrove, and the incredulous expression of his face turned slowly to one of mingled amazement and horror. "Why, yes," he stammered. "Dad had a box of white bone counters just like the one I saw. He used to ask his friends in to play some card game, in which these counters were used. I haven't seen them for a couple of years or more."

Again there was a silence, broken by something that sounded like a sob from Ivy. Ted turned towards her with a despairing gesture. "It isn't true!" he exclaimed. "I can't explain it, but it isn't true! Dad couldn't have done it. Why should he? There's some terrible mystery behind all this. I shall never believe that poor dad had anything to do with it. Why was he killed himself, if he had?"

He turned appealingly to Mr Ludgrove. "You don't believe it yourself, do you?" he said.

"Your father was my friend, and I should be the last to accuse him," he replied. "But, in fairness to you both, I was bound to point out the direction in which any inquiry as to the counters must lead. I do not profess to understand it, but I must warn you that a man like Inspector Hanslet cannot fail to perceive the points I have mentioned."

"But what am I to do if he questions me?" asked Ted distractedly.

"Tell the truth," replied Mr Ludgrove solemnly. "Hide nothing, for if it is discovered that you have concealed anything, it will tell all the more heavily against your father. There is only one true court of justice, the court of our own hearts. A consciousness of innocence is the only support against an unjust accusation. It would perhaps have been better had your father realised this."

CHAPTER 16
CORFE CASTLE

For a couple of days after Inspector Hanslet's last visit to the house in Westbourne Terrace, Dr Priestley's attitude had sorely puzzled Harold. He had hardly spoken a word, and the greater part of his time had been spent in sorting out the mass of documents which had accumulated during the course of years in the massive presses which lined the walls of his study. Harold said nothing, knowing from past experience that it was useless to ask questions. When the Professor was ready to issue his instructions he would do so. Until then, untimely questions would merely be rewarded with a rebuff.

It was therefore with intense eagerness that Harold replied, one morning shortly after breakfast, the Thursday following the death of Mr Copperdock, to an abrupt question by his employer: "My boy, what I am about to say to you must remain a secret between ourselves, until either my death occurs or I give you leave to speak. Is that understood?"

"I undertake not to breathe a word to anybody," replied Harold.

"To nobody," repeated the Professor emphatically. "Not even to Hanslet, however urgent the need may seem. I am going away for a time; how long that time may be I cannot tell. I do not wish my whereabouts to be known, as that would possibly place me in considerable danger."

"You're not surely going alone, sir!" exclaimed Harold. "You'll let me come with you, especially as you say that there is danger attached to your journey?"

But the Professor shook his head. "The danger may exist in London equally," he replied. "It is essential that someone I can trust should remain here. Otherwise, my boy, I should be more than pleased to take you with me. Now, listen very carefully to these instructions. Do not leave the house for long at a time, especially in the evening. Open all my correspondence and deal with it to the best of your ability. Should there be among it any letter of a startling character, put a message in the personal column of *The Times*, 'The asp has struck,' and sign it 'Cleopatra.' Do you follow this so far?"

"Yes, sir," replied Harold simply, but gazing at his employer in bewilderment. There was something theatrical about these extraordinary precautions utterly foreign to the Professor's usual methods of procedure.

"Very well," continued the Professor. "If I find it necessary to communicate with you it will be by letter. The contents of the letter you may neglect. It may be typewritten, or in a disguised hand. You will know the letter is from me by the fact that it will be addressed in the first place to Westbourne Grove. The word *Grove* will be ruled through, and the correct word *Terrace* substituted for it. The envelope will, in fact, convey the message. If the contents of the letter are to be read, which will only be if any unexpected developments take place, the envelope will be stamped with a three-halfpenny stamp. If, on the other hand, it is stamped with a penny and a halfpenny stamp, you will immediately proceed to the Post Office from which it was sent, which you will discover from the post-mark, where you will wait till I join you. If the envelope is stamped with three separate halfpenny stamps, you will go to Inspector Hanslet, explain what I am now telling you, and persuade him to come with you at once to the place indicated by the post-mark. Is that clear?"

"Perfectly clear, sir," replied Harold. "I'll just make a note of that code, if you don't mind, sir."

"No, make no notes!" commanded the Professor. "I have purposely contrived the code so simply that you can carry it in your head. You must realise that our actions will very probably be watched, in fact, I should not be surprised to learn that they have been under observation for some considerable time. Now, the next thing I want you to do is to type out a few copies of this paragraph and distribute them to the news agencies."

He held out a scrap of paper as he spoke, and Harold took it from him. It ran as follows: "Dr Priestley, whose scientific writings have rendered his name familiar to the British public, has received a cablegram begging him to deliver a series of lectures at a number of the Australian Universities. Dr Priestley, who has just completed the manuscript of his forthcoming book, *Some Aspects of Modern Thought*, has accepted the invitation. Since he is anxious to return to England before the end of the year, he has left London hurriedly *via* Southampton and Havre, in order to catch the Celestial liner *Oporto* at Marseilles. He will travel by the *Oporto* to Sydney."

In spite of several attempts upon Harold's part, he could elicit no further information from the Professor. He typed out the paragraph, and took it round to the agencies himself. When he returned, he found the Professor upstairs busily engaged in piling a quantity of clothes, which he was never likely to wear, into three or four large trunks.

"You aren't really going to Australia, are you, sir?" he ventured.

"It would be quite useless for me to announce the fact unless I were to make every appearance of so doing," replied the Professor tartly. "The boat train for Havre leaves Waterloo at half-past nine, I understand. You will arrange for two taxis to be here at a quarter to nine. I always like to give myself plenty of time to catch the train."

The Professor was normally one of those people who travel without any fuss. But on this occasion it seemed that he could not accept anything unless he had seen it done with his own eyes. He stood on the steps of the house for at least five minutes, directing the taxi-drivers where and how to distribute his trunks. When he and Harold arrived at Waterloo, he insisted upon interviewing innumerable officials, to each of whom he gave his name, asking endless and apparently irrelevant questions. Finally, having secured his seat, he walked up and down the platform several times the whole length of the train, instructing Harold as to the disposition of his household in his absence. It was not until the train was on the point of starting that he took his seat.

"Remember what I told you, my boy," were his last words as the train moved off.

The Professor had booked to Paris, where he arrived before noon on Friday. He fussed about the Gare St Lazare for some little time, and finally put his trunks in the cloak-room. He then went to one of the smaller hotels in the Quartier de l'Europe, booked a room, for which he paid in advance, and arranged for the collection of his trunks from the station. He lunched at a big restaurant in the boulevards, and spent the afternoon at the Louvre. In the evening he returned to the Gare St Lazare, ten minutes before the Southampton boat train was due to leave. He booked a ticket for Southampton, and with a directness in singular contrast with the indecision he had displayed on the outward journey, took his seat in the train. He reached Southampton early on Saturday morning, and remained in his cabin until the London train had left the docks. Then, carrying a single suitcase, he walked to the West station and took a ticket to Corfe Castle.

Dr Priestley, although he was known by name to a very large circle of newspaper readers, who were periodically entertained by one or other of his thrusts at some pet nostrum of the moment, such as the craze for brown bread or the discovery of vitamines, rarely or never appeared in public. He had even escaped the doubtful honour of having his photograph reproduced in the evening papers, though this perhaps was a disadvantage, since it would certainly have been unrecognisable. He was therefore in no sense a public figure, in that he was most unlikely to be distinguished from the ordinary crowd of travelling humanity. He sat in the train without any attempt at disguise, studying an ordnance map which he had laid open upon his knees.

It was still early when he reached Corfe Castle. The village, with its commanding ruin perched upon the summit of a conical hill, was in the full flood of its morning activity. Dr Priestley, standing at the station gate, watched the passers-by for a moment with keen interest. Not one of them paid him the compliment of more than a fleeting and incurious glance.

He walked towards the heart of the village, and entered the first inn he came to. Having ascertained that he could have a single room for as long as he liked, he announced his determination of spending a few days, and was finally shown into a comfortable room with a view of the Castle. Here he remained until lunch.

The Professor lunched with keen enjoyment. His adventure was giving him an appetite. In spite of the amount of travelling which he had done during the last couple of days he felt thoroughly fit and well, much better than he had done during the winter in town. The menace which had been revealed to him seemed far away to him in this peaceful spot, it almost seemed to him as though the whole of his discoveries had been merely some impossible dream, the penalty of overwork, and that the fresh country air, tinged with the faintly salt tang of the sea, had swept it from his brain into the realms of the unreal. Perhaps, after all, he was entirely wrong in his deductions. Those mysterious murders in Praed Street might have been the result of some entirely different influence. He had merely conjecture to guide him: somehow, now he had reached the place where alone the corroborative facts could be gathered, it seemed as though his actions and his fears were the effect of a sudden and unaccountable impulse.

He wandered from the luncheon room past the little saloon bar, and glanced in at the open door. The place was empty; it was past two o'clock, and the local habitués had returned to their labours. It was too early in the year for visitors. The Professor walked into the bar, and took a seat by the side of the counter.

The proprietor, who was serving a few belated customers in

the tap-room, came in at the sound of the Professor's entrance, and greeted him with professional courtesy.

"Good afternoon, Mr Deacon," he said cheerfully. (Deacon was the name which the Professor had inscribed in the hotel register —it said much for the proprietor's skill that he had deciphered it correctly.) "I hope you found your room to your liking, and enjoyed your lunch?"

"Yes, thank you," replied the Professor. "I think I shall be very comfortable here for a day or two. I looked in here to ask you for a liqueur after my lunch. Perhaps you will join me in one?"

"Liqueurs ain't much in my line, thankee, sir," replied the landlord. "But I'll take a drop o' gin with you, since you're so kind. What'll be yours, sir? I've got Benedictine, Crême de Menthe——"

"I should prefer some old brandy, if you have it," interrupted the Professor.

"Ah, you know a thing or two, Mr Deacon, I can see that," replied the landlord with a knowing wink. "I've got a rare drop of brandy put away in the cellar. I never had only six bottles of it, and there's still four left. My customers don't hardly ever ask for it, it's mostly beer or whisky with them. Unless it happens to be a gentleman from London like yourself, sir."

He disappeared, and returned in a few moments with a long-necked bottle, from which he poured a glass of pale amber liquid. "There, just try that, sir," he exclaimed proudly.

The Professor picked up the glass and sampled the contents gravely," Excellent, very excellent indeed!" he commented approvingly. "I am quite sure that my doctor would have prescribed this as part of the cure, had he known of it."

"Cure, sir?" inquired the landlord sympathetically. "I hope the illness has not been serious?"

"Oh, no, not at all," replied the Professor. "One could scarcely call it an illness. I have been rather run down, that is all. Men of my age have to take care of themselves, you know, and I have been devoting rather more time and energy than was perhaps wise to my business in the City. I found myself suffering from headaches and loss of appetite, so my doctor ordered me a complete rest. He said it was the only thing to set me up again."

"Well, here's your very good health, sir," said the landlord, tossing off his gin. "You couldn't have come to a better place than this for a rest. I was afraid, when you comes in, that you'd find it too quiet at this time of year. I says to myself, 'Here's a gentleman from London who'll be looking for a band and a promenade and what not!' Why, sir, there isn't even a sharry running at this season."

"That fact adds another attraction to your most comfortable house," replied the Professor. "It was my doctor who recommended me to come here. He motored through on his way to Swanage last year. He recommends me to take a fairly long walk after every meal. I understand that you have some very beautiful heaths around here?"

"They may be beautiful, but they're precious lonely," said the landlord. "They may suit you all right, sir, but for my part I take the bus into Wareham or Swanage when I wants to get out for a bit."

"I shall not be sorry to enjoy the loneliness of the countryside, after the bustle of London," replied the Professor. "But I suppose people do live on these heaths, do they not?"

"Well, there's a few clay pits, and now and then a gravel quarry," said the landlord. "But, take it all round, you can walk a long way without meeting a living soul, so long as you keep off the main road. It is like that all over Purbeck, whichever way you go. Of course, there's a few cottages where the clay-workers live, but that is about all, outside the villages, and there ain't many of them."

"What an ideal spot on which to build a country retreat!" exclaimed the Professor. "Not one of those villa residences, which are growing up so plentifully all over the country, but just a cottage, in the true sense of the word, where one could enjoy without distraction the glories of nature!"

The landlord looked at the Professor with a curious expression. "You wasn't thinking of doing anything like that, was you, sir?" he inquired.

"Why, no, not at present, however much the idea might appeal to me," replied the Professor, artlessly. "I fear that my duties in London would not allow me sufficient leisure."

"Queer thing, now, that you should say that about a cottage, sir," said the landlord, confidentially. "It puts me in mind of an odd thing that happened in these parts, not so many years ago. All along of another gentleman, about the same age as you might be, sir, coming into this very bar and asking me if I knew of a lonely cottage for sale."

"Indeed?" replied the Professor casually. "Perhaps you would refill my glass with that most excellent brandy. And if you will do me the honour of taking another glass of gin with me——"

"You're very kind, sir," said the landlord, filling up the glasses. "I thought you'd take to that brandy. As soon as I sees you taste it, I says to myself, 'Here's a gentleman that knows a good drop of liquor when he sees it.' 'Tisn't every gentleman that takes kindly to the drink nowadays, sir. Why, there's some of them what drops in here for lunch as takes water with it! Can't say I hold with it myself. Well, here's your very good health, sir!"

He consumed his glass of gin at a gulp, and stood with his elbows on the counter, looking at the Professor. "Your saying that about the cottage does put me in mind of that other," he said, reminiscently. "Mind you, sir, not that he was like you at all. Of course I didn't know who he was when he came in, but I says to myself, 'That fellow's no business man, I'll warrant!' And, as it turned out, I was right! But you can always tell, can't you, sir?"

"Usually," agreed the Professor. "He was not a business man, then?"

"Not he!" exclaimed the landlord, contemptuously. "He was one of them scientific chaps, like you reads about in the papers. What good they does I don't know! Always seems to me as though they'd be better employed doing something useful instead of talking a lot of gibberish decent folks don't understand. Well, this poor chap suffered for his folly, anyhow."

"Why, what happened to him?" inquired the Professor

without any great show of interest.

"Burnt to death!" replied the landlord, impressively. "Burnt till there wasn't nothing but a heap of charred bones left, sir. Terrible thing it was, and him all alone out on the heath there. Quiet enough chap he seemed, too. Why, I couldn't believe my ears when the constable told me about him afterwards. You wouldn't have guessed what the chap was really, not if you was to try for a twelvemonth."

"I dare say not," remarked the Professor dryly. "I never was good at guessing. What was he?"

"Ticket o' leave man!" exclaimed the landlord, leaning over the counter confidentially. "If you'll believe me, that man had just served fourteen years hard on Dartmoor for murdering a Duke, when he walked into my bar as cool as a cucumber. Oh, he was a deep one, was that Mr Morlandson! And not a soul bar the super knew a word about it!"

"Burnt to death, was he!" remarked the Professor. "Dear me, what a terrible end. How did it happen?"

"No one knows rightly," replied the landlord. "He lived all alone on the heath, over yonder towards Goathorn. Built himself a concrete place, I can't remember what the super said he called it. Word something like lavatory."

"Laboratory, perhaps?" suggested the Professor.

"Aye, that's it, sir. You can see the ruins of it still, they tell me. I haven't been out that way since it happened. Used to lock himself up in this place of his, and fiddle about with all sorts of inflammable stuff. Bound to go up it was, and sure enough it did. Just after closing time one evening. Old George what lives way out towards Studland, comes knocking at my door and says the heath's on fire. 'Heath on fire!' I says, 'Why, it's been raining for a week. What are you talking about?' 'Tis that for sure!' says old George. 'You can see the flames up along my way.' 'Flames!' I says, 'It's the stuff they gives you at the "Red Bull" over yonder that makes you see flames, and I don't wonder at it!' Well, he keeps on, and at last I goes half a mile or so up the road with him. Sure enough, there was a great pillar of flame coming up from the middle of the heath.

"We hadn't been there more than a minute when the constable comes along. 'What's up yonder?' I says. 'Morlandson's place on fire,' says he. 'Super he's gone off on his bike. You chaps best come along and see what you can do.'

"Well, sir, it weren't no manner of good to take the engine. She's only one of them hand concerns, and last time we'd had her out to practice, she pumped back'ards like into the river instead of out of it. Joe Stiggs, him what looks after her, said he found he'd put the valves in the wrong way. Besides, it would have taken us best part of an hour to push her out there, there ain't no regular road. And, what's more, all the water out at Morlandson's place was a well what ran dry every summer."

"Then there was nothing to be done?" commented the Professor.

"Nothing whatsoever," replied the landlord emphatically. "Mind, we didn't know Morlandson was inside. We expected to find him running round outside chucking water at it from a bucket. However, off we goes, and as we gets close we catches the stink of it. Lord! I shan't forget it in a hurry. It was like the smell what comes from the pits when they burns carcases when the foot-and-mouth's about.

"The super he meets us, and I reckon I hollered out when I saw him by the light of the fire. He was black as a sweep, and all the hair singed off his face. Told us he'd been into the cottage, which was burning like a dry rick, and that he couldn't find Morlandson anywhere. 'I reckon he's in there,' he says, pointing to the lav——labor——what you call it. 'There's a horrible smell of burnt flesh about.'

"He was right there, it fair made me sick. But there was nothing to be done. You couldn't get within fifty yards of the place. We waited till nigh on midnight, but even when the flames went down the walls were red-hot and we weren't no further for'ard. Super, he stays on all night, and in the morning he finds what's left of Morlandson, and that's precious little."

"Dear me, what a terrible thing!" exclaimed the Professor.

"Aye, that it was," agreed the landlord. "They brought back what there was of the poor chap in a potato sack, held an inquest on him, and buried him in the churchyard yonder. And that is what happened to the last gent what fancied a lonely life on the heath, sir."

The landlord glanced up at the clock, the hands of which pointed to five and twenty minutes to three. "Hallo, I must close the bar, or I'll be getting into trouble," he said, reluctantly removing his arms from the counter.

"A visit to the scene of the tragedy would provide me with an object for a walk," said the Professor. "Which is my best way to it?"

"You can't go wrong, provided you don't mind a bit of rough going," replied the landlord. "If you go out of the village towards Wareham, you'll come upon a railway track, what they runs the trucks of stones along. That goes to Goathorn pier, a matter of six mile away or more. Follow the line for nigh on three mile, and you'll come to a clay-pit. Then, about a quarter or half a mile away, on your right, you'll see what's left of the place, standing up among the gorse and heather. There is a track, but it's a long way round and plaguey hard to find if you don't know it. Now, if you'll excuse me, sir, it's past closing time."

CHAPTER 17 THE CLAY-PIT

Dr Priestley walked out of the inn, and down through the village towards the ruined castle, standing upon its curiously artificial-looking mound. He had attained one of the objects of his visit, corroboration of the story of the death of Mr Morlandson, and that without asking questions which might have suggested that he had any interest in the matter. Since the landlord had himself volunteered the information, there could be no reason for his having distorted the truth. Morlandson, by the evidence of those best qualified to speak was dead, and his charred bones were resting in the quiet churchyard which the Professor was at that very moment passing.

He felt a great desire to see the site of the tragedy, but his natural caution prevented him from walking to it immediately. He was most anxious to avoid any suspicion that Mr Deacon, the City merchant, was in any way interested in the fate of the ex-convict. But, on the other hand, there was no reason why he should not visit the ruins of the castle, the scene of the murder of King Edward the Martyr, three-quarters of a century before the Conquest. It was the show place of the district, the natural magnet for any casual visitor like himself.

The Professor climbed slowly up the steep slopes of the natural earthwork, which stands like a fortress guarding the only gap in the long range of the Purbeck hills, and listened attentively while the guide, delighted at finding a sympathetic audience so early in the year, recounted the history of the stronghold and indicated its more prominent features. Then, his inspection over, he sat down on the grass on the north-eastern slope of the hill, and drew his ordnance map from his pocket.

His horizon was bounded by the high land on the southern side of the River Stour. At his feet was a rolling, sandy plain, diversified here and there by clumps of trees, but mostly covered with gorse and heather. This plain stretched away into the distance, and beyond it an occasional silvery gleam betrayed the winding channels of Poole Harbour. Here and there across the plain he could see evidences of human occupation, the white surface of a clay-pit or the roof of a tiny isolated cottage. But, apart from these, the tract of country over which he looked appeared utterly deserted, abandoned to a great silence disturbed only by the note of some hovering bird.

His map told him that no road traversed this expanse. Only a few winding paths, trodden by the feet of rare wayfarers, led away from where he stood in the direction of the thin wisps of smoke which indicated human habitation. Here and there he could see traces of the railway of which the landlord had spoken, which led from the hidden quarries behind him to a pier built upon one of the secluded arms of the harbour. It seemed to be but little used. The Professor, enjoying the quiet of the fine afternoon, sat for hour after hour, his eyes absorbing the subtle beauty of this unharassed land. And, except for the solitary figure of a labourer, tramping stolidly across the waste towards some unknown destination, he saw no sign of life in all the wide extent of country laid out before his eyes. Yet, somewhere, lost among the lonely solitudes of gorse and heather, lay the solution of the mystery which he had set himself to solve.

Dr Priestley smiled as the conviction that this was so came back to him with redoubled force. Utterly contrary to his usual methods of procedure, he had formed a theory based entirely upon conjecture. So far, these facts by which it must be tested seemed to point to the incorrectness of this theory. Yet, were they facts? Was it not even yet possible that some master brain had arranged these seeming facts in order purposely to mislead an investigator like himself? And, if so, what unknown dangers might he not be incurring by the attempt to prove them false?

The Professor had never shirked danger throughout the whole course of his career. And in this case, as he reflected, he already stood in such imminent danger that his present actions could hardly increase it. If his theory were correct, a determined and unknown assassin held in his hand already the weapon which was aimed against his life. Why had he not struck, months ago, when the Professor was in blissful ignorance that his life was threatened? This was one of the aspects of a case which, in spite of the perils which it held for himself, thrilled him as no case had ever thrilled him before.

Sitting here, contemplating the peaceful afternoon, the Professor reviewed his theory for the last time, testing it with all the apparatus of probability. It *must* be correct, there was no other theory which would fit in with all the data before him. Yet, how could it be correct, in the face of the formidable array of facts which seemed to disprove it? This seeming contradiction it must be his task to unravel, and that alone.

For he had realised at once that it was no good calling in the aid of the police, even of Hanslet, whose experience had taught him that the Professor's most extraordinary statements had a way of justifying themselves. The police would merely confront him with their so-called facts, and seek to prove to him that his theory was utterly untenable. He could give them nothing tangible to go upon, could give them no clue which would lead to the capture of the undetected criminal he knew to be at large. Even if they accepted his theory in its entirety, how could they protect him from the dangers which encompassed him? Sooner or later, in some unguarded moment, the shadow would leap out upon him, and the Professor's theory would be proved upon his own body.

No, physical precautions were useless. It must be a battle of wits between them, himself and this mysterious killer. How far had a watch been kept upon his own actions, the Professor wondered? He was almost certain that he had not been followed to Corfe Castle, but he was by no means so certain that his pretended departure from England had imposed upon his adversary. *The Times* of Friday had contained the paragraph mentioning his visit to Australia. So far, so good. But it was almost with surprise that he had failed to find the message in the personal column, which should inform him that the letter which he daily expected had arrived.

The Professor rose to his feet, and walked slowly back to the inn. He had ordered dinner at seven o'clock, and it was already past six. The landlord was standing at the door, and the Professor nodded pleasantly to him as he entered.

"What a beautiful afternoon!" he said. "I have been admiring the view from the Castle. A very fine prospect indeed, is it not?"

"Well, sir, some admires it and some don't," replied the landlord. "I fancies something with a bit more life in it myself. But I dessay it's a change to you after London."

"It is, indeed," agreed the Professor. "Indeed, I am so taken with the look of the heath, that I propose to take a walk across it after dinner."

"Well, don't lose your way, sir. It's a bit lonely out there. You aren't likely to meet anyone who'll put you right, either."

"Oh, it is not really dark till ten o'clock," replied the Professor cheerfully. "I have my map, and the Castle ruins must be visible from a long way off. You need have no fears of my getting lost."

"There's no danger, sir," the landlord hastened to agree. "Only you might happen to wander a bit further afield than you meant to. The bar closes at ten, but if you happen to be later than that, you've only got to knock on the door. I shan't be abed before eleven."

The Professor's dinner was served punctually at seven, and by eight o'clock he was well on the road of which the landlord had told him, and which his map showed him led in the direction of the railway. A short distance beyond the village he found a narrow lane, which, after a few twists and turnings, brought him out upon the track. There was a narrow path beside it, and along this he stepped out, anxious to reach his destination while it was still broad daylight.

The track followed a devious path across the heath, which, viewed from near at hand, was more undulating than at first appeared. The track had been built to avoid the steeper gradients, but every now and then it ran upon a low embankment, or through a shallow cutting. On either side the heath spread out, silent and mysterious, sometimes bare and sandy, with twisted pine trees standing above it at intervals, sometimes covered with low, dense thickets, in which the general silence seemed to be accentuated. When the line rose slightly to cross one of the lesser eminences, the Professor caught a fleeting glimpse of still water, the wandering arm of some unfrequented lagoon among the islands of the harbour. Behind him the sun hung low over the long range of the Purbeck hills, which changed from green and gold to blue and purple as the sun sank ever lower. Against them, the sharp outlines of the ruined Castle stood out clear cut like a beacon.

As the Professor strode on through the silence, devoid of any vestige of human habitation, he noticed how admirably adapted was this barren heath to purposes of concealment. Spread over its surfaces were a series of shallow depressions, shaped like a saucer, and sometimes holding an abandoned gravel pit, now half filled with stagnant water after the winter rains. A man might lie concealed in one of these, secure from observation, for as long as he could keep himself supplied with food. There would be no risk of discovery; those whose business led them to cross the heath kept strictly to the narrow paths, barely a foot wide, which meandered at wide intervals through the close growth of heather. A living man, so long as he avoided observation from these paths, might lie hidden for as long as he chose. And if a living man, why not a dead body? How easy to drag the damning evidence of crime into one of those dark thickets, to sink it into the silent depths of one of those black, unruffled pools!

The Professor shuddered, and increased his pace. This lonely heath was no place in which to indulge in morbid thoughts. His life might be in danger, but somehow he felt that it was not here that the blow would fall. If his theory were correct, if he had gauged aright the psychology of his adversary, it would not be thus that he would meet his death, here where there was none to witness the blow. Despite the almost threatening aspect of the country, deepening in tone every instant as the sun sank lower behind the distant hills, there was no vestige of any real danger. The shadows that lurked amid the gorse and heather were but the shadows of his own fears.

So the Professor reasoned with himself. It would have been folly for him, wishing as he did to avoid any suspicion of his interest in Dr Morlandson, to approach the scene of his death during the day. The very track by the side of which he was walking contained a potential risk of discovery. It must be used sometimes, the rails showed signs that wagons had passed over them not so very long ago. They led only to a pier, or rather jetty, upon which the contents of the wagons were unloaded into a waiting barge. The pier was utterly unfrequented except by these barges. The track, in fact, was a dead end as far as any casual wayfarer was concerned. There could be no rational excuse for following it.

He topped a slight rise, and saw in the distance the white surface of the clay-pit which was to be his guide. From where he stood he could see a considerable distance on either side of him. There was no sign of life upon the heath, except that far away, perhaps a couple of miles, the outlines of a cottage stood out against the grey background.

The Professor reached the clay-pit, and searched the undulating surface of the heath for some sign of the remains of Dr Morlandson's laboratory. For some moments he failed to find it, and then, at last, he made out the jagged tooth of a broken wall thrust upwards from behind a clump of gorse bushes. This, no doubt, must be his goal. There was no path leading to it from the track, but the Professor, using his stick to feel the way, stepped out boldly across the heather, which yielded like a cushion to his footsteps.

The distance from the track to the ruin must have been six or seven hundred yards. It took the Professor some little time to cover it, since he was obliged to make several détours in order to avoid clumps of gorse. But he reached it at last, and stood on the edge of what had once been a clearing, surveying the scene that lay before him.

The cottage itself had completely vanished. All that remained of it was a mound thickly overgrown with weeds and coarse grass, from which protruded here and there fragments of charred beams and rafters. The encroaching heath had hidden any signs of any garden there might once have been, and it was impossible for the Professor to form any idea of what the place had looked like while it was still standing. But the laboratory, having been built of concrete, had defied the utter obliteration to which the rest of the premises had succumbed. Its broken walls, rough and jagged, stood up in a gaunt rectangle, roofless, their foundations hidden deep in the all-effacing vegetation, but still marking without fear of error the site upon which the building had stood.

The Professor pushed through the weeds and undergrowth until he reached the gap in the wall where the door had been. The door was still there, rusty and twisted, lying almost hidden at the base of the wall, where it had been thrown by Dr Morlandson's would-be rescuers. It was a plain sheet of iron, fitted with hinges and a lock. The Professor glanced at it, then passed through the doorway into the space enclosed between the walls. Something, perhaps a grass-snake, rustled among the grasses as he entered.

The laboratory had been a fairly spacious room, about thirty feet by fifteen. Of its interior fittings nothing whatever remained. As the Professor advanced into the interior of the space his boots struck metal at every other step. He stooped and probed with his stick, and brought to light a twisted and shapeless tangle of iron, which might once have been the frame of a skylight. He examined it for a moment, and then cast it aside, with a nod of comprehension. The walls themselves still showed upon their interior surface the signs of having been subjected to an enormous heat. He poked about inside the laboratory for a short while longer, then came out and sat down upon the mound which had once been a cottage.

There could be no doubt that the fire which had destroyed the laboratory had been far fiercer than that which had burnt down the cottage. The charred beams of the latter still existed, while nothing whatever remained of the wooden fittings of the former. And yet, in the case of a concrete built laboratory, one would have expected a fire merely to have burnt out the interior without doing much damage to the structure. The place must certainly have contained a large quantity of substances whose combustion produced great heat, such as thermite. And Dr Priestley knew enough of the methods of research chemists, who as a rule deal in very small quantities, to wonder why Dr Morlandson required such large quantities, and why, even supposing that his isolated situation made it necessary for him to obtain his supplies in bulk, he should store them in the laboratory itself. The suspicion that Dr Morlandson's activities had not been solely concerned with researches into the properties of medicinal drugs seemed to the Professor to be thoroughly well grounded.

To the Professor's mind, there was even something suspicious about the origin of the fire itself. Dr Morlandson had been aware of the danger of such an outbreak; he had warned the police superintendent against smoking in the laboratory. This being so, was it likely that he would lock himself into what had proved to be a regular death-trap, and leave himself with no means of escape? The doubt raised by these queries set the Professor's mind to work upon an entirely fresh train of thought. Had Dr Morlandson's death been as accidental as it had appeared? Or was it possible that he too had had an enemy, who had somehow contrived the whole affair? And, if so, what became of the theory which had brought the Professor to the Isle of Purbeck?

The Professor awoke with a start from his meditations,

suddenly conscious that the light was failing rapidly. It was already past sunset, the ruined Castle which was to be his landmark was now indistinguishable against the universal grey of its background. A faint, silvery mist was rising above the heath, wreathing every object within sight with a curious opalescent halo. The Professor realised that he had already spent long enough contemplating this deserted heap of ashes. Their secret, did they hold one, was not to be wrested from them by further study that night.

He turned his back upon the gaunt skeleton of the laboratory, and walked round to the further side of the mound. Here the stumps of a rotten post or two showed where a fence had probably surrounded the front garden, now long since overgrown. Beyond the posts a white thread caught the Professor's eye, and he made his way up to it. It was a narrow track, apparently disused for years, and had no doubt once been the path by which the cottage was approached.

In one direction it led towards the railway line by which the Professor had approached the place, and rejoined the line lower down than the point at which he had left it. He started to walk down the track, with a muttered exclamation of satisfaction. By following it he might add a yard or two to his journey, but it would save him a slow and tiresome trudge through the heather in the gathering darkness. Of his ability to find his way back to the inn he had no doubt. He had only to follow the railway line backwards until the lights of the village came in sight, and then strike across country till he reached them, even if he missed the lane by which he had come.

The Professor had not gone very far before he stopped dead, and bent down to examine the narrow white strip beneath his feet. He felt in his pocket, and struck a match, which he held close to the surface of the path. It was a still, windless evening, and the flame of the match burnt clear and unflickering, illuminating a narrow circle of fine, white sand. Across the centre of this patch, following the path upon which the Professor stood, ran the sharp and unmistakable imprint of a bicycle tyre.

Somehow the discovery made the Professor's pulses beat quicker than before. This apparently deserted track was in use, then, despite its overgrown appearance. No doubt it formed a short cut between two spots upon the heath, such as a pit and a clay-worker's cottage. This was the obvious explanation, but to the Professor's mind it seemed unsatisfactory. He had studied the map very carefully that afternoon, and knew roughly the location of every human habitation marked upon it. And this particular track seemed to run in the wrong direction to connect up with any of these. Was it possible that somebody beside himself was interested in the ruined cottage which he had just left?

He threw the match away, and strode forward briskly in the direction of the railway line, which he calculated must now be less than a quarter of a mile ahead. He had an uncanny feeling that the rider of the bicycle might have been concealed close at hand while he was investigating the ruins, that he himself might have been the object of close observation all the time he had believed himself to be alone in the vast emptiness of the heath. It was an uncomfortable and a disturbing thought, and the Professor pushed on rapidly, grasping his stick tightly. Of course it was absurd, he was not the least likely to be molested. But he could not keep his mind from drawing ugly pictures of the dark thickets, of those deep, black pools, so admirably adapted as a hiding place for a murdered body——

And then, all of a sudden, with an abruptness which fell upon his ears like a blow, the Professor heard a bell ring sharply behind him. He spun round in his tracks, raising his stick instinctively, as though in self-defence. Coming along the path behind him was a tall figure on a bicycle, indistinguishable but for its outline in the swiftly-falling night. The slight mist magnified it to inhuman proportions.

Dr Priestley stepped back into the heather, and waited for the figure to approach him. As it came nearer he began to distinguish details one by one. It was a man, dressed apparently in trousers and jersey, with a seaman's cap upon his head. The Professor felt a sudden feeling of relief. No doubt this was a man from one of the stone barges which came up to Goathorn Pier to load stone or clay. He would no doubt join the railway, and follow the track beside it down to the pier. He could see the man's features by now, or such of them as were not hidden by the mass of black beard, which grew up in whiskers on either side of his face until it was lost beneath his cap. And then, with a sudden recollection of a certain vivid description which Hanslet had given him, the Professor realised that the man had an angry-looking scar extending the whole length of his right cheek. Even as he realised the significance of the man's appearance, he had dismounted from his bicycle, and stood confronting the Professor.

"Good evening, Dr Priestley," he said pleasantly, but in a curiously harsh and strained voice. And, at the words, the Professor knew that this was indeed the Black Sailor.

CHAPTER 18 THE AVENGER

The Black Sailor stood in the middle of the path, leaning on his bicycle and looking at Dr Priestley with a faint smile of amusement in his eyes. The Professor, for his part, stood his ground and waited for what might come next. He understood quite well that any attempt to escape would be pure folly. If it came to a chase across the heather, the sailor would overtake him in half a dozen strides. And as for shouting for help—well, the nearest inhabited house was nearly two miles away.

Besides, what was there to shout about, after all? The sailor appeared to be unarmed, and his expression was rather one of amusement than of menace. The absurdity of the situation began to appeal to the Professor. He had been accosted by the man whom the police would have dearly loved to lay their hands upon, and he was utterly powerless to take any steps towards his capture.

The Black Sailor broke the silence. "You seem interested in the fate of the unhappy man who ended his days in this lonely spot?" he said, with something that sounded like a short laugh.

"The fate of Dr Morlandson has a particular interest for me," replied the Professor significantly.

"Yes, it would have, naturally," said the sailor conversationally. "It has puzzled me why you have been so long in realising it. I didn't expect it of the others, but you, surely, should have guessed the motive long ago. It would interest me to know what brought the connection to your mind?"

The Professor hesitated. Yet, after all, he was in this man's power. So far as he could see, his only chance of escape lay in gaining time, until by some miracle a belated labourer should come past within hailing distance. It was the most unlikely thing in the world to happen, but there was just a chance. Consequently, since the sailor seemed disposed to talk, it was best to humour him.

"I guessed it first when I heard the name Copperdock again," he replied. "I could not remember at first where I had heard it before, but finally the whole scene came back to me."

"Yes, it is an unusual name." agreed the sailor, "but, if you will excuse my saying so, Dr Priestley, you appear to be not entirely at your ease. Perhaps it will reassure you if I remind you that no single one of the victims of Dr Morlandson's vengeance has come to any harm until he has received the counter with his number on it. Although, as you seem to believe, you are included among them, you are perfectly safe until that token is delivered."

"I have no alternative but to believe it," replied Dr Priestley steadily, "for I was the foreman of the jury which condemned him."

"It is for that reason that you have been reserved till the last," said the sailor solemnly. "It was Dr Morlandson's wish that it should be so, and that, before you died, you should understand the reason for your punishment. Do you remember Dr Morlandson, as you last knew him?"

"I remember him in the dock," replied the Professor. "A slim, tall, clean-shaven man, with an intellectual face, and a pleasant soft voice."

"You remember his appearance," exclaimed the sailor impatiently, "you never knew the man's soul, as I did. Dr Morlandson loved two things in this world with a passion which filled his whole being, his wife and his profession. His sympathy with suffering was unlimited, and his nature recoiled from the spectacle of any pain which could be prevented. And you, twelve good men and true, took it upon yourselves to condemn him to death because he had the courage to put one of God's creatures out of his agony. At one blow you took from him all that he loved and lived for, his profession, and his wife who died under the shock of her husband's conviction. Can you wonder that during those long years of torment in prison, his thoughts turned from sympathy to vengeance? Yet, even in his vengeance he was merciful and killed swiftly."

Dr Priestley nodded. "Yes, I guessed that was the motive," he said in a matter of fact tone. "I took the trouble to look up the names of the jurymen, as soon as I remembered that it was while I was serving on that jury that I had met a man bearing the name of Copperdock. The others were Tovey, Colburn, Pargent, Martin, Goodwin, Thomas, Bailey, Underhill, Abbott and Hewlett."

"Quite right. Thomas, Bailey, Underhill, Abbott and Hewlett were already dead when Dr Morlandson was released. Their punishment has passed into other hands. Of the remaining seven, six have paid the penalty which they wished to inflict upon Dr Morlandson. You only are left, Dr Priestley."

"I had realised that my life was threatened," replied the Professor calmly. "As you have probably guessed, it was for the purpose of verifying the fact of Dr Morlandson's death that I came here."

"Dr Morlandson is dead, but he left his vengeance behind him," said the sailor sombrely. "You killed him as surely as though the law had taken its course upon your cruel verdict. He came here, a broken man, to die in solitude like a stricken animal. I met him, not a hundred yards from this very spot, a few days after he had come to live in the cottage. I was desperate that evening. I had murder in my soul, no matter why. I would have killed him then and there for what he might have had about him, but I was afraid. There was something about him that prevented me from touching him, I did not know what it was. He took me to the cottage with him, and talked to me all night. And at last I found out that he was in the grip of a hate greater than mine.

"I saw him every day after that. I was the only person he spoke to, except that fool of a police superintendent who used to come out to see him. He'd have been glad enough to lay his hands on me, if he had known that I was hiding within a few yards of him. Hour after hour we talked, Dr Morlandson and I, while he fed me and sheltered me. He told me his whole story, and at last, when he knew he could trust me, he made me an offer. If I would become the heir to his vengeance, I should also be heir to a very large sum of money he had safely concealed.

"He explained his plans to me in detail. During his years in prison he had thought over every little thing, and his scheme was complete. But one thing he had not allowed for, and that was the fact that prison life had broken him up. He, who had gone to prison a strong man, came out ruined in health and body. His mind had eaten him up, as he put it. The awful hours of solitude, when his only means of diverting his thoughts from his wrecked life was to perfect his plans for vengeance, had sapped his youth and his strength. He came out an old man, utterly incapable of the task before him.

"I had told him my story, such as it was, and he saw in me the one man who could take his place. I was an educated man once, Dr Priestley, forced by circumstances to abandon my former life, and become what you see me now. In those months I was in Morlandson's company he taught me more than I had ever learnt before. He told me the names of the men who had formed the jury, and showed me how I was to trace each of them. He had thought out dozens of ways of killing them undetected, and he explained to me how each should be employed according to circumstances. In that laboratory which he built he spent long hours working at poisons which should be swift and effective, in preparing weapons which could not fail in the clumsiest hands. He taught me anatomy, where the vital organs of the body lay, how to strike so as to produce instant death. Within a few months I was fitted to undertake the task which he had delegated to me."

The Black Sailor paused, and looked intently at the Professor, as though to assure himself that he was taking in all that was being said to him. "It was Dr Morlandson's wish that you should fully understand the reasons for your punishment before you died," he continued. "You, at least, we had no difficulty in tracing. Your name was frequently in the papers, you were the only one of the twelve who had attained any fame whatever, except perhaps that conceited ass Pargent. It was only fitting that you, as foreman, should be reserved until the last. Morlandson hoped that you would guess the reason for the deaths of your fellow-members, and so realise the fate which was hanging over your own head."

"Yes, I think I understand it all pretty thoroughly now," replied the Professor. "There are, however, one or two points upon which I am not quite clear. I am told that Mr Ludgrove, the herbalist, has received a counter bearing the number VII. I presume that this is not due to you, since Mr Ludgrove was not a member of the jury, nor, to the best of my recollection, was he concerned with Dr Morlandson's trial."

The Black Sailor scowled, and looked fiercely at the Professor. "Ludgrove is an interfering busy-body," he growled. "I do not propose to explain my methods to you, naturally, but this much I will tell you, Ludgrove has on more than one occasion prevented me from carrying out my designs. I have no quarrel with him, and he is in no danger so long as he minds his own business. The counter was sent to him as a hint to keep out of the business altogether. And, by the way, Dr Priestley, when you get back to London, you may give him this message from me. Unless he keeps clear, the counter, which was only a warning, will be followed by something worse."

He laughed harshly as he saw a flicker of astonishment pass across the Professor's face. "Oh, yes," he continued. "You will no doubt go back to London and recount your experiences to your friend Hanslet and the rest of the police. Why not? I have no doubt they will be very pleased to learn the motive for these mysterious murders which have so sorely puzzled them. They may dimly realise that an apparent murder may sometimes be a just execution. But the knowledge won't help them much, and it won't help you, Dr Priestley. In fact, it was Dr Morlandson's wish that the reasons for the deaths of his victims should be fully known. His example may cause jurymen to consider their verdicts more carefully in future. And as for me, what harm can any of you do? Why, from the first there has been a reward upon my head, a reward you will never earn, Dr Priestley."

He paused, and then continued more seriously. "You are a sensible man, and must see how utterly useless any attempt to put the police on my trail must be. It will take you an hour at least to reach the police station at Corfe Castle, and heaven knows how much longer to persuade the police to search for me. Don't for an instant think this meeting is accidental. It is not. I have for some time been seeking for an opportunity of meeting you. It was Dr Morlandson's expressed wish that I should see you and explain matters. Now that I have done so, the Black Sailor will disappear, only to appear once more, when your sentence is to be executed."

"And that sentence is—— ?" inquired Dr Priestley firmly.

"That you should live in the constant expectation of a violent death," replied the Black Sailor gravely. "The time may come soon or late, but you cannot escape the doom which hangs over you. You may take what precautions you please, you may condemn yourself to a life of constant supervision within the walls of a fortified house. If you do, you will know something of the hell which Dr Morlandson endured as the result of your verdict. But at last the moment will come, and you will be stricken with death when you believe yourself to be safest. Copperdock was warned, he was under the special care of the police, he was alone in his own house with the door locked behind him. Yet death found him, as it will find you when the time comes, Dr Priestley."

The Black Sailor put his foot on the pedal of his bicycle. "You will excuse me if I break off this interesting conversation," he said. "I have many things to attend to tonight, and it is getting late. But before I go I will give you this. It will serve to remind you that your meeting with me was not a trick of your imagination. It may also be useful as evidence of your veracity when you tell the story to the police."

He drew something from his pocket and threw it contemptuously at the Professor's feet. Then, before the latter could reply, he had jumped on his bicycle and was pedalling rapidly in the direction from which he had come.

It was quite dark by now, and the Professor watched his retreating form until it was lost in the night. Then he bent down and picked up the object which he had thrown upon the ground, and which glimmered faintly upon the dark surface of the heather on which it had fallen. He knew what it was, without the trouble of striking a match. It was typical of him that he handled it by the edges, and wrapped it carefully in his handkerchief before he put it in his pocket. Then he started once more on his homeward journey, his mind full of this interview with the man who called himself the Black Sailor.

His theory had been vindicated. During the night which had followed Inspector Hanslet's first visit to him, he had racked his brains in the endeavour to recall the circumstances under which he had first heard the name of Copperdock. And then, at last, just before dawn, the scene had come back to him. The gloomy court at the Old Bailey, the voices of counsel, the set tense face of the prisoner in the dock. And finally, the scene when the jurymen, under his direction, had discussed the verdict which was to decide the man's fate. Yes, he remembered the name of the little man who had seemed to share his own merciful views. Copperdock, that was it. The names of the others he did not remember, but they had seemed to be inspired with a stolid common-sense virtue. One of them had implied that if doctors thought they could get away with this sort of thing, there was no knowing what they would be up to. They were a lot of butchers as it was, always cutting people up to find out what was the matter with them.

Yes, he remembered the scene well enough. It had been impossible to argue with his colleagues on the jury. The majority were against him and the man Copperdock; they could only acquiesce in their opinion. The twelve had filed back to the places in court, he could see now the look of awful anxiety in the eyes of the prisoner. And then, in reply to the solemn question of the judge, he had spoken the words, "Guilty, my Lord."

Morlandson had been reprieved, and, according to the notes made by Harold, must by now be at liberty. Was it possible that he had returned to the world with vengeance in his heart? The Professor had obtained permission to examine the official records of the trial, and had thus learnt the names of the remaining members of the jury. Five of them corresponded with the names which Hanslet had mentioned as the victims of the recent mysterious murders. There could be no further doubt.

But Morlandson had died, burnt to death in his laboratory within a year or so of his release. How was this fact to be fitted in with this theory? The Black Sailor had enlightened him upon this point. Dr Morlandson had handed on his vengeance to this mysterious successor, whose true identity he had no means of guessing. It was true that in one direction his doubts had been resolved, but only to be replaced by a series of questions, equally imperative. Who was this man, who called himself the Black Sailor? The Professor had examined his appearance intently while the light lasted, and could see none of the obvious traces of disguise. He could swear that his most striking beard and whiskers had been genuine, and he had worn his clothes naturally, as though accustomed to them. Again, how had he known that Dr Priestley was in the neighbourhood? The professor was certain that he had not been followed during his journey from London. It was impossible that this man should live openly, with the reward for the Black Sailor circulating all over the country. Was it possible that he lived concealed somewhere in this desolate tract of country? And if so, how did he contrive to carry out his murders within the very heart of London?

These problems would wait. A more urgent one seemed to the Professor to require solution. What, he asked himself, had the Black Sailor's object been in seeking this meeting? The

Professor was quite prepared to believe that the reason he had given accounted for part of the truth. He could well imagine Morlandson, his brain turned by his fancied grievance, wishing the effects of his vengeance to become known. This was to be expected, it was merely an example of the curious vanity usually displayed by maniacs. But was there any other purpose in the meeting, which he had not yet understood? And, in any case, what course was he to take?

As the Black Sailor had suggested, to set the local police on the scent would be sheer waste of time. No serious attempt to scour the heath could possibly be made before daylight next morning, by which time the object of the search would be far away. They might find the tracks of his bicycle, but if he desired to elude pursuit all he would need would be to carry it for some distance over the heather. The Professor credited the man who had baffled the London police by the ingenuity of his murders with sufficient acumen to leave no tracks by which he could be followed. No, the police could not help him; if he were to escape the fate that threatened him, it must be by his own efforts.

And so far his adversary had completely outwitted him. In spite of his own elaborate precautions, his investigations into the death of Dr Morlandson were known and had been treated as the most natural thing in the world. For his own part, he had learnt very little that he had not known before. Certainly his theory as to the motives for the murders in Praed Street had been confirmed. This was a small satisfaction to place against the Professor's chagrin. He had also learnt that the Black Sailor, in spite of official scepticism, was an actual person. But of his identity, or the means by which the crimes had been committed, he had learnt nothing. From the police point of view he had failed utterly, since he had failed to secure any information which could possibly lead to an arrest.

It was nearly eleven o'clock when the Professor saw the lights of the village in the distance, and, leaving the railway line, found the lane which led homewards. The sound of his footsteps re-echoed among the silent houses, the whole place breathed an atmosphere of perfect peace and tranquillity. His recent adventure seemed to the Professor as an impossible dream, a trick of his mind, so long concentrated upon the subject. So strong was the illusion of unreality that the Professor was impelled to feel the hard outline of the counter hidden in the folds of his handkerchief. There had been something theatrical about the whole adventure; the time, the place, the man's appearance, his voice, so curiously harsh and rasping, his very words, so utterly at variance with his character of a rough sailor. With something of a shock the Professor remembered that Copperdock had claimed to have seen him at a moment when it was proved that there was no one there. Was it dimly possible that there was something supernatural about the affair? The Professor brushed the suggestion aside as absurd.

The inn was closed by the time he reached it, but, remembering the landlord's instructions, he knocked upon the door, and after a short interval the key turned in the lock and the door opened. The landlord's voice welcomed him. "Bit later than you expected, sir, aren't you?" he said. "Did you lose your way or anything like that?"

"No, the—er—beauty of the night tempted me to stay out of doors," replied the Professor.

"Well, sir, come ten o'clock, and seeing as you didn't come home, I put a drop of that old brandy aside for you. I hope I didn't presume too much, sir."

"You did not indeed, I shall be very glad of it," replied the Professor thankfully.

The landlord disappeared for a moment, and returned with a glass on a tray, which he handed to his guest. "I thought you might be glad of it after your walk, sir," he said. "Did you find the ruins of Dr Morlandson's cottage?"

"Yes, I did," replied the Professor quietly. "A most isolated spot. I noticed that there was a path running past it. Where does that lead to?"

"It doesn't lead nowheres in particular, sir. When the cottage was first occupied, before Morlandson's time, it led out to the

Studland road. That was the only way to the place before that railway line was built. The path's still there, is it? I should have thought it would have been growed over by now."

"No, you can still trace it," said the Professor. "And, curiously enough, there were the marks of a bicycle wheel running along it."

"A bicycle!" exclaimed the landlord. "Well, to be sure! When there's a barge lying at Goathorn the fellows on board sometimes brings bicycles and rides in here by the side of the railway line, but I don't know what could have taken any of them past the cottage there. Perhaps one of them wanted to get to Studland, though there's a shorter way there from Goathorn through Newton. I should have said nobody used that path, not once a year."

"No, I do not imagine that this man Morlandson saw many visitors," said the Professor reflectively. "I suppose people occasionally went to see him, though?"

"I don't believe, bar the men who built the laboratory, that a soul went near the place except the super I was telling you of, sir," replied the landlord. "Leastways, I never heard of any. Morlandson used to come in and fetch everything he wanted. If there was anything heavy, he'd bring a barrow with him. No, sir, if you'll believe me, that man never saw a soul when he was at home, except the super. Didn't care about meeting people, I suppose, with a past like his."

"Well, he certainly chose a lonely place for his retreat," agreed the Professor. "I do not suppose that any strangers were likely to disturb him?"

"Lor' bless you, no, sir. 'Tisn't many strangers as finds their way on to the heath, unless it's a gentleman like yourself, out for a walk, and then they keeps to the paths. It's not overgood going over the heather."

"So I discovered," replied the Professor. "But, on the whole, I have had a most interesting evening."

CHAPTER 19 A DISCOVERY

It was quite evident to the Professor that since his presence upon the Isle of Purbeck was known to his mysterious acquaintance of the previous evening, there was no further need for secrecy as to his movements. As soon as he had breakfasted on Sunday, he put a trunk call through to London, and very shortly had Harold on the end of the wire.

"Yes, it is Dr Priestley speaking," he said. "The asp has struck, Cleopatra. Does that satisfy you? Yes, yes, I know, but circumstances have made it necessary for me to change my plans. Now listen. Put another short paragraph in the papers, to the effect that domestic reasons have made it impossible for Dr Priestley to carry out his projected lecture tour in Australia. He was recalled by telegram from Paris, where he stopped on his way to join the *Oporto* at Marseilles, and will shortly return to London. Having done that, get in touch with Inspector Hanslet, and bring him to Corfe Castle by the train leaving Waterloo at 2.30 this afternoon. I will explain the reasons for asking him to come when I see him. I will meet the train at Corfe Castle station. Is that clear?"

Apparently it was, for after a further word or two the Professor laid the instrument down. He spent the day within the portals of the inn, to all appearances studying the contents of the Sunday papers, but actually trying to solve some of the problems suggested by his incredible meeting with the Black

Sailor.

The train came in to time, and out of it stepped Inspector Hanslet and Harold. They glanced at the Professor enquiringly as they greeted him, but asked no questions until they were outside the station. And even then it was the Professor who spoke first.

"I am Mr Deacon here, to the landlord of the inn, at least," he said. "I will take you there and you can leave your suitcases. Register in any names you like, but do not divulge your connection with the police, Inspector. It would attract undesirable attention."

Hanslet nodded, and the Professor introduced the two to the landlord as the friends he had been expecting. They left their suitcases, and then followed the Professor out into the village street.

"This is a most interesting country," he said conversationally. "I should like to show you the Purbeck Hills from the distance. We have, I think, time for a walk before dinner."

Hanslet nodded. "I should be glad of a stroll after sitting in the train," he replied. "Lead on, Mr Deacon. You know the way."

The Professor took the lane which led towards the railway line. It was not until they were well beyond the outskirts of the village that he spoke.

"I must apologise for my recent actions," he said at last to Hanslet. "I think you will understand them when I have explained my reasons to you. I was anxious to come here without anybody suspecting my presence. I had formed a theory as to the motive of the murders in Praed Street. Harold, my boy, tell Inspector Hanslet, as concisely as you can, the facts about the arrest and trial of Dr Morlandson."

Harold obeyed, and as he finished Hanslet nodded. "I remember the case vaguely," he said. "But I don't see——"

The Professor interrupted him. "I happened to be the foreman of the jury. When you mentioned the name of Copperdock the other night, I fancied that it was familiar to me. Eventually I remembered that a man of that name had been one of the jurymen. More out of curiosity than anything else, I took steps to discover the names of the remainder of the panel. They were Tovey, Colburn, Pargent, Martin, Goodwin, and five others, whom I am informed have since died."

"Good heavens!" exclaimed Hanslet. "Then you mean that this Morlandson, who was released from jail after serving his sentence, is the murderer! Why on earth didn't you tell me so before, Dr Priestley? It will be simple enough to trace him. Our people at the Yard will know all about him."

"They do," replied the Professor drily. "They have a completely authenticated record of his death, which occurred five years ago. In fact, I am now taking you to the place where it happened."

"But he can't have died five years ago if he murdered Copperdock only last week!" exclaimed Hanslet in bewilderment. "There's some mistake. There must have been two Morlandsons and you've got hold of the wrong man."

The Professor shrugged his shoulders. "Ask our landlord, when we return to the inn," he replied. "He is a most communicative man, and will, no doubt, be delighted to tell you the story, as he told it to me. I had the same doubts as you have expressed, and it was those doubts which brought me down here. I inquired for Morlandson's history as tactfully as I could, and I examined the scene of his death, as I shall ask you to."

"I am quite prepared to accept your statement, Professor," said Hanslet. "How did it happen?"

The Professor recounted the facts of Morlandson's life on the Isle of Purbeck, and the circumstances under which he met his death. "All these things can, of course, be verified," he said, as he came to the end of his story. "It was while I was engaged in verifying them yesterday evening that I met with an adventure which can only be described as amazing. You will remember the man described as the Black Sailor, first seen by Wal Snyder at the time of the murder of Tovey the greengrocer, and subsequently by Copperdock?"

"The man Whyland was persuaded to issue a reward for?" replied Hanslet with a smile. "Yes, I remember. We seem pretty generally agreed that he was a myth."

For a moment the Professor made no reply. They had by this time reached the spot where the track from Morlandson's cottage crossed the railway line. The Professor stopped, and turned to Hanslet impressively. "I met him last night, about three hundred yards from this spot," he said simply.

Hanslet stared at him in amazement. "You met him!" he exclaimed. "You mean you saw someone who looked like him, I suppose?"

"No, I met him, and had a most interesting conversation with him," replied the Professor. "He was riding a bicycle, and since there has been no rain since last night, you will see the tracks in a few minutes. Further, he gave me this." The Professor produced his handkerchief, unrolled it, and handed Hanslet the numbered counter.

"Good Lord, this beats anything I ever heard of!" exclaimed Hanslet. "What did the man say to you?"

The Professor gave a careful and detailed account of his adventures on the previous evening, to which Hanslet and Harold listened in silence. He finished by explaining that he had thought it useless to set the local police on the Black Sailor's track, and Hanslet agreed.

"The fellow would have been miles away before you had got them to move," he said. "Of course, I shall have to circulate his description again, in case anybody else saw him. But he can't have gone about openly, with a reward on his head like that. Somebody would have been bound to have spotted him. It's the most amazing story I ever heard. You don't suppose he was pulling your leg, do you?"

"How did he know my name, and the names of the jurymen who served with me?" replied the Professor.

"Well, this case is full of the most extraordinary contradictions. We'd better have a look at these bicycle tracks you speak of, it's just possible we may be able to find out the direction in which he went off. Where did he mount his bicycle and ride away, Professor?"

"About a quarter of a mile along this path. Lead the way along it. Inspector, and I will stop you when we reach the spot."

They proceeded in single file, Inspector Hanslet leading. After about five minutes the Professor spoke. "It was just where you are standing, Inspector."

The party halted, and Hanslet bent down to examine the path. The sand was in admirable condition to receive and retain an impression; firm enough to resist the force of the wind, yet not too hard to take even the lightest imprints. Hanslet, kneeling in the heather by the side of the path, looked at it closely.

"You've mistaken the spot, Professor," he said at last. "There are no tracks here. It doesn't look as if anybody had passed along here for a long time."

The Professor frowned. "I do not usually mistake a spot which I wish to remember," he replied. "However, it was nearly dark when I left it, and I may have made an error of a few yards. As you can see, this track leads straight to those ruined walls, which are the remains of Morlandson's laboratory. It was in that direction that the man made off. If you follow the path, you are sure to find the tracks further along."

They resumed their way, Hanslet examining every foot of the path as they proceeded. It was not until they reached the ruined posts which had marked the limits of the front garden that Hanslet turned and looked anxiously at the Professor.

"You are quite sure that this was the path he followed?" he asked. "I can't see any tracks along it at all, either of your feet or of the bicycle."

"Perfectly certain," replied the Professor stiffly. "I am not likely to mistake it, especially as it would appear to be the only path in the vicinity."

Hanslet nodded, and made his way through the tangled vegetation towards the ruins of the cottage. He walked carefully round the mound, then proceeded to the broken walls of the laboratory. He gazed at these for a minute or two, then turned towards his companions, who had remained on the path.

"I wish you would come here a minute, will you, Mr

Merefield?" he called.

Harold obeyed his summons, and Hanslet led him round an angle of the walls, out of sight of the Professor. "Has he been overdoing it a bit lately?" he asked in a low tone. "Overworking himself, or anything like that, I mean? I thought he looked pretty well done up when I first saw him the other evening."

"Well, he's hardly been outside the house for the last six months," replied Harold. "He's been busy with a new book, and I think it took it out of him a good deal. Why?"

"You heard that extraordinary yarn he spun us just now, about the Black Sailor and his bicycle. If the tracks showed anywhere, it would be on that path. Now here, all round this place, you can see the Professor's footmarks. He was here all right last night, as he says. But it's odd we can't find traces of the other fellow. You don't think he can have dreamt it, do you?"

"It would be most unlike him," replied Harold. "Why should he imagine such a thing, anyhow?"

"Well, you see, if this jury business is correct, he is the only survivor. You remember his telling us the other day in town that there would be one more murder? He meant that his own life was threatened, and I expect it's been preying on his mind. It's the only way I can account for this business."

Harold shook his head. "It is true that he hasn't been quite himself lately," he replied. "But I don't think he's got to the stage of seeing things. Anyhow, how do you account for the counter he gave you just now?"

"How do you account for anything in this blessed case?" retorted Hanslet. "I believe the devil's at the bottom of it, if you ask me. I wish you would follow up that path in the opposite direction for a bit, while I poke about here. If you find the marks of a bicycle wheel, don't touch 'em, but come back and tell me."

Harold followed the path for half a mile or so in the direction of the Studland road, and returned shaking his head. Hanslet had by this time finished his inspection of the ruins. He turned to the Professor, who had joined him. "Well, there's nothing very definite to be seen here," he said, with his usual cheerful smile.

"What do you suggest we do next. Professor?"

"Return to the inn for dinner," replied Dr Priestley. "Tomorrow, if you agree, I propose to return to London by an early train."

"I think that will certainly be the best course," agreed Hanslet. "I will just run round to the local police station after dinner, and have a chat with whoever's in charge. We must certainly follow up this valuable clue of yours."

They returned to the inn, and after dinner Hanslet went round to the police station. The superintendent who had been in charge at the time of Morlandson's death had since been promoted and had left the district, but Hanslet had no difficulty in verifying the story as told by the landlord. He had disclosed his identity, and explained that he had come down in connection with a case in which he was interested, without, however, mentioning the Praed Street murders. In the course of conversation with the sergeant in charge he elicited the information that no strangers had recently been heard of in the district, and certainly nobody in any way resembling the Black Sailor.

"There's a few foreigners and the like comes into Poole, sir," the sergeant had explained. "But they never comes over this way. The barges what goes up to Goathorn are all local craft, and there's never a stranger among them. If any stranger was wandering about the heath, we'd get to hear of it, sharp enough. Why, it's an event in the lives of these clay-workers if they see a strange face."

"Well, if you should hear of a strange man with a bicycle having been seen, you might let me know," said Hanslet. "Good night, sergeant, I won't trouble you any further."

Hanslet left the police station, more convinced than ever that the Professor was suffering from some temporary aberration. He had known such cases before, where overwork had caused the queerest effects. It was quite understandable. The Professor had certainly discovered the motive for the murders; it could not be a coincidence that all the men who had died had served on this particular jury and had been the victims of this mysterious murderer. But, having discovered this, and realising that he was the only survivor, the Professor must have received a shock which had unduly stimulated his imagination. This was all that Hanslet could make of it. Meanwhile he determined to keep a very close watch over the Professor, for, if his theory was correct, his life was undoubtedly threatened. Black Sailor or no Black Sailor.

The party returned to London on the Monday morning, and Hanslet immediately went to see Whyland, whom he had left in charge during his absence. At the police station he was told that he had gone to see Mr Ludgrove, and thither Hanslet followed him.

He found Whyland and Ludgrove seated in the latter's sanctum, and the herbalist greeted him warmly on his entrance. "Come in. Inspector," he said. "Mr Whyland and I are talking about the death of Mr Copperdock. As you see, I am still alive, in spite of my numbered counter."

"So I see," replied Hanslet. "You've seen or heard of nothing suspicious, I suppose, Whyland?"

"Not a thing," replied Whyland. "Mr Ludgrove and I set a little trap, but nothing came of it."

"Oh, what was that?" inquired Hanslet. "Did you wander about Praed Street with counters stuck on your backs, or what?"

"Better than that," said Mr Ludgrove with a smile. "Of course, you realise that five out of six of these deaths have taken place in Praed Street, don't you? Well, another thing is that they have taken place during the weekend. It was a fair inference that if my life was to be attempted, it would be during the weekend, and in Praed Street. Do you agree?"

"Well, it sounds reasonable, anyhow," replied Hanslet. "What about it?"

"I felt as though a breath of country air would do me good," continued the herbalist. "As Inspector Whyland may have told you, I usually try to spend a weekend out of London at least once every three weeks. For one thing, it does me good, and for another my business obliges me to collect herbs from time to time. And I happen to have heard of some particularly fine colchicums growing near Dorchester."

"Mr Ludgrove told me this, and I thought it wouldn't do him any harm to go and look for these collycums, or whatever he calls them," broke in Whyland. "Besides, his suggestion gave me an idea. So we smuggled him off to Paddington, where two of my plain clothes men saw him into a train on Saturday morning. I reckoned he'd be safe enough out of London. Then I stayed here, being careful to keep a light burning in the shop, so as people would think Mr Ludgrove was in residence. Then we met Mr Ludgrove's train at Paddington yesterday evening, and brought him back. But, as I say, nothing happened. I only had one visitor all the time, and that was young Copperdock, on Sunday morning. I explained to him that Mr Ludgrove was upstairs, and he said he would look in again later. But he never came, at least while I was here."

"Well, it wasn't a bad notion, certainly," said Hanslet. "I don't think I should go about alone too much, if I were you, Mr Ludgrove."

The herbalist smiled. "I hardly get the chance," he replied. "I have a habit of taking a brisk walk in the neighbourhood every evening. During this last week I have never gone more than a few steps before being accosted by a charming and talkative individual who insists upon accompanying me. I am not complaining, I have found his conversation most interesting."

"And he yours, Mr Ludgrove," laughed Whyland. "I'm sorry, but what can we do? I don't want to alarm you, but you know there is the chance that an attack might be made upon you. And that attack would give us the clue we want."

"I see. I am to be used as a stalking-horse," said Mr Ludgrove. "Well, I have no objection. I am only too glad to be of service in unravelling this terrible mystery."

Hanslet, who had been silent for a moment or two, suddenly turned towards Whyland. "You say that nobody came near you while you were alone here but young Copperdock. What did he want, I wonder? Have you seen him since you came back from your herbalising expedition, Mr Ludgrove?"

A grave expression spread over the herbalist's face. "I have," he replied. "It was for this reason that I asked Inspector Whyland to come here and see me. I was about to tell him the story when you came in, and I realised that it would be better if you heard it together. Ted Copperdock came here yesterday evening, about an hour after my return."

"Oh, he did, did he!" exclaimed Hanslet. "What did he want?"

"He told me he had come round in the morning to ask me if I would go through his father's belongings with him. Finding me busy, as he supposed, he went back home, and started to go through them by himself. He spent the whole afternoon sorting out Mr Copperdock's papers, and it, was not until late that he began to look over his clothes. In the pocket of one of his coats he discovered something which, as he himself said, terrified him. He came to me at once, and begged me to come back with him. He was so insistent that I broke the promise which I had made to Inspector Whyland, not to go alone into any house in Praed Street, and went upstairs with him into his father's bedroom. There he showed me an overcoat hanging in a cupboard, and in the pocket of it—this!"

The herbalist rose, walked to the bench at the far end of the room, and pointed to an object wrapped loosely in paper. Hanslet and Whyland followed him, and the former unwrapped the paper carefully. As the object appeared, they both uttered a startled exclamation. It was the blade of a knife, and with it a long wooden handle, with a hole running the whole of its length, and fitted with a set-screw.

Whyland bent over it with a look of triumph. "I knew it, all along!" he exclaimed. "Look at this blade! It is exactly similar to the ones found in the bodies of Tovey and Pargent. You see the dodge, don't you? This blade just fits the hole in the handle. It's meant to be pushed through and gripped by the set-screw. But, if you tighten the screw as far as it will go first, then put the blade in, it is held lightly, just by its very end. Now, if you stab a man with the blade fixed like that, what happens? The blade goes in all right, and there it stays, while you walk away with the handle. It's beautifully simple, and you leave no finger-marks behind you."

But Hanslet stared at the knife in silence, his brain a whirl of conflicting theories. If the Professor was correct in his assumption, Copperdock was a victim of the unknown assassin. How did this knife, which, as Whyland said, was exactly similar to those with which Tovey and Pargent had been killed, come into his possession? On the other hand, if Copperdock had been the murderer, what became of the Professor's theory? Why should one of the jurymen wish to murder his colleagues? The problem became more complicated with every fresh discovery.

"This blessed case would drive an archangel to drink," he observed disgustedly, as he wrapped up the knife again and put it in his pocket. "Well, we'd better go across and see what young Copperdock has to say about this, eh, Whyland?"

CHAPTER 20 MR LUDGROVE'S INVITATION

April gave place to May, and May to June, with no further development in the mystery which surrounded the Praed Street Murders. The discovery of the knife in the pocket of Mr Copperdock's overcoat, combined with the fact that although Dr Priestley and Mr Ludgrove had each received a numbered counter, they had not so far been menaced by any particular danger, had convinced the police that the secret had died with Mr Copperdock. A very careful examination of the handle showed that it bore his finger-marks, and his son, although he could not account for its presence where he had found it, was emphatic that it could not have been placed there since the night of his death.

The Professor made no reference whatever to the case, either to Harold or to Hanslet. The latter during his infrequent visits to the house in Westbourne Terrace, made no reference to the case. He was becoming more and more convinced that the Professor's interview with the Black Sailor had been a pure hallucination; that the Professor, having imagined the sequel to his theory of the jurymen, had somehow been under the illusion that the events of his imagination had actually taken place. In his own mind, however, he was by no means satisfied with the official view of the matter, of which Whyland was the principal exponent. It left so much to be explained, chiefly Copperdock's motive, to say nothing of his methods. To begin with, how had he contrived to murder Mr Tovey, when at the moment of the latter's death he was sitting comfortably before his own fire? And, if the answer to this was that he had accomplices, who and where were they?

However, his superiors appeared to be satisfied, and towards the beginning of June Hanslet went off upon his long postponed leave. The Professor's time was fully occupied in correcting the proofs of *Some Aspects of Modern Thought*, which were now coming in from the printer, whose reader, appalled by some of the Professor's strictures upon his contemporaries, had scattered here and there across the margin the ominous words "Query libellous?" To each of these the Professor added the note: "Nonsense!" in letters half an inch long at least. It was perhaps fortunate for the conscientious reader that he was beyond the reach of the Professor's tongue.

The rigid police protection which had at first been imposed upon both the Professor and Mr Ludgrove had been gradually relaxed until now it had dwindled to nothing more serious than a casual glance at their houses by the constable on beat when he happened to pass them. The Professor himself appeared to have forgotten the warning given to him by the Black Sailor, and to have acquiesced in the official view that, since the perpetrator had committed suicide, nothing further would be heard of the murders.

It was while matters were in this state that Dr Priestley received one Saturday morning a letter which obviously caused him some satisfaction. It was signed "Elmer Ludgrove" and was written in a curiously neat and clerkly hand. The contents of it were as follows:

"DEAR SIR. I should not venture to write to you, but for the fact that I know that you are as interested in the recent affair of the numbered counters as I am myself. I have recently come across, wholly by accident, certain curious facts which may serve to throw an entirely fresh light upon the deaths of six men, which, to my mind, have not yet been satisfactorily explained. I am not anxious to approach the police, at least until I have consulted you. The police, as is perhaps natural, could scarcely be expected to welcome disclosures which would completely upset their official theory. They believe, as I confess I did at one time myself, that the late Mr Copperdock was guilty, and that his mania finally culminated in his own suicide.

"If I am correct in my deductions from the new evidence which has come into my hands, I can prove beyond question that Mr Copperdock was innocent, indeed, that he himself fell a victim to the agency which committed the other murders. I must ask you to respect my confidence until you have allowed me to put my evidence before you. When this has been done, I shall ask your advice as to the best means of laying it before the authorities. You, I have reason to believe, are on friendly terms with Inspector Hanslet, and perhaps you will agree, when you have examined the evidence I shall put before you, that it will be best to call him into consultation.

"I suggest, as the various exhibits to which I shall be compelled to refer are at present at my house, and as it may be necessary for me to point out to you certain peculiarities of the locations in which the murders took place, that your examination be carried out there. As I believe that as little time as possible should be wasted, I suggest, if it meets with your approval, that you should do me the honour of calling upon me this evening. As, in the light of recent events, you may not care to come to Praed Street alone, I propose to call upon you after your dinner this evening, and to learn your wishes in the matter. If you agree to my suggestion, we can then walk to my house together. I am, sir, yours faithfully,

"ELMER LUDGROVE."

The Professor read this letter through twice. His final conclusion was that this man Ludgrove had in some way discovered that the dead men had all been members of the Morlandson jury.

After all, he knew from the Black Sailor's words that Ludgrove had made inconvenient enquiries, and it was possible that he had somehow stumbled upon the truth. Anyway, there could be no harm in going to see him and hearing what he had to say. Besides, he had never conveyed to him the Black Sailor's warning. Hanslet might have, but the Professor, who had penetrated the ill-concealed scepticism of the Inspector, considered this unlikely. In any case, by comparing notes with this man, who had been living in Praed Street throughout the period of the murders, he might derive a hint which would lead him to his goal.

For Dr Priestley, although he appeared to have put the whole affair out of his mind, was in fact determined to find the solution of the problem. He felt that so far the part he had played had been a distinctly ignominious one. Both his theory of the motive of the crimes and his account of his meeting with the Black Sailor had been disregarded. And although Dr Priestley affected to regard his excursions into the solution of criminal problems with half-amused tolerance, his ill-success hitherto in this instance was a secret, but none the less bitter, blow to his pride.

Yes, he would certainly go to see this man Ludgrove. His letter showed him to be a man above the ordinary standard of education in his position. Hanslet had spoken of him as a man of considerable intelligence. The Professor, considering the matter, felt that he might well have got into touch with him before. He began to think that he had been too ready to rely upon the police descriptions of the events which had taken place, and had neglected an alternative source of information which might contain many details of value. And, his determination made, the Professor fidgeted all day until, having hurried through dinner and found himself in his study earlier than usual, he could expect his visitor.

Mary had been instructed to show him straight in, and, when he was at length announced, the Professor rose at once to greet him. Mr Ludgrove, seen for the first time, was certainly an imposing and dignified figure. His snowy white hair and beard gave him a patriarchal appearance, produced an almost severe impression, which was only modified by the kindly smile which habitually hovered at the corner of his mouth. His eyes were screened by his powerful spectacles, but one guessed them to be direct and piercing in their expression.

"I am delighted to meet you, Mr Ludgrove," said the Professor warmly. "Yes, I am Dr Priestley, and this is my secretary, Mr Merefield. I received your letter, and am much obliged to you for your suggestion, which I shall be very glad to fall in with."

"Thank you, Dr Priestley, you are very kind," replied Mr Ludgrove, in his deep and pleasant voice. The Professor glanced at him in astonishment. Neither the voice nor the intonation were such as he would have expected of a herbalist in Praed Street.

"It is a beautiful evening." continued Mr Ludgrove. "Shall we walk to my house, or would you prefer to call a taxi? I know that the vicinity of Praed Street has a bad reputation as a result of these deaths, but although, as you probably know, I received a numbered counter some weeks ago, I have so far come to no harm. You need have no apprehensions once we reach my house. The police still display considerable concern for my safety."

Mr Ludgrove smiled, and even the Professor's set features relaxed a little. "I am not afraid to walk to Praed Street, especially in your company, Mr Ludgrove," he replied.

"And coming back?" persisted the herbalist. "I fear I have no telephone, and it may take me some minutes to find you a cab. I should be happy to walk back here with you."

The Professor made an impatient gesture. "Believe me, Mr Ludgrove, I am no more afraid of Praed Street than you are. If you insist upon walking home with me, I shall be very glad of your company. If not, I am perfectly capable of taking care of myself."

"It will be late, I am afraid, that is, if you have the patience to listen to me for so long," replied Mr Ludgrove. "I shall be compelled to inflict upon you a long and possibly tedious tale. However, you shall decide how much of it you wish to listen to."

"I am usually considered a good listener," said the Professor. "Shall we walk to your house, Mr Ludgrove?"

The herbalist assenting, they left the house and walked down Westbourne Terrace together. Mr Ludgrove's shop was scarcely half a mile away, and they covered the distance in a few minutes, conversing about anything but the matter uppermost in their thoughts. The Professor found Mr Ludgrove a most entertaining companion, and found himself wondering what such a man was doing to be compelled to keep a shop in such an odd neighbourhood.

They walked down Praed Street without adventure, and Mr Ludgrove unlocked the door of his shop with his latchkey. They passed through it into the inner room, the window of which was already curtained and the gas lighted. Dr Priestley cast a swift glance round it, noting with interest the scientific instruments on the bench, the cases full of books, and the two comfortable arm-chairs. "This is a very comfortable room of yours, Mr Ludgrove," he remarked approvingly.

"It has heard some queer stories in its time," replied Mr Ludgrove with a smile. "You can form no idea of the extraordinary confessions which some of my clients force me to listen to. But I can assure you that it has heard nothing more amazing than the story which I am about to unfold to you this evening."

"May I ask a question before you begin, Mr Ludgrove?" said the Professor quietly.

"Certainly, pray ask as many as you please," replied Mr Ludgrove with a smile.

"How did you learn of my interest in this affair? So far as I am aware, it is not common property."

"I am afraid that Inspector Hanslet was indiscreet," replied Mr Ludgrove. "When he first took over the case, he came here and had a long talk with me. He said then that he would put the facts before one whose powers of deduction were unrivalled. When I next saw him, he happened to mention your name, which I already knew as that of the boldest and most enterprising scientist of the age. It required very little intelligence on my part to infer that you would be interested in these extraordinary happenings, and that you were scarcely likely to accept the official explanation of them."

"I see," said the Professor. "Well, as it happens, your inference is correct. I am greatly interested, and I have a theory of my own as to the motive for the murders, which the police have been pleased to reject. I am all the more anxious to hear the evidence you have to put before me. There is still one more point in which I am interested. I am informed that, sometime before his death, Mr Copperdock reported that he had met an individual known as the Black Sailor. Upon this being reported to you, you stated that you happened to have Mr Copperdock under observation at the moment when he stated the meeting took place, and that no Black Sailor was present. Is this correct?"

"I can assure you, Dr Priestley, that at that moment there was nobody in sight but Mr Copperdock and myself," replied Mr Ludgrove simply.

"Thank you," said the Professor. "Now, I am prepared to examine the evidence you have to show me."

Mr Ludgrove rose from his chair. "Will you excuse me for a few minutes. Dr Priestley?" he said. "Before I begin my explanation, I should like to fetch certain things which I have put in a place of security upstairs. I will not keep you very long."

He passed into the shop as he spoke, and the Professor could hear the sound of his footsteps as he climbed the stairs. The Professor, left alone in the room, proceeded to examine the titles of the books in the shelves. They were mainly botanical works, such as one might expect to find in the library of a herbalist. But here and there among them were a few volumes of general scientific interest. Dr Priestley smiled as he saw, lying inconspicuously at the end of one of the shelves, a work he had published a year or so before, *Fact and Fallacy*. No doubt this had given Ludgrove the cue to his own interest in a problem so intricate as that of the Praed Street murders.

Lying next to it was a book bearing the name of an author

well-known in the scientific world, which the Professor had never heard of. He took it up and began to turn over the pages with interest. His eye caught a passage dealing with one of the subtler mathematical problems raised by a particular aspect of relativity. He became absorbed in this, forgetting all about Mr Ludgrove and his promised demonstration. So he remained for several minutes, until he had read the passage from beginning to end. Then, all at once, he became conscious that he was no longer alone in the room, that somebody was standing just inside the door, awaiting his pleasure.

The Professor laid the book down, and turned on his heel, an apology upon his lips. But the words died in his throat, and he stood for an instant staring at the figure with unbelieving eyes.

It was the Black Sailor.

CHAPTER 21 AN EXPLANATION

The Professor's first startled thought concerned the manner in which the man had entered the room. He had heard no sound of his entry, and he remembered that Mr Ludgrove had been careful to lock the door of the shop when they had come in together. His second was a sudden thrust of anxiety for Mr Ludgrove's safety. In the complete silence of the little room, into which no sound penetrated but the faint low rumble of the traffic outside, he listened for the sound of his footsteps above. But, even to his keen ears, the house seemed as quiet as the grave.

It was the Black Sailor who broke the silence. "Sit down, Dr Priestley," he said gravely. "I have much to say to you. You will recall that this is our second meeting."

But Dr Priestley took a step forward, and stared into the man's face, at his jet-black beard and hair, at the scar which gleamed angrily upon his cheek. He wore a woollen cap, drawn down over his face, and a blue pilot coat over his jersey. But for these details, he was dressed as he had been when the Professor had met him upon the Isle of Purbeck. And the tones of his rasping voice sent a thrill of fear through even the Professor's determined heart.

"How did you get in here? Where is Mr Ludgrove?" The Professor found his voice at last.

"Mr Ludgrove is dead," replied the Black Sailor, almost gently. "Surely you remember the warning I gave you when we last met? Mr Ludgrove, the herbalist of Praed Street, is dead. Nobody on this side of the grave will ever see him again. But you shall not be disappointed, Dr Priestley. He was to have explained to you many things that seemed obscure, but were in reality very simple. It is only fitting that I should take his place."

And then at last the Professor understood. Perhaps it was some note in the man's voice that gave him the clue. The solution was so simple that he could have laughed aloud at his own lack of perception. "You are Mr Ludgrove," he said simply.

The Black Sailor laughed quietly, and the laugh and the voice in which he replied were those of the herbalist. "So you have guessed at last, Dr Priestley!" he exclaimed. "Oh, but it was so simple! A little dye, which could be applied or removed in a few minutes, a little grease-paint for the scar, an artistic disarrangement of my beard and hair, a change of clothing, and who would recognise Mr Ludgrove the herbalist? Still, the Black Sailor was careful only to appear in the half light. His disguise might have been penetrated under more searching conditions. But I flatter myself that it is effective."

The Professor, looking at the man, was forced to agree. Even now that he knew, he found it difficult to recognise the venerable Mr Ludgrove with his well-kept, snowy beard, his kindly smile, and his large spectacles, in this wild-looking sailor with the fierce face and the tangled black hair which seemed to cover it. The disguise was undoubtedly effective, but—how simple!

"Mr Ludgrove is dead. His mission is completed, and you will never see him again," continued the Black Sailor. "Let us do his memory the justice of saying that he told the truth. When Copperdock saw the Black Sailor, it was perfectly correct for Ludgrove to say that he and Copperdock were alone in the street. Ludgrove was the Black Sailor that evening. But this is beside the point. Pray sit down, Dr Priestley, and we will enter upon the explanation which I have to give you."

Dr Priestley's mind had been working rapidly while the man spoke, and it appeared that he had guessed the Professor's thoughts.

"Perhaps I should explain the conditions," he continued. "All the entrances to this room are securely fastened. The door is locked, and, as you see, there is a heavy curtain across it. The window is boarded up, and there are no other openings. If you were to shout as loud as you cared, no one could possibly hear you. Please do not think I wish to threaten you, Dr Priestley, but I would point out that if you were so unwise as to attempt personal violence, I am a very much more powerful man than you, and I am armed. I am afraid that there is no alternative for you but to listen to what I say. And after that will come release. Now, surely you will sit down, Dr Priestley."

The Professor, after a glance round the room, perceived the helplessness of his position. The man was clearly mad, but his mania was strictly limited. Upon most subjects he was as sane as he was himself. He must perforce listen to what he had to say. Perhaps, during the time which this would occupy, he might be able to evolve a scheme for his capture. He walked across the room and sat down in the chair which the Black Sailor pointed out to him.

The man immediately took the chair opposite. "Artists are naturally vain, Dr Priestley," he began, "and I think my exploits entitle me to consider myself an artist. I have long promised myself the pleasure of recounting them to one who would appreciate their ingenuity, and you are the very man for such a purpose. I have, I believe, read everything that you have written, and I have understood a nature which revels in ingenious methods. I flatter myself that what I have to tell you will, at least, not bore you."

"I shall be extremely interested to hear it," replied the Professor quietly.

"Before Dr Morlandson died, he furnished me with a list of his intended victims, and a very fine collection of lethal apparatus," continued the Black Sailor. "My first concern was to find some spot in London from which to operate. I made careful inquiries as to the present addresses of the surviving jurymen, and found that most of them came from this part of London. This, of course, was not coincidence, since juries are frequently called by districts.

"I therefore determined to establish myself in this neighbourhood. I knew enough of the properties of herbs to set myself up as a herbalist, and I was fortunate enough to find this empty shop, almost opposite the premises of one of my intended victims. Once in possession of it, I set myself to develop a business which should bring me into contact with all the gossip of the neighbourhood, and to study the habits and circumstances of my intended victims. My own apparent vocation I tried to make as open as I could. My shop was available to any who cared to enter it, and from the first I accustomed the acquaintances which I made to my habit of spending occasional weekends in the country, and of taking a walk every evening, since I foresaw that these would be essential to my purpose. And in Mr Copperdock I found a simple and not over-intelligent personality who would serve me admirably as a dupe upon whom suspicion might be cast.

"You will, I think, understand the task which I had been set. I was to execute the vengeance of Dr Morlandson upon the men who had condemned him to so many years of agony. But this must be done in such a manner that their deaths would not be attributed to pure chance, but must eventually be made to appear as acts of justice, as indeed they were. I could not employ the same methods in each case, but at the same time I wished each death to carry the same distinguishing mark.

"I was at first puzzled to think of any such mark. And then, during a visit to Mr Copperdock, the idea came to me. I saw a box full of white bone counters lying on his table, and I managed to appropriate a dozen or so of these. At the same time I carefully noted the envelopes he used in his business, and by a casual question learnt where he had obtained them. I bought three thousand of these, all the remaining stock, giving the name of Mr Copperdock. There was very little chance of their being traced, but if they had been, the result of inquiries would have shown that they had all been sold to the tobacconist.

"I also discovered that the typewriter recently purchased by

Mr Copperdock was a Planet, and I took a careful note of the brand of pen and red ink he habitually used. I next made inquiries among the envelope addressing agencies, until I found one which employed Planet machines. To this agency I sent my envelopes, together with a telephone directory in which I had marked some two thousand names, among which were those of my intended victims who happened to have a telephone. To this list I added one of my own, containing a thousand additional names, among them the jurymen I had not found in the telephone book. I instructed the agency to type these names and addresses on the envelopes. It was a safe assumption that a year later, when I began operations, the agency would not remember having typed the names of the dead men among so many thousands of others. The counters I numbered myself, as required.

"Last November, I felt myself in a position to seek my first victim. I decided that it should be Mr Tovey, a personal friend of Mr Copperdock, from whom I had learnt all I required to know about his habits. I had among my other weapons, a paper-cutter's knife, with half a dozen blades. These blades I had sharpened along both edges until they resembled daggers, and I had discovered a means of fixing them lightly into the handle, so that they would remain in the wound, leaving me free to carry off the handle.

"That evening, Mr Ludgrove took his usual walk, returning by way of Paddington station. From there he telephoned to Mr Tovey, giving him the message that he was wanted at St Martha's. Mr Ludgrove then walked back here, and took on the character of the Black Sailor. Behind this shop is a piece of ground which was once a garden, and that in turn is separated by a low wall from a yard, deserted after business hours, with gates and also a small door leading into a back street. I had made myself a key to the small door, and it provided me with an alternative means of access to this house.

"The Black Sailor went out this way, waited in the shadows at the corner of the back street until he saw Mr Tovey pass, then followed him and caught him up among the crowd outside the Express Train. The knife required no violence in its use, merely a firm push in one of the spots which Dr Morlandson had shown me. The actual stabbing was a very simple matter, and the Black Sailor disappeared in the crowd, to return here by the way he went out and transform himself into Mr Ludgrove.

"But I realised that this method, although it had served its purpose once, was inartistic and dangerous. There was always the risk that the Black Sailor might be recognised, and traced back here. As a matter of fact, Wal Snyder had noticed him, but his evidence was discredited. The police, however, were compelled to offer a reward for him, and I determined that the Black Sailor must be reserved for special purposes.

"In the case of Mr Colburn I adopted quite a different method. I had become a customer of his, and had encouraged his son to confide in me. From him I gradually learnt his father's habits and peculiarities, particularly that of smoking a pipe in the shop after lunch, and, when he had finished it, of refilling it and putting it away on a shelf. I examined the pipe in young Colburn's absence, and noticed that it was cracked. That evening, I visited a tobacconist at some distance from here and bought a pipe of similar make and shape.

"Within a few days, as I had expected, I saw Mr Colburn enter Copperdock's shop. It was a fair assumption that he had gone in to buy a new pipe to replace the old one, since I had learnt that his tobacco was always delivered to him. I took a very small splinter of glass, covered it with a preparation which Dr Morlandson had given me, and drove one end of it into a notch I had made in the mouthpiece of the pipe I had bought. I then went to Colburn's shop, on an errand which necessitated young Colburn's going to the bakehouse and leaving me alone. I saw, as I had expected, a new pipe lying filled on the shelf. I substituted mine for it, put Mr Colburn's pipe in my pocket, waited until young Colburn came back with my purchase, and left the shop. I was in the country when Mr Colburn died, but I heard the details later, as no doubt you have heard them, Dr Priestley."

"Yes, the deaths of Colburn and Martin strengthened my theory that Dr Morlandson was at the bottom of the affair," replied the Professor calmly. "I guessed that there was extensive medical knowledge behind both of them." His one idea was to prolong this recital as much as possible.

"You will agree, however, that it would have been impossible to trace Mr Colburn's death to me. By this time I had come to the conclusion that it would be as well to stage the scene of my executions as far as possible in Praed Street. I wished to concentrate attention upon this particular district, since I knew that the obvious effect on the police would be to suggest to them an inhabitant of it. As soon as they did this, I was ready to supply a number of hints and inferences. I was thus able to become on confidential terms with Whyland, and, by making a friend of him, to put myself above suspicion. And all the time I was influencing his mind in the direction of Mr Copperdock. It was a most interesting psychological study, I can assure you.

"Pargent, whom I determined to tackle next, presented an entirely different problem. He lived some distance from Praed Street, and though I might have devised some means of killing him in his own home, I was most anxious to adhere to the rule I had laid down. It was not until I had carefully considered his habits that I saw my way clear. During the years which I had spent observing my victims, I had discovered the regularity of his visits to his sister at West Laverhurst. And in this regularity I saw my opportunity.

"One Saturday morning, when he was due to go to West Laverhurst, I went down from Waterloo to Penderworth, for which the station is Wokingham, ostensibly to collect plants. I went to Waterloo by way of Paddington and the tube, the most obvious way of getting there. But at Paddington I called at the booking-office, and took a ticket to Reading. Having arrived at Penderworth, I made myself as conspicuous as possible at the inn, in the character of Mr Ludgrove, and then went out with a suitcase, with the declared intention of collecting plants. In the suitcase were my dyes and paints, also a change of clothing.

"Now, Penderworth is four miles from Reading, where the train stopped by which Pargent habitually returned home. I found a convenient coppice, in which I got myself up as a man with iron grey beard and hair, and a conspicuous mark upon my face. I left my suitcase in the coppice, carefully hidden, and in it Mr Ludgrove's clothes and spectacles. Then I walked to Reading and caught the train in which Pargent was travelling. On our arrival at Paddington I followed him through the station, and was by his side when he made his dash across Praed Street to catch the bus. My opportunity came on the refuge, and I employed the same method as I had done in the case of Tovey.

"I had ascertained that a train left for Reading ten minutes after the arrival of the train by which I had travelled up. I had just time to catch this—I already had the ticket which I had purchased in the morning. As the train neared Reading, I went to the lavatory and removed the dye and paint. From here I stepped out on to the platform and passed the barrier unremarked. Even had I been noticed in London, and my description circulated, I thus ran very little risk. The most noticeable thing had been the 'port-wine mark,' and this of course had vanished. I walked to the coppice, buried the clothes I was wearing, resumed the apparel of Mr Ludgrove, and returned to the inn with my suitcase full of the first plants I could lay my hands on. I had apparently an excellent alibi.

"With the death of Pargent, the curious coincidence that all three victims had received counters came to light, as I had anticipated it would. I thought it wise to suspend my operations for a while, while I prepared my plans for dealing with the remainder of the surviving jurymen. Goodwin presented the greatest puzzle. He was confined to his house, almost to one room, and I despaired of being able to reach him. I had nearly decided to leave him alone, knowing that his death could not be delayed very long in any case. But I had a sudden inspiration. The numbered counters had attracted a good deal of attention, and the sequel to their receipt was well known. It was quite possible that Goodwin, to whom any shock was likely to be fatal, would die as the mere result of finding one in his post. I made the experiment, and it was successful. But I claim no great credit for this exploit. I might well have failed, had fortune not favoured me, and I was compelled to abandon Praed Street as the scene of his death. I have always considered that the execution of Goodwin was not up to my usual standard.

"But I have omitted the case of Martin, upon which I rather pride myself. Put yourself in my position, Dr Priestley. Here was a man, living in the suburbs, and having an office in the City. How was I to lure him to Praed Street, and ensure his death when he arrived there, at a time when Praed Street had already gained notoriety as the scene of three mysterious deaths? I knew quite a lot about Martin, more than most people, in fact. I knew that he had once been in business in Praed Street, and that he had prospered there rather more rapidly than his apparent business warranted. My connection among the shadier classes in the neighbourhood helped me there. I discovered, hint by hint, that he was a well-known fence, a receiver of stolen goods, that is, Dr Priestley, and that discovery, coupled with the fact that the premises he had once occupied were again changing hands, gave me an idea.

"My first move was to make the acquaintance of the builder who was carrying out the alterations to Number 407, and from him I learnt in the course of conversation the name of the new tenant. He asked me to come and look at the place, an invitation which I accepted without too great a show of eagerness. In the next few days I visited the place again, more than once. I wanted the builder's men to get accustomed to the sight of me. For this purpose I was Mr Ludgrove the local resident, of course. As a matter of fact, most of the builder's friends went to have a look at the place. There is always interest in vacant premises in a street like this."

"Dr Morlandson had provided me with a number of celluloid capsules, containing pure prussic acid. I took an ordinary electric lamp, broke it, and connected the ends of the leading-in wires by a piece of fine foil, which would become red hot on the passage of a current. Round this I wrapped a few strands of nitrated cellulose, and to this I fixed the celluloid capsule. The action of this device was very simple. If a current were passed through it, the cellulose would inflame and set fire to the capsule, thus releasing the prussic acid. Some of the vapour of this might catch fire, but enough would be left to be fatal to anybody breathing it in a confined space. And I knew of a confined space most suitably adapted to the purpose.

"I wrote a letter to Martin, which I knew could not fail to bring him to Number 407, and to bring him alone. It suggested that somebody had discovered his true occupation, and was prepared to keep the matter secret, for a consideration. Then, on the Saturday morning, just before the men were due to leave, I walked openly into Number 407. I had kept an eye on their habits, and knew that before they left they packed away their tools in the back room on the ground floor. I could hear them there as I went in, and I made my way down to the cellar without anybody noticing me. All I did there was to put my poison device in the lamp-holder in the small cellar—I had heard the electrician tell the builder that the current would be connected that day—hang the numbered counter on the switch, and remove the string by which the swing door could be pulled open from within. The trap was set, it remained only to ensure that Martin should have easy access to it.

"I knew about the arrangement whereby the keys were kept at the sweet shop. I had announced that I was going into the country that day, travelling into Essex by the London, Tilbury and Southend from Fenchurch Street. I took the Underground, apparently to Aldgate, but got out at Aldersgate Street. From here I walked down the Barbican, saw Martin leave his office, go to lunch, and finally book at Aldersgate Street to Praed Street. I immediately telephoned from one of the boxes there to Mr Briggs, who had the keys, saying that I was the tenant of Number 407, and asking him to look out for a Mr Martin, and give him the keys. I then went on to Fenchurch Street, spent a happy and profitable day in the country, and returned home to hear of the death of Mr Martin. I was, I confess, slightly annoyed to find that it had been attributed to suicide. But then, I had never anticipated that Martin would bring an automatic with him. But perhaps I weary you with these details, Dr Priestley?"

"Not in the least!" replied the Professor fervently. He glanced furtively at the clock. It was already past ten o'clock.

CHAPTER 22 THE DEATH CHAMBER

"What I have to tell you now may interest you more clearly, Dr Priestley," continued the Black Sailor. "Having disposed of five of my intended victims, I had to remove Copperdock. But I wished first of all to concentrate as much suspicion as possible on him before his death. You will perceive the idea, no doubt. If the murders were to cease with Copperdock's death, there being already a vague suspicion that he had caused them, further enquiries would not be pursued very briskly.

"For this reason, I appeared to Copperdock that evening as he was coming out of the Cambridge Arms. The disguise was very imperfect, since I had merely smeared the dye on my beard in the street, and the scar was made of sticking-plaster. It would not have borne a moment's close inspection, but it was good enough for Copperdock, as I felt sure it would be. I escaped from him without difficulty, and, having taken a wet sponge with me, removed the scar and dye at the first opportunity and came quietly home. I beat Mr Copperdock by about five minutes.

"As I had expected, he told Whyland the story of his adventure, and I was in a position to swear that he and I had been alone in the street. The result was to discredit his veracity still further. I then thought it time to act. You will remember that Copperdock said he found a numbered counter on his bed? That was the exact truth, although it seemed impossible, and nobody believed him. But it was capable of the simplest explanation in the world.

Look here."

The Black Sailor rose from his chair, and walked across to the bench, from which he picked up an apparatus made of wood and India rubber, not unlike a miniature cross-bow. "I amused myself in my spare time by making this," he said. "As you see, it has a holder which just takes a counter. You would be surprised to see how far and how accurately it will project it. I have frequently practised with it in the country, and I have attained sufficient skill in its use to be able to place a counter where I like at any range up to a hundred feet or so.

"Now, above my shop is a room, which I use for storage purposes. From the window of this room you can see into the window of Mr Copperdock's bedroom. I had merely to wait for a windless evening, fine enough for Mr Copperdock to leave his window open, and seize my opportunity when I knew his house was empty. The opportunity came, and I took it.

"It might have been thought that by delivering the counter in advance I had increased my difficulties. But, on the contrary, I had diminished them. The obvious improbability of Mr Copperdock's story, that he had found a counter on his bed at a time when it was demonstrable that nobody had entered the house, was merely another link in the chain of suspicion which I was forging round him. I allowed a few days to pass, and then, the following Saturday, I took the final step.

"Now, even you, Dr Priestley, failed to read the riddle of the broken hypodermic needle and the incrustation of potassium carbonate round the puncture. Yet it was ridiculously simple. I secured a piece of metallic potassium, and moulded it into the shape of a bullet to fit an air-gun which I possessed. Into the head of this bullet I inserted the broken end of a hypodermic needle, which I had already charged with the same drug as had been so effectual in the case of Mr Colburn. Keeping this prepared bullet in paraffin, to avoid oxidation, I placed the air-gun ready upstairs, and waited for Mr Copperdock's return from the Cambridge Arms. He brought two friends home with him, and I was afraid at first that I should be compelled to postpone my attempt. It was essential to my scheme that he should be alone in the house when I fired the gun.

"However, the two friends left after a while, and Mr Copperdock entered his bedroom and proceeded to undress. I could just see the washing-stand through a gap in his curtains, and I waited until he was bending over this. Then I loaded the gun with my potassium bullet, and pulled the trigger. I saw Mr Copperdock spin round, and then he passed out of my line of vision. But I knew I had succeeded, and I came quietly down here.

"The bullet had possessed sufficient velocity to drive the needle well into Mr Copperdock's body, and I knew I could trust it to destroy its own evidence. I need scarcely explain the properties of metallic potassium to you. Dr Priestley. On exposure to the air it oxidises, as you know, first to the hydroxide, which is caustic potash, and then to the carbonate. The doctor who was called in quite correctly stated that the presence of the carbonate showed that caustic potash had been applied. But he never guessed that the caustic potash had itself been derived from potassium.

"I had expected that Ted Copperdock's first act upon discovering his father's body would be to call me. I thought that this would furnish me with an opportunity for adding yet another mystification for the police to solve. I placed a numbered counter on my own mantelpiece, and waited. Sure enough, young Copperdock came across to me. I met him in the shop, and we went over together, I taking care not to close the door behind us. I have no doubt that the scene in Mr Copperdock's room has been described to you in detail. But there is one incident which seems to have escaped everybody's recollection. I was left alone in the room while Ted went for the doctor and Waters telephoned to Inspector Whyland.

"I had meant all along to contrive to be alone in the room sooner or later, and was prepared for the opportunity. I had in my pocket the handle of the paper-maker's knife and one of the blades. I placed the handle in Mr Copperdock's right hand, and pressed the fingers round it. Then I put the blade and handle in the pocket of one of his overcoats, satisfied that sooner or later it would be found there, with his finger-prints upon it. A few minutes later, a chance remark of Inspector Whyland's gave me a further idea. If the suicide theory were correct, the hypodermic syringe ought to be found. I had, I confess, overlooked this point, but it was easily rectified. Directly he left me, I looked out an old syringe, fitted the other half of the needle to it, and dropped it by the side of the road under Mr Copperdock's window. Waters found it within half an hour.

"Meanwhile, Inspector Whyland had returned here at my suggestion. He was the very witness I required to my finding of the counter. The door left open afforded an obvious suggestion of the means by which it had reached my mantelpiece. I did not care what theory he evolved as to the identity of the person who had entered the house. My only object was to confuse the issue as much as possible.

"Then, Dr Priestley, Inspector Hanslet came upon the scene, and I knew that the real battle of wits had begun. As I have told you, I had spent years studying the characters of the members of the jury, and among them I had devoted a large part of my time to observing you. I soon discovered that Inspector Hanslet consulted you upon his principal cases, and I knew as soon as Hanslet appeared, that I was at last pitted against the most acute brain in England. I may say, without exaggeration, that the knowledge gave me the keenest pleasure which I had known for years."

The Black Sailor paused, and smiled at his auditor benignly. "You see, Dr Priestley," he continued, "I was in rather a delicate position, where you were concerned. I had purposely left you until the last, because, as foreman of the jury, Dr Morlandson wished you to have special treatment. You were to be warned, but your fate was to be left hanging over your head as long as possible. I was afraid that you would not attach much importance to the mere receipt of a counter. You are not the sort of person to be so easily frightened. Yet how to deliver a personal warning without giving you a clue which would be fatal to the execution of my design, I could not see.

"I knew Inspector Hanslet had discussed the Praed Street murders with you. Or rather, in deference to your well-known insistence upon exactitude, I will say that I believed it to be in the highest degree probable. During one of my evening walks, accompanied, I may say, by one of Inspector Whyland's charming young men, I passed your house, and saw Inspector Hanslet enter it. It was rather more than a mere guess to infer that he, who had just taken charge of the case, was about to consult you upon it.

"Then, a day or two later, I saw in *The Times* the announcement of your hurried departure to Australia. Believe me, Dr Priestley, I had a higher opinion of your courage than to imagine that you had hastened to seek a place of safety. I reasoned, and events proved that I reasoned correctly, that you alone had connected the names of the dead men with those who had served on the jury at Dr Morlandson's trial. You were therefore aware that your own life was threatened. But one thing puzzled you. If Dr Morlandson were dead, how could the murders be accounted for? You would naturally wish to verify his death upon the spot, but you would endeavour to do so with the utmost secrecy. Hence, I thought, the announcement of your visit to Australia, which would mislead your antagonist, and account for your absence from London. The place in which to find you alone was obviously the Isle of Purbeck.

"So I suggested a scheme to Inspector Whyland, and here my chance thought of delivering a counter to myself came in useful. I was to go to Dorchester for the weekend—I was thankful for the evidence I had already laid that the fatal period and place were the weekend and Praed Street—and he was to remain here on the watch for the assassin who threatened me. It amused me to think that the solution of the whole mystery would lie under his very eyes, for the cross-bow was on that bench, and the air-gun stands in a rack in my bedroom. But, since I had invited him, I knew that he would attach no importance to these things, even if he noticed them. I left him in possession, and went to Dorchester. But from there I took a train to Wareham, and walked across the heath to Dr Morlandson's cottage, where I most artistically converted Mr Ludgrove into the Black Sailor.

"You must remember that I lived on that heath for a year, during Dr Morlandson's lifetime. I have been there frequently since. There is a disused clay working not far from the cottage, and in this I had secreted a number of useful articles, among them a bicycle. With this I watched in the heather, feeling certain that you would not disappoint me. You did not, and our most interesting interview took place.

"After you had started for home, I made my preparations for departure. It was just possible that you would set the local police on my track, and I was taking no risks. I rolled a round and heavy stone over the path, which gave the sand a level and untrodden appearance, and effectually removed all traces of my bicycle. Then I walked to a spot on the shores of Newton Bay, where I knew that a punt, which is very rarely used, was drawn up. In this I rowed across through the backwaters to a point on the Wareham channel above Lake. I left the punt here, turned myself back again into Mr Ludgrove, and in the morning walked to Hamworthy Junction, whence I caught a train to Dorchester. I was in plenty of time to dig my colichicum bulbs and return to London.

"Now, Dr Priestley, I feel that I owe you some apology. Matters have turned out very differently from what I had expected, owing to circumstances over which I have no control. I had intended that you should survive for months, even perhaps years, in daily expectation of death leaping out at you from some unexpected corner. You are a determined man, but I think you will agree that even your iron will would have broken down at last under the strain. Every now and then, when you were most absorbed in your labours, a warning would reach you, a hint that the sands were running out, that you might not be allowed time even to finish the immediate task. I think in time you would have known something of the horror and despair which grips the innocent man condemned ruthlessly and without mercy, as you condemned Dr Morlandson, Dr Priestley."

The Black Sailor's voice had become harsh and menacing, and the Professor started from his chair to meet the attack which he anticipated. But the Black Sailor waved him back again with an imperious gesture.

"Sit down. Dr Priestley!" he commanded. "I have not yet finished what I must say and you must hear. You need fear no violence, unless you attempt to escape from this room. But you are far too sensible to make any such attempt, which, as you see, would be futile. I could overpower you in an instant, and I should then be compelled to bind you hand and foot and gag you. A most humiliating situation for you, Dr Priestley, and one uncomfortably reminiscent of the methods of the hangman, to whose care you delivered Dr Morlandson, you remember."

The Professor sank back into his chair. He realised that the Black Sailor was right, that in any struggle he must inevitably be overcome, and that resistance would probably lead to his immediate death. If he were to leave this room alive, it must be by strategy rather than force. It was unthinkable that the Black Sailor would release him now that he had confessed the full details of his murderous campaign. He could only bide his time, seeking some means of extricating himself from this desperate situation. But what did the man mean by his assurance that he would employ no violence?

Meanwhile the Black Sailor had continued, in the deep, pleasant voice which had been one of the most striking attributes of Mr Ludgrove.

"This is the vengeance which I had planned for you, Dr Priestley. But, unfortunately, my plans have been thwarted. Long ago, when Dr Morlandson was alive, he warned me that, well set up and healthy as I appeared to be, my heart was affected by organic disease. He told me frankly that it might be many years before it seriously affected my health, and that, with reasonable care, I might expect to attain the average term of years. But at the same time he warned me that my trouble might at any time become acute, and he described to me the symptoms which would be my signal to prepare for death.

"Those symptoms developed last week, Dr Priestley, and I knew that I had only a short while longer to live. But I was determined not to die leaving the vengeance which had been bequeathed to me unaccomplished. I had sworn to be the instrument of justice upon those who had destroyed Dr Morlandson's life, for that life had been destroyed just as surely as though his original sentence had been carried out. And of those who had incurred the guilt, only you remained. Dr Priestley.

"I could have shot you in your own house, and then turned the weapon upon myself. In any case I am to die very shortly, and I much prefer death at my own hands and under my own control to the anxious waiting for the uncertain hand of nature. It would have been the easiest way, perhaps, but it was not in accordance with the methods which I had so carefully developed. How much more fitting it would be that you should die in Praed Street, that your death should be the culminating point in the history of the murders in Praed Street! I believed that it could be done, and I set myself to work out the details.

"The police, as you are aware, have rather lost interest in you and me. The discovery of the knife in Mr Copperdock's coat pocket seems finally to have convinced them that the secret died with him, and, whatever the secret might have been, no further murders were to be anticipated. Detectives are busy people, they have no time to spare for academic research. I am sure that they are convinced that no actual danger menaces either Dr Priestley or Mr Ludgrove, although both of them are known to have received numbered counters. They were not likely to interfere with my schemes.

"You are aware of the steps which I took to bring you here. Had you refused to accompany me this evening, I should have shot you outright in your own study. But I knew that you would not refuse. The solution of the mystery had become a point of honour with you, and, besides, you had a message for me which

I was sure that you would be glad of the opportunity to deliver. Surely you would not have hesitated to give the innocent Mr Ludgrove the Black Sailor's message, Dr Priestley?"

The Professor forced a smile. "I had intended to do so, but—he died, to use your own expression, before I had the opportunity."

"Yes, that was unfortunate," agreed the Black Sailor pleasantly. "But still, the fact that you had the message to deliver served its purpose. It was an added inducement to you to accept my invitation. And, by carefully emphasising the possible danger which lurked in Praed Street, I worked upon your pride. You would not have refused to come with me, after that. And I told you the truth. I had revelations to make which I knew would interest you, and I think you have not been disappointed."

He paused for a moment, and then continued, a sinister purpose in his voice: "And now the end has come. It is not the end I sought, but I welcome it as well as any other. We two will pass out of this world together, Dr Priestley, you the last victim of my justice, and I the executioner. It is but anticipating my own death for a short time, and the means I shall employ will render even deeper the mystery which surrounds me. On Sunday morning the world will hear of two more strange deaths in Praed Street. I think your secretary will come round here before the night is over, and, being able to obtain no reply, will call in the police to his aid. How much of the riddle will they solve, I wonder?"

The Black Sailor stretched out his hand, and switched on a small electric hand-lamp which stood on a table by his side. "That will give us sufficient light for our purpose," he said sombrely. Then, before the Professor could guess his intention, he suddenly leapt from his chair, turned out the gas which was burning at a bracket by the mantelpiece, and with a powerful wrench tore the bracket itself from the wall. It fell with a crash into the fire-place.

Then the Professor understood. He, too, leapt from his chair with a shout, and dashed blindly for the door. But the Black Sailor was there before him. "It is useless, Dr Priestley," he said menacingly. "The door is fastened securely, as is the window. The chimney is blocked, and there is no possible escape for us. I doubt if you would be heard if you call again for help, but I cannot risk it. Will you give me your word to wait quietly, or must I gag you and tie you up? Would you care to meet death bound like a criminal, Dr Priestley?"

For a moment the two men stood face to face, the powerful form of the Black Sailor towering threateningly over the Professor. Behind them, with a faint hissing sound, the gas poured into the room through the broken bracket. Already the pungent smell of it caught Dr Priestley by the throat.

And then, suddenly, the idea came to him. It was a forlorn, desperate hope, a scheme almost as dangerous as waiting supinely for the fatal vapours to overpower him. Yet—it was worth trying. He nodded his head almost briskly. "I will not call for help," he said, and, turning on his heel, he sat down again in the chair he had just quitted.

The Black Sailor followed his example, and so the two sat in silence, waiting, waiting. The atmosphere of the room grew thick and heavy, difficult to breathe. The Professor found his thoughts floating away to trifling things, he imagined himself a boy again, at school— With a mighty effort of will he recalled them, forcing his mind to concentrate upon the thing he had to do. Yet, was it worth it? Death, in that comfortable chair, would be so easy. A pleasant languor crept over him. He had only to close his eyes and sleep——

Again his will triumphed. He must wait yet a few seconds longer, wait till the whole room was full of gas. But could he, dare he? His senses were slipping away fast. Yet he must retain consciousness, if only for those few seconds. The Black Sailor was glaring at him with baleful eyes, eyes that suddenly seemed familiar, as though they stared out of him from the past, many, many years ago. Where had he seen those eyes before?

The Professor's strength and energy were failing him fast. He knew that, even if the Black Sailor offered no opposition, he could not reach the broken pipe and stop the rush of the gas.

He felt his muscles failing him, his brain refusing to struggle any longer against the luxurious sleep which enticed it. He must make his effort now, before he yielded to that sweet, enthralling sleep which could know no awakening.

Stealthily he felt in his pockets, forcing his reluctant fingers to their work. Then, even as the Black Sailor struggled to his feet, and stood there swaying dizzily, the Professor slid to the floor, and struck the match which he held in his hand. There was a roar as of the heavens opening, a bright, scorching sea of flame, and the Professor knew no more.

CHAPTER 23 THE WILL

He came to himself slowly and confusedly. A strong light was glaring into his eyes, and he could hear voices, voices which he did not recognise, all about him. He seemed to be lying on the floor, his shoulders supported in somebody's arms.

Gradually he began to distinguish words and sentences. "This one's coming round, I believe." "All right, the doctor'll be here in a minute." "T'other one's gone, I'm afraid. I can't feel his pulse at all." "Here, help me to clear this plaster off him, somebody. The explosion seems to have brought the ceiling down. It's a wonder it didn't blow the roof off. Have you got that gas turned off at the main yet?" "Ah, here's the doctor. Been a bit of a smash here, doctor. Gas explosion, from what I can see of it. Two hurt, one of 'em killed, I fancy. Take this one first, will you?"

The Professor saw a face peering into his own. "Well, my friend, what's happened to you? Blown up, eh? Let's have a look at you. Any bones broken? Doesn't look like it. Can you move your legs? Good. Any pain anywhere?"

"No. I was stunned, I think, when the explosion took place." Dr Priestley's senses were returning rapidly. The whole scene flashed back to him, the feeble glimmer of the little hand-lamp, the figure of the Black Sailor, formidable, immense, swaying towards him——

Before the supporting arms could prevent him, he had struggled to his feet. Something about his head felt unfamiliar, and he passed his hand over it. Every particle of hair had disappeared. He was bald, clean-shaven, without eyebrows or eyelashes.

"Steady, steady," came a voice soothingly. "We'll soon get you out of this. Here, sit down in this chair, or what remains of it."

He let himself be guided to the chair. The outlines of the room, illuminated by the rays of two or three bull's-eye lanterns, began to be visible to him. He hardly recognised it. Everything it had contained was swept into inextricable confusion, as though a tornado had passed through it. Where the window had been was a square of dim grey light, the distant reflection of a street lamp. A whitish gritty dust covered everything, the debris of the fallen ceiling. And stretched out in front of the fire-place was the dim outline of a man's figure, prone and motionless.

One of the men in the room came up to him. "Feeling better, eh? Narrow shave you've had, I should say. Do you remember who you are?"

"I am Dr Priestley, of Westbourne Terrace," replied the Professor.

The man gave a low whistle of incredulity. "Dr Priestley? Well, you don't look it."

"I have letters in my pocket which will serve to identify me," replied the Professor shortly.

He put his hand in his pocket and produced a packet of papers. The man took them, glanced through them and handed them back. "I beg your pardon, sir," he said respectfully. "But—I didn't know you without your hair, and with your face blackened like that. Perhaps you could tell us who this is, sir?"

He flashed his lamp upon the features of the figure lying upon the floor. The Professor leant forward in his chair and gazed at them in silence. This man, too, was hairless as he was himself, as though he had been shaved by some expert barber. Beneath the grime which covered his face, beneath the lines which age and suffering had graven upon him, the Professor recognised the features which had graven themselves upon his memory so many years ago. He saw again the prisoner in the dock, the handsome clean-shaven face with its look of awful anxiety. And he knew where he had seen before those eyes which had stared into his before he had lost consciousness.

"That is Dr Morlandson," he replied gravely.

*

Dr Priestley was removed to Westbourne Terrace, at his own urgent request, but it was a couple of days before his doctor would allow him to receive visitors. He was pretty badly shaken, and the poison which he had inhaled was having its usual after effects. But his brain was as active as ever, and he insisted that Hanslet, who had been waiting with what patience he could summon, should be admitted without further delay.

"Well, sir, you seem to have been right as usual," he said. "But I don't profess to begin to understand, although I have a document here which clears up a good many points. If you feel well enough, I should be very glad if you would tell me what happened in that room. I've arranged for the inquest on this Dr Morlandson to be adjourned until you are well enough to attend. As a matter of fact, I don't see how an inquest is going to be held at all. There's been one already, on the same man, at Corfe Castle, years ago."

The Professor told his story as simply as possible, outlining his actions and repeating the Black Sailor's story, up to the moment when it had occurred to him that his only chance of escape was to produce an explosion. "It could not make things any worse, as far as I was concerned," he said. "I was bound to be overcome by the gas in a very few minutes. But I had to wait until I judged the mixture of gas and air to be correct, and I was very doubtful whether this would take place before I became unconscious. I guessed that I should feel the force of the explosion least by lying on the floor, and, as it proved, that saved me. Morlandson, who was standing up when the explosion took place, bore the full brunt of it, and it killed him."

"Well, it's a most extraordinary case altogether," replied Hanslet, as the Professor concluded his account. "This man Morlandson, or Ludgrove as we called him, displayed the most amazing ingenuity, and there was no reason why we should ever have suspected him, any more than we suspected anybody else in the neighbourhood. And the way he gradually concentrated our attention on poor Copperdock was masterly.

"No doubt you will like to hear our side of the story. It's fairly simple. About ten minutes before midnight the constable on duty outside Ludgrove's shop heard a terrific crash and a noise of breaking glass. He hammered at the door, and, getting no reply, had the sense to make his way round to the back, eventually reaching the place by much the same route as the Black Sailor used, according to what you have just told me. He found the window blown out of the back room, a terrible mess inside, and a jet of burning gas coming out of the broken bracket. He blew his whistle, and by the time that two or three of our fellows had got inside, you came to, Professor.

"Of course, when I heard that you had identified the dead man as Dr Morlandson, I thought you were still dizzy with the shock. We couldn't make out who he was; he was dressed as a sailor, but we couldn't recognise his face, black, and with all the hair burnt off. It couldn't be Ludgrove, yet, if it wasn't, what had become of the old herbalist?

"We next set to work to search the house. The first thing we found, lying on the dressing-table, was a most interesting document, which I should like you to read, Professor. It was in a sealed envelope, addressed 'To all whom it may concern.'"

Hanslet produced a sheet of paper, covered with writing which the Professor recognised as being the same as that of the letter which Ludgrove had sent him. He beckoned to Harold, who had been listening from the farther end of the room. "Read that to me, my boy," he said.

Harold took the paper and opened it. It contained no heading, but started abruptly.

"I, known now as Elmer Ludgrove, and practising as a herbalist in Praed Street, am in reality Ernest Morlandson, late a Doctor of Medicine, found guilty in the year 1906 of murdering Lord Whatley by the administration of an overdose of morphia. This

235

statement can be verified by an examination of my finger-prints, and by a comparison of certain marks upon my body with Dr Morlandson's record, in the possession of the prison authorities.

"I was found guilty, by a jury of men incapable of appreciating my motives, of wilful murder. My defence is that put forward at the time of my trial, that I believed, and do still believe, that my action was one of mercy rather than crime. As to the motives imputed to me, I affirm that, until shortly before my trial, I had no knowledge that my name had any place in Lord Whatley's will.

"I have spent fourteen years in a convict prison, and have seen all that I loved and honoured languish and die, my beloved wife, my professional status, my good name. I have descended to the uttermost depths, I have drunk the cup of bitterness of its dregs. The iron has entered into my soul. I was condemned to death for an act of mercy; I have lived for an act of justice.

"Justice has no quarrel with those who prosecuted me. They did their duty. Nor is her sword pointed against the judge who sentenced me, or the prison authorities who held me in durance. They too but did their duty. It is upon those who condemned me, who, ignorant and careless, disregarded justice as a thing of no account, that the sword of justice has been turned. I have been her swordbearer.

"Prison has been to me a hard and bitter school, a grinding University of crime. Here I have learnt the thousand devices by which men deceive their neighbours, the change of appearance, of voice, of character; the discarding of one personality and the assumption of another. I left prison fully prepared to execute the design which I had formed during the long horror of seclusion.

"As Dr Morlandson, I lived in seclusion upon my release. My plans were made; I had leisure and means in which to carry them out. Dr Morlandson must die, and another must take his place. I sold most of my former possessions, and carried to my retreat only the few things I still required. Among these was a skeleton, which I had acquired many years before. I built my laboratory, and filled it with highly combustible substances.

And meanwhile I experimented with new and hitherto unheard-of drugs.

"When I was ready, I staged my own death. I entered my laboratory, locked the door on the inside, and arranged the skeleton in such a way that it would become a mere charred collection of bones, but would not be utterly consumed. With it I placed all the incombustible means of identification that I could find, chief among them a gold ring. Then, having lit a fuse, and placed my combustibles round it, I made my escape by a ladder through the skylights of the laboratory. I should add that I had collected a quantity of meat from the butcher and placed it where the fire would reach it. The smell of burning flesh was a useful element of suggestion.

"My plan succeeded. Dr Morlandson died and was buried. I retired to a hiding-place which I had prepared and provisioned, a disused clay-working 846 yards South 23 degrees East (true) from my laboratory. My hair had turned white during my imprisonment. I had only to allow my beard to grow, and I became the venerable herbalist, Elmer Ludgrove, seeking premises in which to practise his trade.

"By the time that the contents of this letter become public, the justice of which I shall have been the instrument will be accomplished. This is my last will and testament, given before my appearance at the Court of the Eternal Judge, Who has greater mercy than any earthly jury. The remains of my fortune are contained, in the form of Bank of England notes to the value of fifteen thousand pounds, in a tin box deposited in the clay-workings whose position I have already indicated.

"I have wielded unsparingly the sword of justice. But true justice makes amends to the innocent at the same time as it punishes the guilty. I therefore bequeath all my possessions to the relatives of those who have fallen by my hand, to be apportioned in such shares as the Public Trustee, whom I hereby appoint as my trustee, shall decide."

"The work of a madman," commented Hanslet, as Harold

finished his reading.

"A madman? I wonder," replied the Professor slowly. "If a man who gets a fixed idea into his head, and pursues it through every difficulty, is a madman, then I agree. But in that case some of the greatest names in history must be convicted of madness. I believe that Morlandson really believed that he was executing justice. Perhaps he was. Is that document valid, Inspector?"

"I suppose so," replied Hanslet. "It is signed and witnessed. The signature is 'Ernest Morlandson,' and below that 'Elmer Ludgrove.' The witnesses' signatures are opposite the latter, and the paper has been folded, so that the witnesses could see nothing but the Ludgrove signature."

"And who are the witnesses?" asked the Professor.

Hanslet smiled. "One of them is Elizabeth Cooper, his charwoman. The other is Samuel Copperdock; the document is dated a week before that unfortunate man's death. I think you will agree that this last touch was I typical of the methods of the Black Sailor."

*

A few weeks later, when the Professor had sufficiently recovered to resume his normal occupations, Mary, the parlourmaid, announced to him that a lady and gentleman wished to see him on business.

They proved to be Ted and Ivy, very shy, and apparently wholly unable to express the object of their visit. At last, by strenuous efforts, the Professor and Harold between them got Ted to the point.

"It's like this, sir," he said. "You know all about that will of Mr Lud——, Dr Morlandson's, I should say, sir."

"Yes, I know all about it," replied the Professor. "I must congratulate you upon receiving some compensation at least for that man's crimes."

"I'm sure it's very good of you, sir," said Ted, obviously ill at ease. "We were wondering—that is, Miss Tovey and myself, sir, seeing that we're not so to speak familiar with these lawyer folk —if you'd be so good as to help us, sir."

"Help you? Of course I will help you to the best of my ability," replied the Professor heartily. "What is it that you want me to do for you?"

The direct question was too much for Ted, who flushed scarlet and stammered feebly. It was Ivy who stepped into the breach.

"We want to arrange that our shares should be put together in one lump, Dr Priestley," she said. "We don't either of us quite know who to ask about it. I think it could be managed, don't you?"

The Professor's eyes twinkled. "I feel sure it could," he replied. "That is, of course, if there were a sufficiently good reason for such a procedure."

Ivy suddenly became intensely interested in the pattern of the carpet. "There is a—a very good reason," she said, in a voice hardly above a whisper.

The Professor glanced from one to the other and smiled with the smile of an old man who has not yet lost his sympathy with the dreams of youth.

"Will you tell me the reason, Miss Tovey?" he asked.

"We're going to get married," replied Ivy, blushing prettily.

THE END

JOHN RHODE'S DR PRIESTLEY DETECTIVE NOVEL BIBLIOGRAPHY

1. *The Paddington Mystery* (Geoffrey Bles, London 1925/no US edition). Spitfire Publishers 2021.

2. *Dr Priestley's Quest* (Geoffrey Bles, London 1926/no US edition).

3. *The Ellerby Case* (Geoffrey Bles, London 1926/Dodd, Mead & Company, New York 1927). Spitfire Publishers 2023.

4. *The Murders in Praed Street* (Geoffrey Bles, London 1928/Dodd, Mead & Company, New York 1928). Spitfire Publishers 2024.

5. *Tragedy at the Unicorn* (Geoffrey Bles, London 1928/Dodd, Mead & Company, New York 1928). Spitfire Publishers 2024.

6. *The House on Tollard Ridge* (Geoffrey Bles, London 1929/Dodd, Mead & Company, New York 1929).

7. *The Davidson Case* (Geoffrey Bles, London 1929). US title: *Murder at Bratton Grange* (Dodd, Mead & Company, New York 1929).

8. *Peril at Cranbury Hall* (Geoffrey Bles, London 1930/Dodd, Mead & Company, New York 1930).

9. *Pinehurst* (Geoffrey Bles, London 1930). US title: *Dr Priestley Investigates* (Dodd, Mead & Company, New York 1930).

10. *Tragedy on the Line* (W. Collins & Sons, London 1931/Dodd,

Mead & Company, New York 1931).

11. *The Hanging Woman* (W. Collins & Sons, London 1931/Dodd, Mead & Company, New York 1931).

12. *Mystery at Greycombe Farm* (W. Collins & Sons, London 1932). US title: *The Fire at Greycombe Farm* (Dodd, Mead & Company, New York 1932).

13. *Dead Men at the Folly* (W. Collins & Sons, London 1932/Dodd, Mead & Company, New York 1932).

14. *The Motor Rally Mystery* (W. Collins & Sons, London 1933). US title: *Dr Priestley Lays a Trap* (Dodd, Mead & Company, New York 1933).

15. *The Claverton Mystery* (W. Collins & Sons, London 1933). US title: *The Claverton Affair* (Dodd, Mead & Company, New York 1933).

16. *The Venner Crime* (Oldhams Press, London, 1933/Dodd, Mead & Company, New York 1934).

17. *The Robthorne Mystery* (W. Collins & Sons, London 1934/Dodd, Mead & Company, New York 1934).

18. *Poison for One* (W. Collins & Sons, London 1934/Dodd, Mead & Company, New York 1934).

19. *Shot at Dawn* (W. Collins & Sons, London 1934/Dodd, Mead & Company, New York 1935).

20. *The Corpse in the Car* (W. Collins & Sons, London 1935/Dodd, Mead & Company, New York 1935).

21. *Hendon's First Case* (W. Collins & Sons, London 1935/Dodd, Mead & Company, New York 1935).

22. *Mystery at Olympia* (W. Collins & Sons, London 1935). US title: *Murder at the Motor Show* (Dodd, Mead & Company, New York 1936).

23. *Death at Breakfast* (W. Collins & Sons, London 1936/Dodd, Mead & Company, New York 1936).

24. *In Face of the Verdict* (W. Collins & Sons, London 1936). US title: *In the Face of the Verdict* (Dodd, Mead & Company, New York 1940).

25. *Death in the Hop Fields* (W. Collins & Sons, London 1937). US title: *The Harvest Murder* (Dodd, Mead & Company, New York

1937).

26. *Death on the Board* (W. Collins & Sons, London 1937). US title: *Death Sits on the Board* (Dodd, Mead & Company, New York 1937).

27. *Proceed with Caution* (W. Collins & Sons, London 1937). US title: *Body Unidentified* (Dodd, Mead & Company, New York 1938).

28. *Invisible Weapons* (W. Collins & Sons, London 1938/Dodd, Mead & Company, New York 1938).

29. *The Bloody Tower* (W. Collins & Sons, London 1938). US title: *The Tower of Evil* (Dodd, Mead & Company, New York 1938).

30. *Death Pays a Dividend* (W. Collins & Sons, London 1939/ Dodd, Mead & Company, New York 1939).

31. *Death on Sunday* (W. Collins & Sons, London 1939). US title: *The Elm Tree Murder* (Dodd, Mead & Company, New York 1939).

32. *Death on the Boat Train* (W. Collins & Sons, London 1940/ Dodd, Mead & Company, New York 1940).

33. *Murder at Lilac Cottage* (W. Collins & Sons, London 1940/ Dodd, Mead & Company, New York 1940).

34. *Death at the Helm* (W. Collins & Sons, London 1941/Dodd, Mead & Company, New York 1941).

35. *They Watched by Night* (W. Collins & Sons, London 1941). US title: *Signal for Death* (Dodd, Mead & Company, New York 1941).

36. *The Fourth Bomb* (W. Collins & Sons, London 1942/Dodd, Mead & Company, New York 1942).

37. *Dead on the Track* (W. Collins & Sons, London 1943/Dodd, Mead & Company, New York 1943).

38. *Men Die at Cyprus Lodge* (W. Collins & Sons, London 1943/ Dodd, Mead & Company, New York 1944).

39. *Death Invades the Meeting* (W. Collins & Sons, London 1944/ Dodd, Mead & Company, New York 1944).

40. *Vegetable Duck* (W. Collins & Sons, London 1944). US title: *Too Many Suspects* (Dodd, Mead & Company, New York 1945).

41. *Bricklayer's Arms* (W. Collins & Sons, London 1945). US title: *Shadow of a Crime* (Dodd, Mead & Company, New York 1945).

42. *The Lake House* (Geoffrey Bles, London 1946). US title: *The Secret of the Lake House* (Dodd, Mead & Company, New York

1946).

43 *Death in Harley Street* (Geoffrey Bles, London 1946/Dodd, Mead & Company, New York 1946).

44. *Nothing But the Truth* (Geoffrey Bles, London 1947). US title: *Experiment in Crime* (Dodd, Mead & Company, New York 1947).

45. *Death of an Author* (Geoffrey Bles, London 1947/Dodd, Mead & Company, New York 1948).

46. *The Paper Bag* (Geoffrey Bles, London 1948). US title: *The Links in the Chain* (Dodd, Mead & Company, New York 1948).

47. *The Telephone Call* (Geoffrey Bles, London 1948). US title: *Shadow of an Alibi* (Dodd, Mead & Company, New York 1949).

48. *Up the Garden Path* (Geoffrey Bles, London 1949). US title: *The Fatal Garden* (Dodd, Mead & Company, New York 1949).

49. *Blackthorn House* (Geoffrey Bles, London 1949/Dodd, Mead & Company, New York 1949).

50. *Family Affairs* (Geoffrey Bles, London 1950). US title: *The Last Suspect* (Dodd, Mead & Company, New York 1950).

51. *The Two Graphs* (Geoffrey Bles, London 1950). US title: *Double Identities* (Dodd, Mead & Company, New York 1950).

52. *The Secret Meeting* (Geoffrey Bles, London 1951/Dodd, Mead & Company, New York 1952).

53. *Dr Goodwood's Locum* (Geoffrey Bles, London 1951). US title: *The Affair of the Substitute Doctor* (Dodd, Mead & Company, New York 1951).

54. *Death at the Dance* (Geoffrey Bles, London 1952/Dodd, Mead & Company, New York 1953).

55. *Death in Wellington Road* (Geoffrey Bles, London 1952/Dodd, Mead & Company, New York 1953).

56. *Death at the Inn* (Geoffrey Bles, London 1953). US title: *The Case of the Forty Thieves* (Dodd, Mead & Company, New York 1954).

57. *By Registered Post* (Geoffrey Bles, London 1953). US title: *The Mysterious Suspect* (Dodd, Mead & Company, New York 1953).

58. *Death on the Lawn* (Geoffrey Bles, London 1954/Dodd, Mead & Company, New York 1955).

59. *The Dovebury Murders* (Geoffrey Bles, London 1954/Dodd,

Mead & Company, New York 1954).

60. *Death of a Godmother* (Geoffrey Bles, London 1955). US title: *Delayed Payment* (Dodd, Mead & Company, New York 1956).

61. *The Domestic Agency* (Geoffrey Bles, London 1955). US title: *Grave Matters* (Dodd, Mead & Company, New York 1955).

62. *An Artist Dies* (Geoffrey Bles, London 1956). US title: *Death of an Artist* (Dodd, Mead & Company, New York 1956).

63. *Open Verdict* (Geoffrey Bles, London 1956/Dodd, Mead & Company, New York 1957).

64. *Death of a Bridegroom* (Geoffrey Bles, London 1957/Dodd, Mead & Company, New York 1958).

65. *Robbery with Violence* (Geoffrey Bles, London 1957/Dodd, Mead & Company, New York 1957).

66. *Death Takes a Partner* (Geoffrey Bles, London 1958/Dodd, Mead & Company, New York 1959).

67. *Licensed for Murder* (Geoffrey Bles, London 1958/Dodd, Mead & Company, New York 1959).

68. *Murder at Derivale* (Geoffrey Bles, London 1958/Dodd, Mead & Company, New York 1958).

69. *Three Cousins Die* (Geoffrey Bles, London 1959/Dodd, Mead & Company, New York 1960).

70. *The Fatal Pool* (Geoffrey Bles, London 1960/Dodd, Mead & Company, New York 1961).

71. *Twice Dead* (Geoffrey Bles, London 1960/Dodd, Mead & Company, New York 1960).

72. *The Vanishing Diary* (Geoffrey Bles, London 1961/Dodd, Mead & Company, New York 1961).